NEVER LET YOU GO

CALEB CROWE

INKUBATOR
BOOKS

Published by Inkubator Books
www.inkubatorbooks.com

ISBN (eBook): 978-1-83756-512-2
ISBN (Paperback): 978-1-83756-513-9
ISBN (Hardback): 978-1-83756-514-6

Caleb Crowe has asserted his right to be identified as the author of this work.

NEVER LET YOU GO is a work of fiction. People, places, events, and situations are the product of the author's imagination. Any resemblance to actual persons, living or dead is entirely coincidental.

PROLOGUE

Someone is suffocating her.

Ariana's eyes snap open. Her hands grasp at the pillow pressed against her face. But there is no pillow.

Disoriented and terrified, it takes her a moment to remember where she is. On the sofa, in the study. She gasps for breath. Her eyes widen, searching for any sign of light, for anything at all. But all she sees is darkness.

But if she's not being suffocated, why can't she see? Why can't she breathe?

She recognises the acrid smell of smoke. The darkness above her moves like a living creature. Smoke swirls and clings to the ceiling, dense and toxic, pressing down on her like an angry black cloud.

The house is on fire.

She tumbles from the sofa to the floor and presses herself down onto the stripped boards. The wood is hot to the touch. The air is clearer here.

"Help! Somebody help me!" she cries out, her voice

strained and hoarse. She's terrified. She shouts. She screams, over and over.

But she knows that no one is coming to save her.

No one knows she's here.

The heat intensifies around her, and the smoke sinks lower. Her throat burns with the taste of it, and her shouting gives way to uncontrollable coughing. She can hear the fire now, somewhere outside the room, rumbling and growling. She hears the snap of some wooden piece of furniture, the fire destroying it as easily as someone stepping on a branch. She thinks it must be the chair outside the room, and crawls across the scorching floor towards the sound, to where she thinks the door is. But instead of the door, she finds herself against a wall. She has lost her bearings. She is lost in the black void.

Panic rises. There's no escape. The realisation settles on her, heavy and suffocating like the thick blanket of smoke. No one is looking for her. She is utterly alone, as she has been always. And that is how she is going to die. Alone, unloved, unlooked for.

Jeffrey. Jeffrey has done this.

There is a deafening crash and a bright mass of shimmering glass, like a million stars being born. There's a sudden rush of air. The room flashes with the dazzling orange glow of flames, like the birth of the universe.

She feels something fall against her shoulder and leaps away instinctively, believing it's the ceiling caving in. The thing has hold of her. She imagines herself trapped beneath burning wreckage. But as the thing squeezes tighter she realises it's a hand. Someone has burst into the room.

Before she can see who, she feels a blanket thrown over her head, soaked in water. The hand drags her to her feet and moves her blindly across the room. She can see the orange glow of flames through the fabric and feel the blanket getting hot as the water begins to evaporate. She lurches forward sightlessly, banging into furniture. A searing pain shoots through her hands as they make contact with the burning surfaces. Panic rises. She tries to breathe, but smoke is bleeding through the blanket and making her choke.

The hand keeps pulling her into God knows what, stumbling into the heart of the flames. Blind and lost, she staggers as the stranger pulls her forward.

Her breaths come in short, ragged gasps, each scorching inhalation more painful than the last.

And then, just when it seems inevitable the fire will claim them both, Ariana feels it – a cool breeze on her face, a fading of the orange light penetrating the blanket. Fresh air. Salvation. Her body trembles from adrenaline and shock. She's alive. She's safe. Sirens wail, growing steadily louder. She hears shouting voices and then one softly spoken word.

"Ariana."

The hands release her and she collapses on the ground, gulping in air, coughing, pulling the hot blanket from over her. She can smell smoke and the scorched ends of her wiry burnt hair. Her hands are throbbing and raw. Her eyes grate where the tears have been boiled in her head.

She blinks in the darkness, gets her bearings. She's outside, on the grass verge, looking at the burning house engulfed in flames. Three fire engines, blue lights flashing. Firemen in bulky suits and helmets rush about, their faces grim. Two paramedics hurry away from her, carrying something draped in black. A fireman is beside her, his uniform smeared with soot. He holds her shoulders and looks intensely into her eyes. He begins to lift a mask to her face.

"Wait!" she gasps through her coughing. "How do you know my name?"

He doesn't answer, but places the mask over her face. She gulps in lungfuls of fresh, cold air. A wave of relief washes over her. She looks at the house, a ball of fire, expanding, like a galaxy being born or the sun dying, the fire spreading to the adjoining houses. Raw, primal chaos.

Neighbours stand on the opposite side of the road, in pyjamas and dressing gowns, huddled together, clutching crying children. She scans the faces but doesn't recognise anyone.

Vivian. Poppy.

Daniel.

They're nowhere to be seen.

She looks back at the house. She was inside that. She came out of the fire. Her thoughts swirl like the black smoke pluming into the night sky.

She should be dead.

Somebody saved her.

PART 1

1

NOW

Sometimes, when I look in a mirror, I have no idea whose face is staring back at me.

Jesus. Who the hell is this person?

The girl in my head isn't the woman I see on the other side of the glass: A mid-twenties, slender, allegedly attractive brunette, with good bone structure and green eyes. And that placid, confident, self-assured expression – looking like she knows what's going on. Like she has it all sorted. Like she doesn't have a care in the world.

It's like I'm out in the street, peering through a window at a different person entirely. Staring in at someone who looks like me, but isn't me. That isn't who I am.

"Ariana, darling, have you seen my cufflinks?" Henry calls from the room next door.

I pull myself away from studying the dressing table mirror and call out to him.

"Have you checked inside your good shoes? You said you'd put them in the shoes last time so you wouldn't lose them."

"Did I? That sounds like a ridiculous thing to do."

I hear him clattering away in his wardrobe, tossing his clothes upside down. He's probably lost the good shoes as well. I turn back to the mirror and begin to apply lipstick. I select a pair of simple silver earrings, slender teardrops with filigree patterns that catch the light. I slip them into my ears.

There she is, the elegant stranger.

Henry comes in, holding cufflinks out towards me in the palm of his hand, like he's offering sugar lumps to a pony.

"Bloody good idea of mine, that. Could you help me put them in?"

He proffers the flapping cuff of his crisp white shirt and I fold it over, line up the four buttonholes and thread the end of the cuff through the layers of material.

"Keep our fingers crossed for a full house tonight," he says. "And not just a herd of bloody art students along for a free drink. Some seriously loaded collectors."

"Keep your arm still. You're all twitchy."

"Thanks. I like these cufflinks. The gallery wouldn't be the same without them."

Henry's funny. It's one of the things I love most about him. But tonight I wonder if joking is a defence mechanism. He seems nervous. He's been buzzing in and out for the last half hour, agitation radiating from him, like a comet looping around me in dizzying circles.

I finish the second cuff. "Tonight will be great."

He grins and bends down to kiss me. His salt and pepper hair is clipped short at the temples, but his public schoolboy fringe flops down as he leans over. He kisses my forehead so as not to smear my lipstick.

"Not too much, is it, the suit? Should I just wear jeans? Shorts and a poncho?"

"You look handsome," I say. He does.

"Thanks."

He lurches off, a kinetic bundle of nerves in a well-cut suit.

"Nice arse," I say.

I see him in the mirror, pausing in the doorway. He catches my eyes in the reflection, and for a moment, he's still.

"You look beautiful," he says, holding my gaze. Then he disappears.

The dance before the storm.

I adjust the necklace at my throat. I stand and go to the wardrobe, to give myself a once-over in the full-length mirror. I've gone for something elegant but not too dressy. Smart but arty. I consider putting my hair up, but leave it falling at my shoulders. I like what I see, the dark hair, the shock of red lipstick. But I still can't shake the feeling that I don't know who's looking back at me, this stranger in the mirror.

I smooth my dress and catch sight of the scars on the back of my hand. I shouldn't complain. I'm lucky to be here at all.

The door bursts open and Henry bustles in again.

"The caterers just called. They're lost." He rakes a hand through his hair. "What sort of idiot doesn't have a satnav? Christ, what a balls-up."

"We'll stop on the way," I say. "We'll get some Twiglets and cheesy footballs. No one will give a fuck. They're not coming for canapes."

"You're right, as always. I'm going to load the car."

It's late afternoon, and beginning to get dark. I can see from the window that the sun is low over the horizon, casting an orange glow that lights the street below. I watch Henry, loading boxes of beer and wine into the boot of the car. Beer for the guys who like to keep it real, and good wine for the wankers who think the value of the drink reflects the value of the art. Shouldn't Cassandra be doing this, lugging boxes about? What's the point of having a gallery assistant if you do all the donkey work yourself? The air's heavy with the threat of rain, and there are some nasty-looking clouds over central London, where we're heading. I hope rain doesn't keep people away.

I can't say I'm looking forward to tonight. I feel a sense of unease creeping in. The swanky gallery crowd is Henry's world, not mine. He's comfortable with that art mob. He always manages to charm the room, moving between the prickly artists and the distant collectors. Unlike me. I usually hang back, feeling out of place, skulking on the sidelines in a corner and drinking too much. I make a mental note to lay off the booze in case my tongue gets the better of me and I tell some gobby city boy to shut up and piss off. I won't make that mistake again.

These people, with their money and their privilege, assuming I'm the same as them. I wonder what they'd think if they knew where I really come from. Who I really am. Sometimes I'm glad the woman in the mirror isn't the real me.

Truth be told, I'm dreading it. The bubbly laughs and pretentious chatter grate on me. The whole charade reeks of superficiality and excess. These people don't know real strug-gle, real loss. I can't stand all the bullshit, having to smile and be nice to people I think are arseholes. It makes my skin crawl. Most of them are rich kids who never had to struggle to make anything of themselves. What do they know about the real world?

I catch myself in the irony of what I'm thinking, standing in the elegant bedroom of my lovely North London home. The wonderful life Henry and I have made together. But that's the stranger in the mirror again. On the surface I look like one of them. But I'm a stranger in a strange land. Sometimes I marvel at the chance connections that led me here, to this life that feels like someone else's. I guess that's another lucky escape, given where I came from. In some senses no less miraculous than my escape from the fire.

I look at the burns on my hands, really study them. The scars are a network of pale, uneven skin, etched like a roadmap of the past, smooth and shiny like the material of my dress, as if a pool of wax has been poured and allowed to set. It's almost ten years to the day. Ten years I lucked into this second chance. I owe Henry so much. He's been working hard putting this show together. He hasn't been around as much as usual. All those late nights at the gallery. There's been an increasing distance between us, a slightly bumpy six months. No major drama, just a quiet drifting apart. He's seemed more on edge than usual, just like he seems on edge tonight. Maybe it's because he feels this show could be something big, the culmination of a lot of hard work. We've come a long way since he moved the gallery from Bermondsey to Cork Street. I hope things will go back to how they were. Maybe we're on the cusp of something momentous. Nothing is set in stone. At any moment, everything could change. Tonight could be the start of that.

I'm pulled out of my thoughts by a loud noise.

Even before I've identified what it is, I know something bad is coming, like a spooked animal just before the earthquake hits. A noise, outside the window, shattering the calm of the room.

My brain pieces the jigsaw together. A sickening crunch followed by screeching tyres. A yell. Screaming, of an engine or a person. I'm moving to the window even before I fully know why.

I grip the sill until my knuckles turn white.

Henry lies crumpled on the pavement, his limbs twisted at unnatural angles. He must have been thrown there. He's several houses down the road now. I hear a faint, speeding car engine, and assume it must be the driver who hasn't stopped. They will have been going fast for Henry to have travelled so far. A woman on the pavement screams. She must have come out of her house, drawn by the noise.

The sky is much darker now. I notice the boot of our car is still open, and worry about the things inside getting wet if it rains.

I step back from the window. I feel the edge of the bed pressing against my legs and I sit down. After a while I hear the distant approach of a siren. It must be the police, or an ambulance. That's good. I'm not really thinking what I should do, but now I don't have to do anything, because someone has phoned and I'm relieved I don't have to do it. I continue to sit on the bed.

Even though I'm away from the window, I can still see Henry's body, as clearly as if I was staring at it, his limbs all bent and twisted impossibly, lying on his back, his head turned strangely to one side, his crisp white shirt a mass of red.

I wonder if he left the front door open as he went in and out with boxes. I hope so. In a minute, someone in uniform is going to come into the house and up the stairs to tell me Henry is dead. If he has left the door open it will make it easier for them to find me, and I won't have to get up. I can just sit here.

I'll just sit here and wait.

2

TEN YEARS AGO

I'll just sit here and wait.

Nothing else I can do really.

Bollocks.

I'll be in trouble now. Not that I give a shit about that. I've been in plenty of trouble. But now I'll have to listen to a bloody earful of preachy telling-off. Julie nagging away at me. So bloody booooring.

Or Rob. That's worse. Hopefully it'll be Julie.

This must be a stockroom or something. It's all boxes over that side, but there's nothing interesting like crisps or chocolate. It's all washing powder and dog food and bog rolls. I dunno why this bench is here. I guess this must be the staff room, where they take breaks or something. Though why anyone would want to take their break in here, right next to that toilet, I've no idea.

I need the loo, but I looked in there and it's filthy. No way I'm putting my bare arse on that toilet seat. It's probably all men who work here, pissing and hitting the seat and the floor. You could probably make a biological weapon out of the germs in that bog.

There's a sink with a big chip that's made a big spidery black crack, like a dead tree branch, where the dirt's gone in the gap and never been cleaned out. There's a horrible grubby tea towel hung up by the sink, which they probably use to dry their pissy hands as well as smear it round their filthy coffee mugs.

There's graffiti on the back of the door. Not just in pen either. People have scratched it into the paint with a key or something.

Arsenal are wankers.
Sod off Mackenzie.
I done a massive poo.
Russell.

Shows the class of people they have here. What sort of genius does graffiti of their own name where they work? Way to get fired, Russell. That's probably why there's no choco-late and crisps in here. I bet the staff would nick it.

I'm bloody starving. I knew a boy in one home who ate cat food for a dare. I'm not that hungry though. Not yet.

I only took a manky old cheese sandwich. It's not like I nicked the crown jewels or anything. I'd have paid for it, only I'm saving up. I dunno why they have to make such a fuss about it. It's just a poxy corner shop. The sandwiches are all overpriced anyway. That cheese was sweating more than a jogger's armpit. They probably make them in here out of yesterday's stale bread. Wankers.

I give the door another tug but it's locked. Never mind

me nicking stuff, is it even legal for them to lock up a seven-teen-year-old? That's kidnapping, isn't it?

"Kidnappers!"

I give the door a kick. I look up and try to work out if I can climb through the window if I push the boxes of bog rolls closer. I'm thin, but even I wouldn't get through that.

Jesus, who'd want to work here? It's like a prison cell.

Julie'll be coming soon, I bet. Rob wouldn't be arsed. The security guy asked my name and I told him Ariana Simpson, but he grabbed my bag off me and went through my stuff until he found my ID with my real name, Tracey Jones, which I hate. He took my bag away and my phone and every-thing. He even took the poxy sandwich, the wanker.

Christ, I'm starving. Maybe the security guard is Mackenzie from the bog graffiti. He looked like the sort of wanker who'd have a wankerish name like Mackenzie.

"Sod off, Mackenzie!"

It was all just an excuse to feel me up anyway. He grabbed my bag and threw me in here and got too bloody handsy if you ask me. Probably a paedo. I bet he volunteers for the after-school shifts so he can catch kids nicking sweets and give them a full-on body search. I bet it gives him a right hard-on. He won't try that again with me, not after the kick on the shin I gave him. Never mind nicking me for shoplift-ing, the police should give me a community medal or some-thing for kicking that fucker's leg.

"Paedo!"

I kick the door again and then have a listen.

I can hear voices outside. I think one of them might be Julie.

I think of getting a cup from the bathroom and pressing it against the door like they do in movies, but I'm not sticking

my ear into one of those rancid Petri dishes. I wipe the
scuzzy grease marks off the door with the elbow of my jacket
and press my ear against it.

"...*very sorry she kicked you. That does look nasty. I'm
afraid she has anger management issues.*"

Yes. It's Julie.

"*She's drawn blood, look!*"

That must be Mackenzie. Sounds like I really hurt him.
Good.

"*As I say, I'm very sorry.*" Julie again.

"*Pull your trouser leg down, Carl.*" That must be the
owner. "*What I want to know is, what are we going to do
about this sandwich?*"

"*Obviously, it goes without saying I'll pay for the
sandwich.*"

"*And this drink.*"

What drink? I never took a drink! The thieving bastards.
I kick the door again.

"Thieving bastards!"

"*Yes, of course, and the drink. How much is that?*"

"*Five pounds. And the crisps. Six pounds.*"

Crisps? I never took any crisps neither! I wish I had. My
bloody stomach is doing somersaults with hunger. There's a
bit of a pause and I listen harder. I guess Julie must be
getting some money out of her purse.

"*I should call the police, you know. Kids in here all the
time, taking stuff.*"

The owner. He's had his money, he's got his sweaty sandwich back, and he still wants to get me locked up.

"*I understand your frustration.*" Julie again. "*But if
there's any way we could not do that I'd be very grateful.
Tracey's a troubled girl, but she's a good kid. I'm her foster*

mum. She's had a tough time in care and the good kids like her learn a lot of this stuff from the older ones. I'm sure she's sorry for any trouble."

"My cousin's son was in one of those places for a while." The owner again. "The schools round here are no good for kids. No morals. They're all in gangs, drinking in the park. Hanging round my shop swearing at the customers."

Moan, moan, moan.

"Yes, it's hard for kids these days. I appreciate you giving Tracey a second chance." Julie's really laying it on, making me out to be a right charity case.

I hear steps and move back to the bench.

The door opens. Mackenzie or Craig or whatever his name is stands there, his face like a miserable bulldog that's been kicked in the nuts. He jerks his head to one side, meaning I should come out.

"You're lucky," he says as I pass.

"Oh yeah," I say, "I was born lucky, me. I won the lottery last week. That's why I came in here, to spend my big winnings on one of your delicious sandwiches."

"Come on, Tracey," says Julie. She's got that tone on her, like she's tired of life.

"It's Ariana!" I say. How many times do I have to tell her?

"Alright, whatever your name is, get in the car."

I turn and grab my bag and give Mackenzie the finger as we go out. He'll think twice before he gropes any more schoolgirls.

On the drive back, Julie doesn't say anything. She's not in the best of moods. I think of asking if we can stop at McDonald's on the way, but I know she'll get pissy about it so I don't. If there's bread at the house I'll have some toast.

Hot toast with butter and strawberry jam, if there's some in the fridge.

I wonder if Julie's told Rob. I hope she hasn't. I can cope with the silent treatment. Rob's a different story.

I look out of the window and think about toast.

Then I don't think about anything.

3

NOW

I just look out of the window.

I don't think of anything.

"We're gathering CCTV right now."

I'm jolted back by the voice of the policeman standing in my living room. He's half silhouetted against the window, blocking out the light like a human eclipse. He's enormous, in his complicated uniform of pockets and flaps. It's not the first time I've been spoken to by the police, but for once it's not me who's in trouble.

Though in a more profound sense, I am in terrible trouble.

A female officer sits on the sofa next to me, her knees turned towards me, head cocked on one side, her face resting in the sort of sympathetic smile they must teach them on victim liaison courses.

"We've been going door to door with your neighbours for the last few days," he goes on. "There are several security cameras around, and it's amazing what we can get from people's doorbells."

The female officer nods and smiles. She's trying to be encouraging and sombre at the same time. It's weird. I wonder if she practices this mealy-mouthed face in the mirror.

"What we know so far," continues the other one, "is that a couple of witnesses saw a dark vehicle strike your husband, then head off at speed. There's been a spate of joyriding in this area over the past week. We recovered a vehicle about a mile away that's been burnt out. This may be the car that struck your husband. That vehicle is with a forensics team now."

He keeps saying *struck*. He's avoiding saying killed.

"We're doing everything we can to find out who did this to your husband," says the female officer. She's put her hand on top of my hand, which seems like a bold move. I wonder if I'm supposed to be more upset than I am. Should I be crying? I feel numb.

"Is there anyone we can phone for you?"

Eventually, they leave.

I have friends, but there isn't anyone I want with me now. I want Henry. I'm not sure what I'd say to anyone anyway. And not just now. I've never really felt other people are any use. When the chips are down, you can only rely on yourself. I'm better off on my own.

I can't remember the last time I cried. Years ago. It doesn't do any good. I'm not sure I'd know how to now.

I haven't slept for two days. I'm exhausted, but going to bed and falling asleep seems like such a weirdly normal thing to do under the circumstances. I tried going to bed, but it's just so obvious all the time that Henry isn't there. And seeing the bedroom window makes me think of the last time I looked out of it.

I throw myself into other things. It's busy when someone dies. I field endless calls from people on my mobile, letting everything go to voicemail. I'd practically forgotten we had a landline. Now I am getting calls on that too; long, rambling, awkward messages of sympathy. Henry's sister Anne, who lives in Canada and agonises tearfully about whether she can get back over or not, what with the kids' schooling and exams coming up. I sense she wants me to give her permission not to come, which I do. Even five minutes on the phone to her is exhausting. I turn the volume on the answerphone down, so I just hear occasional rings and clicks.

My phone rings and comes up with a name. *Perry & Sanders Solicitors.*

"Hello. Is that Mrs Ariana Clough?"

"Yes."

"Hello, Mrs Clough. It's Nigel Perry here from Perry and Sanders Solicitors. We prepared Henry Clough's will."

Henry made a will not long after we got married. He got me to put their number in my address book.

"First of all, can I say, Mrs Clough, how very sad I was to hear of Mr Clough's death. I'm very sorry for your loss."

"Thank you."

"I understand what a difficult time this must be for you, but is now a convenient time to talk? I can always call you at a later occasion if now isn't good?"

"No, now is fine." It would be good to have something to focus on. I've been walking round in a semi-coma.

"As you'll recall, we were appointed co-executors with yourself in Mr Clough's will. We're here to help as much as possible, as it's perfectly understandable you have a lot of things to think about."

"Yes. Thanks." I'm not really sure what I have to think

about. I haven't been able to think about anything. The house. The police. The gallery, I suppose. God, and a funeral. I realise that all these things are building up like water in a dam.

"I wanted to let you know that we have notified the Probate Registry of Henry's death. That's standard practice and a legal requirement. We've also taken the liberty of obtaining a death certificate. And when you feel ready, it would be good for us to arrange a meeting to go through the details of the will."

So polite. I can't help noticing how nice people are to you when your husband has just been killed.

"I have an appointment on Thursday at 11 a.m. if that works for you."

"Yes, sure," I say. It's not like I have a full diary. "It's all pretty straightforward, though, right?"

"It will be good for us to go over everything in person."

There's a pause. He hasn't answered me.

"Sure, but we were married. I have a copy of the will. It all comes to me, right?"

Another short pause.

"Yes, that's right..." He sounds evasive. "But there are some details it would be better to go over in person."

"Please, tell me now if there's anything I should know about."

"As I say, I think it would be better to meet in person and—"

I interrupt the slippery little fucker mid-lecture. "Right, in person it is. I'm coming in now."

I grab my coat and keys.

I start the car and swing it out onto the road. I turn hard and hear a rumble behind me as a bottle of wine rolls around in the boot. It's the first time I've been in it, since Henry. As I pull away, I hear the chinking of beer bottles. I drive fast, away from the house, and focus my gaze ahead as I pass the section of pavement where Henry's broken, twisted, lifeless body got thrown like a bit of fly-tipped rubbish.

THE RECEPTION AREA OF PERRY & Sanders looks more like an advertising agency than a solicitor's. It's airy and bright, with trendy Scandi mid-century chairs, one of which I'm sitting on now. They must have a lot of arty clients, and this space is their way of trying to look trendy and creative and fit in. It's pathetic that they're lawyers who don't want to look like lawyers.

I scan the walls to see if any of the artwork is by one of Henry's artists, but I don't recognise anything. I don't know his artists well enough anyway. The art was his thing, not mine.

After five minutes a balding man in his mid-forties – Henry's age or thereabouts – comes out of an office laughing with another man of about the same age, bearded and wearing large, boxy glasses. They look more like the crowd you'd expect at one of the gallery openings. I try to work out which one is the lawyer and which is the client.

After a brief handshake goodbye, Glasses leaves through the door and Balding comes over to me. His face shifts impressively from jovial to sombre in an instant.

"Mrs Clough? Thanks for coming in. I'm Nigel Perry."

He's completely unfazed by me hotheadedly barging in. His bedside manner is impeccable.

"Marina, hold my calls. Thanks." He flashes a smile at

the receptionist and then extends an arm, inviting me into the boardroom.

It's a massive room, all glass on one side with the glass door we've just come through, and has a vast oak table with about thirty chairs. I note a laptop and a pile of papers.

"Please, take a seat."

I sit at the seat that's already been pulled out and Nigel sits by the laptop, one seat down from me. He angles himself towards me to make it feel more intimate in this huge space. I'm reminded of the policewoman and how she sat, trying to calm me down with her pathetically rehearsed body language. Perhaps she and Nigel have done the same course.

"Mrs Clough –"

"Ariana."

"Ariana, as we were discussing earlier–"

"Listen, Nigel," I say, "I'm sorry to interrupt you again, but you don't have to pussyfoot around me. I know I'm a lot younger than Henry was, but I'm a big girl. I've seen a lot of stuff. I won't go into detail, but the short version is, you can tell it to me straight."

Nigel gives me a look and takes me in. He nods his head slowly, weighing things up. It occurs to me he may think that because I'm twenty-seven and Henry was forty-five I was just in it for the money. He's wrong. I think of telling him that, about our ten happy years. I think of opening my phone and showing him photographs of our honeymoon in Italy, our incredible trips to India and Japan and Laos. I could tell him about Henry crying in my arms after his father's funeral, or our plans for children. But it doesn't make any difference either way, so I don't say anything.

Neither does he. He just sits there, looking at me. I get the same feeling he's not telling me something.

"So, what's the problem?" I ask.

"I'm not sure whether you're aware that Henry's liabilities, in relation to the value of the estate, are quite considerable?"

I feel a wave of panic take hold, like a stomach cramp.

"Liabilities?" I repeat, as neutrally as my panic allows. No. I'm not aware of any considerable liabilities.

"Yes," says Nigel. "Debts. Essentially, you inherit Henry's assets, but you also inherit Henry's debts."

"I didn't know he had debts," I say. "How much?"

Nigel looks at me again. I've told him to be straight with me, and something about his manner tells me he's just about to be. He reaches his hand out and pulls the pile of papers and the laptop towards him. He's got that mealy-mouthed look on his face the WPC had.

It's not going to be good news.

4

TEN YEARS AGO

It's not going to be good news.

Julie's told me Rob wants 'a word with me' when he gets home. She's told him about the stuff with the shop. Apparently, he isn't happy. No shit, Sherlock! He's never happy, the miserable twat.

Jesus. All this over a poxy cheese bloody sandwich.

That's why I'm here, in Belinda's room, under her bed. I've used most of the obvious hiding places in the house and he knows where to track me down, so I'm trying somewhere new. It's disgusting under here. Has Belinda even heard of a vacuum cleaner? There's about four million years' worth of dust, like some creepy old haunted castle. When I first crawled in I started some massive sneezing fit. We did a thing in science once, looking at dust under a microscope. It's mainly bits of human skin. That means I'm lying here breathing in bits of Belinda. Bleaurgh. It's enough to make me want to gip.

There's all sorts of junk under here. A plate with some

kind of sauce on it that's dried on like cement. Fossilised baked bean juice or something. And she's shoved her diary under here too, a stupid kiddie-looking book with a picture of a Flutterbye Fairy or something. I know I shouldn't read it, but after ten minutes I'm so bored I open it and take a look. But it's just stuff about what she's had for dinner and how much she misses her home and her mum and brother and her cats. She does little circles with smiley faces over the 'i's, but I don't know why, as it's all ultra sad and depressing. After a few pages I'm so bored I want to pull my eyes out so I close it.

I don't miss my home, or my mum.

This place is nicer than my home, but it's still just a foster home. I've been here a while and it's okay, but I've been moved before, so I think of it like I'm just passing through. I can't get attached, like that bean juice.

Craig says I can stay here 'til I'm eighteen if I want. Craig's my personal adviser. I had a meeting with him last week about my action plan for leaving the care system. I'm eighteen in six months. He says I could stay here until I'm twenty-one, or even twenty-five if I go to college. He's a prat who talks to me like I'm an idiot. Why would I want to stay here any longer than I have to?

It would be nice to have somewhere I thought was home.

I know I'm clever, but I mess about. That's what they always tell me at school, and it's true. I can't concentrate in lessons. I find them so boring. Mr Jenkins, the year head, says if I concentrated and listened, I'd find it interesting. But who the hell can listen to someone going on about potassium permanganate crystals for forty minutes? I'd rather kill myself.

So no, I won't be going to college, thanks very much. But I don't say that to Craig, because he's a chippy little twat and he can proper get the face on him if stuff doesn't go how he wants it. I argued with him once, and he said he could make my life easy or he could make it difficult. I bet he would too. Bet he gets a real hard-on pushing kids about, like that security guard.

And I can see he keeps looking at my tits and he thinks I don't notice.

Sometimes when he's yabbering on I think I could fly across the room and attack him, but I don't. I just bite my tongue and let him talk. Having someone like Craig in charge of what happens to me makes me feel sick.

"Tracey!"

Shit. That's Rob looking for me. He sounds pissed off. He'll go round all the usual places looking for me now. Maybe he won't find me. When he tries a few places and can't find me, he might think I've gone out and give up. Honestly, how much effort is it really worth over a sandwich?

It's quite peaceful under here. I wonder if Belinda ever comes under here to get away from it all and imagine she's back with her mum and her brother and her cats.

I'm an orphan. That's how I think of myself anyway. Even if he's alive, I don't know who my dad is and I don't care. Fuck him, the loser. My mum fell in with the wrong people when she was young; that's what she used to say. I did love her, I suppose, and she loved me, probably. She just messed up. I was in care first while Mum was in prison. Then she died. I got fostered by a few different families. In some ways it's maybe better here than where I was with my mum. I don't like to think about those days. They were good people who took me in, most of them. But it's a job, not love, not like in a real family. They get *paid* to look after me. It's not like someone who loves you for you.

"Tracey!"

He sounds farther away. If I lie under the middle of the bed I reckon I can see Rob's feet if he comes in the room without him seeing me. I have a quick shuffle to the edge of the bed and look round the room. I guess I could get in the wardrobe, but that's so obvious. There's the window, but the moth-eaten curtains only just reach the sill, so I'd be an obvious lump, with my feet poking out under the curtain like some robber in a cartoon.

I can see the posters on Belinda's wall of her favourite pop star, Ariana Grande. Belinda really likes her, and now I like her too. I've got one of the same posters, the one where she's kneeling on a white stool and she's wearing white stilettos and a lacy black top and knickers and she's got her head tilted to one side on her hand, and her eyes are closed, like she's sleeping, or thinking about something peaceful. Ariana's beautiful and talented and her life must be perfect. All the things Tracey Jones's life isn't. I bet Ariana doesn't have to go through a care plan with some twenty-five-year-old with bad breath and acne. I bet she doesn't get felt up for nicking a cheese sandwich.

I'm going to see Ariana in concert at the O2 with Belinda in a few months. I'm excited. It'll be brilliant. Belinda's not bad actually. She's already got her ticket. I've got £35 saved so far. I have to save a bit more to get the £50 ticket from the resale site. It's a lot, but like Belinda says, it's a once in a life-time opportunity and you can't put a price on that.

I get £2 a week allowance and I have to do shitloads of

washing up and cleaning to get that. It's a sodding joke. Slave labour.

I was in one home with a girl called Claire. She was into crystals and all sorts. She did tarot readings with a ratty old deck of cards she got off her dead nan. She just made it all up, I reckon. I don't believe in any of that stuff. But sometimes I wonder if it's my fault. It can't be coincidence that so much bad stuff happens to one person. Maybe the universe doesn't want me to be happy. Maybe I'm being punished for something bad I did in a past life.

"Tracey?"

I can see Rob's feet in the doorway. The horrible shapeless jeans he never washes and his gopping white TK Maxx trainers. I pull myself back from the edge of the bed and hunch under the springs of the bedframe. It's hopeless. He doesn't even bother to look in the wardrobe or anywhere else, he just leans over and peers under the bed. His face is all red from where he's been stomping round the house, the unfit fucker. He's found me, but it's not a nice surprise. It's like some twisted horror movie version of hide and seek and he's the hunter tracking down his prey.

"Get out!" he says.

I don't. I shuffle farther under the bed. I don't know what I'm thinking. It's not like I believe he's going to go away.

He stands up and makes a noise that's a cross between a sigh and a growl. Next thing I know, he's got hold of my ankle and he's dragging me out from under the bed. I kick out at him as hard as I can, but he's got a real hold of my jeans and keeps pulling me out across the carpet.

"Get off me!"

He's not allowed to lay a hand on me. I should have the police onto him, but they'd just take his side. Once I'm in the middle of the room, he lets go of my leg and grabs a big fistful of the collar on my jacket and hauls me onto my feet. He starts marching me out of the room while I helicopter my arms at him, trying to catch him a good wallop. I manage to land one thump on the side of his head, but he grabs hold of my wrist as well and twists my arm behind my back. It really hurts. The skin burns on my wrist and my shoulder feels like it's going to rip apart, like when you pull the leg off a roast chicken.

"I'm absolutely sick of you causing trouble," he says as he marches me up the landing. I see Julie standing at the top of the stairs as we go past. She doesn't look happy, and I don't know if it's because of what I've done or because of what Rob's doing now. Either way, she just stands there like a gawping scarecrow, doing nothing.

Rob swings me into my room, letting go of my wrist as he does. Ouch. It really hurts and my shoulder feels like it's on fire, but I don't rub it as I don't want to give him the satisfaction. He goes over to my desk and starts going through my stuff, shoving my make-up about and knocking my college bag on the floor. My pencils and pens roll across the carpet but he ignores them. He goes into my drawer and pulls out the tin with my Ariana money. He takes the lid off and takes the notes out, six five-pound notes I've folded in half in a little bundle. He throws the tin on the desk and I hear the pound coins inside rattle. A couple of them roll out and onto the floor with the pencils. Rob peels two five-pound notes off the bundle and throws the others down on the desk. He comes over and waves the notes in my face.

"This is for the food you stole. Next time you pull a stunt like that, we'll let the police deal with you."

He goes out of the room.

Once he's out, I fly across the room after him. I grab hold of the door frame.

"Bastard!" I yell into the landing corridor at the top of my voice. I grab hold of the door with both hands and slam it as hard as I can. It makes such a draught my Ariana poster comes away from the wall on one side and flaps about on two bits of Blu Tack before falling on the floor. The door noise echoes a bit and then it all goes muffled and quiet.

I won't cry.

I kneel down and pick up the pound coins and put them back in the tin with the other coins and the five-pound notes on my desk. Twenty-five pounds. I'll never get that Ariana ticket in time now.

I stick the Ariana poster back on the wall. I put the other stuff on the floor back in my college bag, and sit back down on the bed. I don't know what to do now. I have literally nothing to look forward to in my future. My past is shit and my present is shit and my future is shit.

Fuck this.

I go round the room and grab whatever else I might need and shove it in my bag. I don't have much. Then I wait. They call me for dinner an hour or so later but even though I'm starving I don't go down. No one comes up for me. I listen to everyone else in the house do whatever they're doing, and just wait, for hours.

Eventually it's quiet and dark.

I go out onto the landing and down the stairs. I go into the kitchen and raid the fridge for whatever I can find. There's some cold sausages and ham. I eat some and put the rest in a bag in my pocket. There's half a loaf of Warburtons sliced white bread and I spin the neck of the bag closed and take that too.

I unbolt the front door as quietly as I can and step out onto the street.

It's dark and quiet. The sky is black. There aren't any stars.

I'm never going back.

5

NOW

I'm never going back there.

Poverty.

Even before my mum was in prison we were poor. We lived in a horrible council flat, with no decent heating and barely decorated, like squatters. My bedroom had black mould spores all up one wall and across a corner of the ceiling. Everything smelled of damp. Even when I went into school, I could smell it clinging to my clothes. The electricity was on a pay-as-you-go meter and quite often it would run out in the middle of me watching cartoons on the bashed-up telly. The electric cooker wouldn't work and we'd have to eat cold beans or spaghetti hoops. That's if we were lucky enough to have any food in at all.

I pull into the underground car park and squeeze the car into a space by a pillar. Twenty pounds for two hours. It's eye-watering, but I just couldn't face being with people on the tube. I emerge onto Saville Row and walk past the line of swanky gentleman's tailoring shops. The window displays are full of wool and tweed suits with faceless mannequins in deerstalker hats. The bays on the road are marked for loading only, but are full of dark, sophisticated limousines with their engines running and chauffeurs chatting to each other while they wait for their bosses inside.

I duck into a small coffee shop and pick up a flat white and an apricot Danish to go, then out and round into Cork Street. The uncluttered shopfronts, with barely anything on show, make it clear you've entered the gallery district. I hate all this elitist bullshit. The suit shops may be snobby, but at least they put bloody suits in the window. All these gallery windows say is *Keep Out*.

I arrive at Clough's, unlock the door and go in.

Home with Mum was defined by poverty, but when I went into care it wasn't much better. There was wallpaper and carpets. I had a bed and not just a mattress on the floor. The sheets and blankets didn't feel wet with cold when I got in them. But I never owned anything. Never had anything I could call my own. The houses weren't mine, the bedrooms weren't mine, the families weren't mine.

I go through the gallery and into the office space at the back. I sit at Henry's desk. It's a beautiful leather chair and I can feel the shape of it, feel it hug me in all the curves and contours where Henry sat. The space that Henry has left. I take a bite of my pastry and a gulp of hot coffee and boot up the laptop.

Things changed when I met Henry. I was only seventeen and he was thirty-five. He had a house and a life. I was embarrassed, because he'd built a life around him and all I owned fitted into one small rucksack. But he invited me into his home in a way that wasn't like the other homes I'd been in. And his home became my home, we got stuff together, we got married and it all became ours. We loved each other.

Now Henry's dead and our stuff has become my stuff. Except it hasn't.

What Nigel Perry took me through in exhaustive, painful detail was how much financial trouble Henry was in. And now how deep in the shit I am.

Henry had secrets. He remortgaged our house without telling me. The first time to finance the move to the gallery. The second time to bail out the gallery when it started haemorrhaging money. This fabulous chair, this beautiful heavy oak desk, this polished concrete floor reflecting the light from this exquisite Italian light fitting. Everything oozing quality. The idea is that the environment bolsters the price of the art. But if that doesn't work, what you're left with is a load of expensive shit in a big room on a posh street where you can't afford the rent. The phone call I had with the accountant yesterday confirmed it. Things have been going downhill for the past ten years. The accountant compared it to a gambler at a table, throwing good money after bad.

I miss Henry more than anything, and at the same time he's done something that's made me so bloody angry. He should have talked to me. He must have been embarrassed, I suppose. Typical Henry, too bloody embarrassed to make a fuss, like one of those old-fashioned gentlemen too embarrassed to elbow people out of the way in the queue to the lifeboats and who goes down on the Titanic, disappearing under the waves without a grumble.

Well, that's not me. No way. I'm not going back to all that poverty and misery. I've clawed my way up to the life I have now and I'm determined to keep hold of it.

The accountant suggested I close the gallery. I've inherited the millstone round Henry's neck, and I could get dragged under with it. He used words like *insolvency* and *bankruptcy,* which felt like buckets of cold water being thrown in my face. But what's clear is if I stop now, I'll lose most of it. The personal savings are gone. I'll have to sell the house to pay off the debts. I'm carrying a big mortgage. I'll have nothing.

The only way out is to keep going. The ship's sunk, the lifeboats have gone, but I somehow have to make a go of what I have now and hope something changes. I refuse to give up and roll over.

I hear the front door open and feel a sense of dread that it's a customer. The show is still up in the gallery, the one we never had the opening for the night Henry was killed. But I don't know a thing about the work. I can't even remember the artist's name. I urgently scan the desk for a copy of the exhibition handout.

Fortunately, it's Cassandra, the gallery assistant.

"Oh God!" is all she says, as she scampers across the office and grabs me in a hug.

I've only met Cassandra twice before. She's been at the gallery for six months or so. Henry had a series of gallery assistants, almost always the young and absurdly pretty daughters of wealthy parents. Cassandra seems perfectly nice, but oozes old money and ponies. As far as I understand it, her job is to run out and get coffee, or man the stand at art fairs while Henry tries to sell things to investors over boozy dinners.

She hangs onto me in a teary cuddle. Aren't I the one who's supposed to need comforting? "Oh God, Ariana, I'm just so sorry." Cassandra detaches herself from me and steps back.

She's thin and waif-like, with sharp elfin features and the most incredible red hair that hangs down in ringlets. I think it's natural. I'd kill for that hair. She's in a tailored suit with a tartan jacket and miniskirt and model-thin legs. She could have stepped off the cover of *Vogue*. She stands there awkwardly, like an urchin who's been blown in here by a strong gust.

"I can't fucking believe it," she says in the way that only posh people can swear, like it isn't swearing at all, like she's just broken a heel or something. "Henry was lovely. Just lovely. I can't believe he's not here anymore. How are you? You must be a wreck. Can I get you a coffee?"

Christ, she's confident. Where does that come from? I was gobby when I was her age, but I didn't have an ounce of that confidence. I like her. I hold up my coffee cup to show her I don't need one.

"Right," she says, pulling up another chair to the desk and sitting down, pressing the pleats of her skirt down against her thighs like a conscientious schoolgirl. "What do you need?"

CASSANDRA SPENDS the next hour giving me the most comprehensive summary of the gallery business I've ever had. I feel like a complete arsehole for prejudging her as window-dressing. She's smart and switched on and I learn more from her in sixty minutes than I've picked up in ten years of being with Henry. She gives me a rundown on all the artists the gallery represents and tells me who's good, who's dead wood, who should get ditched and who's in danger of leaving if we don't hang on to them.

"Look, Cassandra," I say, "that's all great, really helpful. But you know I'm in trouble, right? Do you think I've got any chance of turning this business around?"

She stops talking and looks directly at me, with a slightly puzzled expression.

"Of course you bloody well have," she says with enthusiasm. "You're not interested in art, are you?"

"Not really," I say, apologetically. Does she spot me as a fraud?

"That's good," she says. "Henry was a lovely man, but his problem was that he was too interested in art. You don't need to be interested in art. You need to sell it."

I think I'm in love with this girl.

"Go on a charm offensive with the artists," she says. "Do a bit of fluffing, blow some smoke up their arses. They'll be terrified you don't know what the fuck you're doing, but shitting themselves they might not have a gallery. Artists are like racehorses. They're skittish. You have to massage their egos with a bit of carrot but they love it when you give them a bit of whip and show them who's boss."

It all sounds a bit S&M. I knew she was the sort who understood ponies.

"I'll do you a list," she says. "The ones who'll be fine with a coffee, which ones will expect a decent lunch, and who should be tackled in the pub."

"Thanks," I say. It feels like a plan is forming.

"Trouser suits for the women, skirts like this one for the men," says Cassandra. "You've got bloody amazing legs," she says, giving me the once-over, "so let's put them to work."

This girl is amazing. For a moment I feel good about myself and stop thinking about the miserable mess I'm in. For the first time in days, I feel positive about something. This might work.

6

TEN YEARS AGO

This might work.

I knock on the door again. There are lights on inside the flat and music playing, but I've knocked three times and there's no answer. Maybe they've gone out and left music on to fool burglars. I peer over the balcony of the open walkway down three flights to the ground below. Bits of scrubby grass. An empty Tesco's shopping trolley. A potholed patch of tarmac where a car's been burnt out. What a shithole.

Someone moves behind the glass and the door opens a crack. A pair of frowning eyes peep round the edge. They brighten up when they recognise me.

"Tracey!"

Shaniqua opens the door and looks at me.

"Rah, girl, what you doin' here? Ain't seen you in time."

She notices the bag I'm holding and sucks her teeth.

"Hi," I say. "Can I crash on your sofa for a couple of days?"

Shaniqua rolls her big brown eyes and doesn't say

anything, but she swings the door open and steps back down the corridor, allowing me in.

Shaniqua throws herself down on the couch in the living room. It's a bashed-up green thing and has a big rip on the arm that's patched with gaffer tape. It's probably been rescued from a skip. She used to be fostered with Rob and Julie but left last year when she turned eighteen. We got on okay, and she gave me her address when the council found her a flat. We haven't spoken since then. I wasn't sure she'd still be here.

Shaniqua got a hairdressing job at a place that gives her day release to study hair and beauty at college. She's got shiny straightened hair now, instead of the big afro she had before, which I used to like to squash and boing out like a sponge. *Get offa me. Girl, what is with you white girls and my damn hair?* She's fatter than when I last saw her.

There's a boy on the sofa watching the TV with the sound turned down while the music's playing from a speaker on the table. He isn't wearing a top and his skinny bare chest is smooth and shiny. He's maybe twenty or so, or a bit older. It's hard to tell. Maybe he shaves it. He has his feet crossed on a wooden box that's being used as a coffee table. His feet are bare. The soles of his feet are almost black, like maybe he never wears shoes at all. He hasn't looked up at me at all since I came in.

"Tracey's gonna stay here for a couple of days, a'ight?"

The boy looks me up and down with an expressionless face and goes back to his silent telly. I guess that means it's okay. It's not even football or snooker that makes sense with no sound. It's some kind of drama, all shadowy and car chases and shootouts.

"Liam stays here too," says Shaniqua. "You can have the

couch when we go to bed. You left Rob and Julie's? How old you now?"

"Seventeen. I left tonight. Rob was doing my head in."

Shaniqua sucks her teeth again. She's been in care for years, like me. She gets it.

"It's Ariana," I say.

"Say what now?"

"I'm not called Tracey anymore. It's Ariana. Ariana Simpson."

"Safe."

She slides up the sofa towards Liam, making space for me. I sit down on the other end with the gaffer tape. My new home for a couple of days at least.

I END UP STAYING LONGER. The flat is a bit rough and it's scuzzy and there isn't much furniture, but I've definitely lived in worse, and at least I don't have to put up with Rob giving me shit all the time.

Shaniqua's out at college or work most of the time, so I hang out at the flat mostly, watching daytime TV. One night me and Shaniqua and Liam go out to McDonald's and Shaniqua gets me a Bacon McDouble and fries and a strawberry milkshake and she doesn't ask for the money or anything. There isn't much food in the flat, just pasta and tinned tomatoes and stuff like that, but she tells me I can eat what I want.

Liam comes and goes and doesn't say much, just watches the telly. The flat's small and at night I hear them shagging in her room. I kind of want to listen but also I try not to. I wake up early because there aren't any curtains and just lie there on the sofa until the others get up. I only have three lots of underwear, so most mornings I wash a pair of knickers and a t-shirt out in the bathroom and hang them on the back of a chair to dry.

One day Liam comes back with a fake ID for me which says Ariana Simpson and has a birthday on it that makes me nineteen. He's used a photo of me Shaniqua took on her phone. He tells me I owe him twenty quid, but it's worth it. I say the date over and over in my head so if anyone asks me it I won't look like I have to think about it for a second. So long, Tracey Jones. I'm Ariana Simpson now.

One night we go for a drink and Shaniqua gets herself, me and Liam drinks and crisps. I just have a half of cider. I've been here four days now and I know it can't last. I've no idea where I'm going to go after. I have five pounds. Five sad little pound coins rattling around in a tin. I'm so fucked.

After the pub we get in Liam's car and drive back. It's a silver Ford Fiesta with all rust up one side and a massive dent on the back where he must have reversed into something. He drives fast and he doesn't indicate. Shaniqua sits in the front with him and I sit in the back. I look out through the windows at all the houses we drive past, with cars in the drives and lights in the sitting rooms. I think about all the families inside, having dinner together and sitting down to watch Eastenders. I look at the lights on upstairs and wonder about all the mums and dads tucking their kids in for the night, reading them stories and giving them teddies and leaving the landing light on while they go to sleep.

Suddenly there's a burst of sound and a flash of light from behind. Even before I swing round to look I know it's a police car. Liam immediately floors it and the engine screams in protest. We accelerate fast and I reach for the seat belt I've forgotten to put on. Only there isn't a seat belt, just a frayed bit of black where it's been cut through with a knife.

Liam swings the car round a narrow turning onto some estate or other. I'm thrown sideways across the back seat and bang my head on the passenger door before sliding down onto my back. I watch the streetlights flash past through the windows above me like a kid being driven on holiday. The car brakes hard and I'm thrown forward face-first into the passenger seat before I fall onto the footwell. I sniff and taste blood. I must have a nosebleed where my face hit the seat. At least down here I don't roll about so much, but I can't see what's going on. I just hear the car engine and the police siren and Liam and Shaniqua laughing.

I'm scared. It feels like we're going to crash and die at any minute. I don't want to be here. It's like one of those horrible rollercoaster rides where you know you've made a mistake and it goes on forever.

Eventually I can't hear the siren anymore and we slow down. It turns out Liam hasn't passed his test and doesn't have insurance. Laugh, laugh. Yeah, fucking hilarious. You guys laugh it up while I suck down mouthfuls of bloody snot and try to get over my heart attack.

That night I lie on the sofa listening to the shagging through the wall and think about how to find some way out of this place. But to get away I need money.

In the morning I ask Shaniqua whether they maybe need someone in the salon she works in, to make coffee or sweep up the hair or something. She says she'll ask.

I don't wanna spend another day in the flat with Liam, not after the car thing. Plus he never has a shirt on when he's inside, and his feet make me want to puke, and I sometimes catch him looking at me funny. I dunno. I just get a bad feeling. So I go out and hang about in the park. It's boring but it's okay. The weather isn't too bad, and there's a pond that has ducks and geese and some swans in it. The swans have three babies, and they all float around in a little line.

There's a cafe there and at lunchtime I go in and get a croissant. Five quid isn't going to get me anywhere, so I might as well spend two quid and not starve to death. I sit on a picnic bench and take my croissant out and lay the paper bag down like a kind of plate so the food doesn't go on the table. I eat slowly and chew every tiny mouthful and swallow before I have another one. I read somewhere if you eat slowly you feel more full up, but I still feel hungry when I've finished.

A little bird lands on the end of my table. It wants the crumbs on my bag, but it's too nervous to come near. I think about pushing the bag towards it, but then I decide not to. I sit there really still and wait. The bird hops about a bit, then forward, then back. It flies off and flies back. After about five minutes, it gets the nerve up to grab a little flake of croissant from the edge of the bag and scamper to the end of the table with it. I watch it eat, looking round nervously. It's only the length of my finger. It's got an amazing orange body and it's blue on the top. It's got this long black line that goes from its beak across each side of its face, with its eyes in the middle, like it's put black eye makeup on to go to a goth club or something.

Once it's finished eating it comes back for another crumb. Then another. I sit there for about half an hour watching it get more confident and come farther and farther onto the bag for more flakes of pastry. It's so close I could touch it, only I couldn't because it would fly off if I moved.

Then it finishes the last crumb and flies off.

I don't think I've ever felt so lonely in my life.

THAT EVENING SHANIQUA tells me she can't get me a job at her salon.

"They got bare girls makin' coffee and sweeping hairs. Damn, that's what I do half the time."

Shit. Now what am I going to do?

"This lady, right? I help with her hair, yeah? She got two kids and I watch them when she needs. She wants someone tonight, but I's seeing Liam. I telled her you could do it. Said you're nineteen, like on your ID. She needs you round seven-thirty. A'ight?"

"Great. Thanks."

She writes the address down for me on a scrap of paper in her big looping handwriting.

Vivian Willens. She sounds posh. I look at the address. North London. Even the street name sounds posh. Maybe this is where my life changes, going through that door with my new name where nobody knows the old Tracey. A new start and a new me.

Just through that door.

7

NOW

Just through that door. That's where they all are. I feel a terrible stirring in my chest, a shortness of breath that borders on panic. I know people will think it's grief, and excuse it, but weirdly it's not grief – it's nerves. The nervousness of having to stand up in front of people and deliver Henry's eulogy.

There's something vaguely ridiculous about people gathering together with the sole purpose of being as miserable as possible. I can hear them next door in the chapel, the low murmur of conversation and the occasional inappropriate laugh, quickly stifled.

Henry's parents are both dead, and he only has Anne and her family in Toronto. As expected, they haven't come over. Cassandra helped me put together a list of art people to invite, artists and other gallery owners and some of Henry's clients and investors. I thought it was going to be a relatively small gathering, but from the noise bleeding into this small back room there are loads of them. A big art world works outing.

It isn't just nerves. Of course I'm sad. I'm devastated. Henry is the only person I've ever really loved, and who has ever really loved me, unconditionally. But being in care makes you grow a thick skin. It makes you feel you can never rely on anyone but yourself. You learn to hold a bit of yourself back. People will always let you down eventually and you have to be okay when they do. You have to be okay on your own. But with Henry I let that guard down. I let him in.

I notice I'm fidgeting with the folded paper in the pocket of my jacket. I've spent nights writing this speech, getting the words exactly right, going over all the memories and anecdotes, the happy times and the sad ones. Writing that speech, on my own, in private, was my real grieving. Today is just me rehashing it all for public consumption.

There's something else too, something I haven't written down and won't say. The anger. Angry with the person who ploughed into Henry with that car and left him smashed and broken at the side of the road. Angry at the police for still not having caught someone.

"I'm sorry, Mrs Clough." That's what the officer said. *Sorry!* As if an apology was somehow helpful. This was two days ago. Sitting awkwardly at the kitchen table, a mug of tea in front of him, which I'd made out of some bizarre instinct to make it all seem normal. "We still don't have any solid leads."

"How the hell is that possible?" I almost shouted. "How can someone get run down and be *murdered* in broad daylight in the middle of London and no one knows anything?"

I was up and striding round the room. I could see how awkward the policeman looked, not knowing whether to get up as well or stay sitting. He decided to stay sitting down, probably to defuse the tension. Probably another technique they teach them on those sodding courses.

"We've established the burnt-out car we found is the one that struck and killed your husband, but the vehicle was stolen and I'm afraid we haven't recovered any useful CCTV of the driver."

He took hold of the cup handle and turned the mug on its coaster, but didn't lift it up.

"Forensics are back, but frankly we're struggling to find anything useful. The car was burning for a long time at a high temperature and that's destructive for any DNA evidence."

"What about fingerprints?" I stood over him, hectoring like a mother scolding a naughty child. It felt good to vent.

"Fire isn't good for fingerprints either, I'm afraid. The heat evaporates oil deposited by the fingers. We were hopeful we'd recovered some prints on one window, but these turn out to have been smudged. The driver must have been wearing gloves, which is quite unusual for joyriders, but it does happen."

He looked guilty. Like it was his fault.

"That's it then, is it? Case closed?"

"Definitely not. We're hoping someone might come forward with information. People often do, when there's a death involved."

He shifted awkwardly. He's probably not supposed to say *death*.

"We haven't given up, Mrs Clough. But the joyriding has stopped for now and it seems like they've gone to ground. If I'm honest, right now the trail on your husband's killer has gone cold."

He left the undrunk tea on the table.

So the whole mess is unresolved. It's hard to know what to do with the anger when I don't have someone to direct it against. Some little joyriding shit I can look at in a courtroom and imagine pummelling to death with my fists.

And that's not the only anger. The worst of all is that I'm angry with Henry. Angry with him for leaving. Angry with him for the situation he's put me in, the secrets, for not talking to me. We shared everything, so why didn't he share the things he was most worried about? He probably thought he was protecting me. But now he's abandoned me and left me to face it all on my own. I feel guilty having these emotions, but I just can't put them aside.

"God, it's like an exhibition opening out there!" Cassandra comes into the room, closing the door behind her. She looks at me. "Christ, you look fucking amazing in that outfit. Is that inappropriate? Sorry. You do though."

I'm wearing a black Chanel suit I bought for a formal gallery dinner a couple of years ago. I felt guilty this morning, bothering about how I look. I got the same familiar feeling of not being myself, that elegant stranger in the mirror looking back at me.

Cassandra looks amazing too, of course, in her figure-hugging tube dress and cardigan. "Look at us," she says. "We could be off to cocktails, not a bloody funeral."

She gives me a warm smile and squeezes my arm. It *is* all a bit inappropriate, but it puts me at ease.

"Come on," she says, taking my hand and leading me towards the door, like a parent guiding a nervous child on the first day of school. "You'll be fine."

. . .

THE ROOM HUSHES slightly as I come in, like a polite version of a Wild West saloon when the sheriff arrives. I'm met with a sea of black outfits. People haven't sat down yet, and swarm about like beetles, chatting to one another. It suddenly occurs to me that maybe they all know what I didn't – that Henry's gallery was in terrible financial trouble. Maybe that's what they're all whispering about.

I don't recognise most of the faces. A few people look at me with pitiful eyes, or a sort of pursed-lip half-smile. Somehow it's all toe-curlingly embarrassing. I don't know what the rules are. Am I supposed to talk to people, thank them for coming? That happens afterwards, surely. Or am I thinking of a wedding? Maybe they're supposed to come over to me... How does the whole thing start? Have they been waiting for me to come in? I guess they could hardly begin without me. Am I supposed to call them to order now, ask them all to sit down, like a headmaster in assembly? I scan the room again, hoping I'll get some kind of sign from someone's face, some clue on what happens next.

That's when I see him.

The shock of his face, so different after ten years, after everything, nearly knocks the wind out of me. And yet he's so familiar, so instantly recognisable. The two times collide, ten years ago and now. It's such a strange coming together it feels like the room has been hit by a bolt of energy, and I'm forced to steady myself against a table. For the first time in as long as I remember I no longer feel like a stranger. I'm me, at seventeen, thrown back into my body like a teleporting time traveller, jolted into reality like a comet crashing to the ground.

By him. By this unexpected face from the past.

Daniel.

8

TEN YEARS AGO

"Daniel!"

The woman, Vivian, shouts upstairs as she leads me through the hallway. It's the nicest house I've ever seen. The hall is about as big as Shaniqua's entire flat. The stairs end with a massive post with a big wooden ball on top. There's a big photo of Vivian and a man I guess must be her husband, and two children – a pretty, smiling girl and a grumpy-looking boy who's definitely not happy about being photographed. He's got a right face on him. The others have cheesy grins, but the expressions look fake. The room they're in looks fake too, one of those sets in a photography studio. The only real thing in the photograph is the boy's angry face.

We go into the kitchen. It's really nice.

"Please, sit down. Would you like a drink, Ariana? I was just making one."

"Yes, please." I sit at the big wooden breakfast table. There's a vase of flowers in the middle. It feels like the sort of perfect set-up you see in an advert or an American sitcom on the telly. I say the birthday date on my fake ID in my head, in case she asks me about being nineteen and not seventeen. It looks nice here and I don't want to muck it up.

"Tea or coffee? Or something else?"

"Um, have you got any Coke, please?" I never drink tea or coffee. I don't like them. Vivian goes over to a huge silver fridge the size of a wardrobe. It's the first time I've seen a fridge that isn't white. She gets me a Coke and a glass and goes over to a fancy-looking coffee machine. It coughs and splutters when she puts a pod in. She brings it over and sits down opposite me at the table.

"So, Ariana, Shaniqua tells me you know each other from school?"

"Yeah, that's right." It's a lie. Shaniqua's like me. You don't tell people you've been in care. They assume things about you. Not good things.

"It's very good of you to help us out at late notice. Jeffrey and I will head out as soon as he comes back with our daughter Poppy, and then we'll leave you in charge with Poppy and Daniel, if he ever comes down from his room, that is. Daniel!"

She yells out again in the direction of the hallway.

"Getting him out of his room these days is like getting blood out of a stone."

She laughs to herself, but it's one of those laughs people do when they don't actually find anything funny. Daniel's the son then.

"We'll be back by about midnight. Is that okay?"

"Sure. No problem."

"And is ten pounds an hour okay? Did Shaniqua mention that?"

"Yeah, that sounds right."

Jesus. Ten pounds an hour? I thought I was getting ten pounds for the night. I have to practically stop myself from dancing round the kitchen.

We make a bit of small talk while we wait. Vivian's an accountant. Jeffrey runs a building firm. Poppy's thirteen and likes gymnastics and ice skating and is out at a birthday party at a friend's house. I think she's just filling the silence until the others get back. She doesn't mention Daniel at all.

There's the noise of a key in the lock.

"It's Jeffrey and Poppy." Vivian jumps up, gulps her coffee down and puts the cup in the dishwasher. Jeffrey comes into the kitchen. He's a stocky little bloke. He looks flustered.

"Getting those girls to say goodbye to each other is a major number," he grumbles. He flicks a look at his watch and barks at Vivian. "We're running late. Are you ready to go? Come on."

His tone is nasty. He's a thuggish bully of a man. He hasn't looked at me once yet, even though I'm a complete stranger sitting in his kitchen. I guess I'm just staff, not a real person.

"I'll just get my coat," says Vivian. "This is Ariana," she says as she goes out into the hallway. "She's babysitting."

Now he looks at me. "We'll be back by midnight, alright?"

"Yes. That's fine."

The girl from the hallway photo comes into the room. This must be Poppy. "Hi," she says, giving me a smile. She goes to the fridge and gets a juice box, then sits at the kitchen table texting on her phone in its pink, fluffy case.

Vivian comes back in, holding a coat over her arm.

"There's pasta bake in the fridge for the kids. It just needs heating up. You'll work out the oven. Help yourself if you want. There's enough. Try to get Daniel down for some if you can."

"Right, let's go," says the husband. He grabs Vivian by the elbow and steers her towards the kitchen door. I've seen enough bullies in my time to know his type. I don't like him.

ONCE THEY'VE GONE, Poppy chats to me a bit but she's more interested in her phone. I need the loo, but I was too embarrassed to ask Vivian. Poppy points me upstairs, and I head up. The bathroom's massive too. It's like peeing in a palace. I wash my hands and look at myself in the mirror. I try to imagine this is my house, that I live here, that this is just what I normally do every day when I go for a wee. But my brain won't let the idea stick. Instead, I just look like an intruder.

I'm about to go downstairs when I think I'll have a quick look around. Most of the doors are open. I peek into one of them, keeping my feet on the landing and leaning round the door frame. I know immediately this is Poppy's bedroom. It's done out in pastel shades and the bed is a kind of mini four-poster that a princess would sleep in, with all netting and stuff hanging down from a canopy. It's girly and a bit young for a thirteen-year-old. There's clothes on the floor. She has more clothes in this floor pile than I owned in my entire life.

The next room I peep into is Vivian and Jeffrey's. It's dark and luxurious, with dark brown wood on the walls and a thick grey carpet and smart grey bedding. It looks like the comfiest bed in the world, like I could lie down on it and sleep for a month. It takes all my willpower not to go in there and give it a try.

The rooms are huge. Plus, there's a staircase going up to another level, but it feels too risky going up there, in case Poppy finds me sneaking about. On this level I can just look like I'm coming out of the loo.

There's one more room on this floor, and it's shut. I'm guessing this must be Daniel's bedroom. I stand really still outside it to see if I can hear anything, music or something, but there's no noise at all. I could just go downstairs, but the way Vivian talked about him, I feel a bit sorry for Daniel. I know what it's like when you just want to lock yourself away from everything. Anyway, I'm in charge and I should probably make sure he's okay.

"Hello?" I knock on the door gently. There's no answer.

"Hello?" I try again. Still no answer. "Daniel? Do you want some dinner?"

"Go away," a surly voice comes from somewhere deep inside the room.

"It's pasta bake," I add, wondering if it might be one of his favourites.

"Leave me alone." He's angrier now, but there's something else in his tone I recognise. He's not just angry. He's sad.

If someone wants to be left alone you should leave them alone. When you're in care you're in places rammed with people and you're never alone. And when you want to be alone, they assume something's wrong with you and make you talk about it, which is the absolute bloody opposite of what you want.

I decide to leave Daniel alone.

I feel sorry for him though. I reach into my pocket and

pull out a Twix I bought earlier, which I was saving for later. It's okay, I guess. I can have some pasta instead. Very quietly, I stoop down and put the Twix on the floor just outside Daniel's room.

I wonder if I'll ever see him.

9

NOW

For years I've wondered if I'll ever see him.

The last time I saw Daniel, he was twelve.

Not that I *could* see him. Not properly. His poor face was covered in bandages, and his hospital bed was surrounded by a vast tent of plastic curtains, to stop infections, they said. I was still in hospital myself then, being treated for the burns on my hands, but they were about to discharge me. Daniel was going to be in there for a long time. I felt so sorry for him. I promised I'd see him soon.

But that was a lie.

I didn't know at the time. I genuinely thought I'd see him again. But it never happened. Weeks turned to months. Then to years. Every now and then something random made him pop into my head, or I'd be surprised by the sight of the backs of my hands, and think maybe he'd show up. Sometimes I thought about trying to get in touch with him. But he never appeared, and I never made the call.

And now here he is, ten years later.

I've felt guilty all this time. Guilt I've never shaken, no

matter how long passed, or how deep I buried it. Guilty, because he rescued me and I abandoned him.

His father Jeffrey was a nasty piece of shit who set fire to their home, and the whole family died, except Daniel. He managed to escape – but when he heard me trapped and screaming in the building Daniel went back in and dragged me out. Twelve years old, and he literally walked into fire for me. He pulled me from a burning building and saved my life.

He was a brilliant kid. Literally. He was the cleverest person I'd ever met in my life. Genius-brilliant. But other than that, he was just a normal boy. Slim, dark-haired and serious. He had dark, brooding eyes in his pale face. Though he did go outside sometimes, he spent a lot of his time in his room, with the blinds drawn, living in the weird half-light of heat lamps from the tanks for his spiders and snakes.

Whatever guilt I've felt about it before, that's nothing compared to how I feel seeing him now.

His face has changed – obviously; he's ten years older. He's not looking directly at me, but off to one side, talking to one of the funeral directors about something, pointing towards a chair at the back. It's only when the person he's talking to leaves and Daniel turns to face the other way that I can see them.

The scars.

Oh God, the scars.

The right side of his face is unnaturally smooth in places and horribly cratered in others, like the surface of the moon. His right ear is misshapen and slightly pointed where half of the top part missing. His nose from the side looks pointed and angular, where they must have rebuilt it in surgery. It looks fake somehow, sharper than a normal nose. The pointed nose and ear remind me of a cat.

I jump in surprise as someone touches me on the shoulder, and I turn to look at them. It's a woman I don't recognise. She's offering me a tissue, and for a moment I don't understand. Then I realise there's a tear rolling down my cheek. I take the tissue and wipe it away.

I can't remember the last time I cried. It must be ten years. It won't look out of place here.

But it's not Henry I'm crying for. It's Daniel.

I need to talk to him.

I start to move through the mass of people who step back like they might catch the misery from the grieving widow. As I get nearer, I see the right side of his face in more detail. It's a patchwork of skin grafts. The area around his eye has a web of fine stringy lines. His mouth pulls slightly to one side where the scar tissue tugs at the corner of his lip. His forehead is higher on the right where the hair can't grow. He's grown it long on the left, and it flops across his forehead in an attempt to hide some of the scarring. But it forms a curtain that only partly veils the unsettling damage.

Just as I'm about to get to him, someone steps in my way.

"Hello. Phillip Tench."

A squat, balding man in a vulgar navy pinstripe suit thrusts a hand towards me. I instinctively shake it.

"I've never had the pleasure of meeting you before, Mrs Clough, and now when I do it's on this terrible occasion. I'm so sorry for your loss. Henry was a giant in the art world."

Anyone would look like a giant to this hobbit. He's about five foot nothing. I feel awkward, staring down onto his little bald head while his face is eye level with my breasts.

"Thank you," is all I can manage.

"Henry's gallery was one I truly admire. Will you be continuing his legacy? I'd be more than happy to offer any assistance over the next few weeks. It's quite the shark tank out there." He's already talking about the gallery in the past, like it died with Henry. Maybe he knows all about my financial trouble.

He thrusts a business card my way.

Tench Fine Arts.

As I'm reading it, he takes hold of my hand again, then cups it in his other hand, like one of those drawings of some Victorian tosser in a cheesy romance. I half expect him to go down on one knee. He gives me a look that's meant to be sympathetic but just comes over as smarmy. He's so greasy you could fry him.

"Truly, I mean it. Anything I can do to help. *Anything.*"

He squeezes my hand a couple of times like he's trying to get toothpaste out of it. At last he lets it go. I smile thinly and make a point of putting his card in my jacket pocket, hoping if he sees me do this he'll leave me alone. He smarms me a smile again and steps back, walking backwards while still looking at me, like a waiter kowtowing in a cheap Japanese restaurant.

At last, I can get back to Daniel.

But when I look round the room, there's no sign of him. He's disappeared.

TEN YEARS AGO

"She can't have just disappeared!"

I'm hiding in Shaniqua's living room, while she's at the front door, listening to Craig drone on in his pathetic nasal voice.

"What the hell you axin' me for?" says Shaniqua. "I ain't seen the girl."

"Look, I know she doesn't have anywhere else to go. She's here, isn't she?"

He must be desperate to come round here looking for me on a hunch. I bet his arse is really on the line for losing track of a kid. Maybe I'll write to his boss and say it's coz of him I ran off. That'll make him think twice before he looks at girls' tits in counselling sessions.

"Listen, Shaniqua, Tracey's only seventeen. She's vulnerable. She can't be running around with no one looking out for her."

"No, *you* listen, bruv. If she WAS here she wouldn't be runnin' round with no one to look after her, coz I'd be lookin' after her. Which I ain't, because she ain't here, see?"

Puzzle your way through that one, Craig, you whiny shithead.

"Is that her bag?"

Bollocks. I've left my bag in the hallway. It's a stupid Hello Kitty one I've had since I was fourteen. I used to think it was cute, and now I just think it's stupid but I can't afford another one. Craig's seen me with it loads of times.

"Nah, fam," says Shaniqua. "It's mine. I'm all about that Hello Kitty life."

"Look, Shaniqua..." He's trying to come over all nicey-nicey now. "You're doing really well here. If you're harbouring a runaway, I'd hate to have to report it to my boss. He's a real tightarse about these things, and I'd be gutted to see you lose this flat."

There's a pause. I strain to hear what's going on. Is Shaniqua going to give me up?

"Listen, you stringy piece of shit," she says quietly, "if you come round here again I'll get my man and his boys to mess you up big time. They'll bury you, fam. Now fuck off."

She slams the door really hard. Shaniqua comes back into the room, grinning. She high-fives me. Phew. I'm safe.

But only for now.

I need to get more money. I need to get to somewhere Craig can't track me down.

LATER THAT DAY I get a text on my mobile. It's Vivian, the woman I babysat for the other day. She wants to know if I can come round again tonight.

"Go for it, girl," says Shaniqua. "I don't even like it round there anyways. They're a weird family, but if you okay with it you can go there again for sure."

When I get there, Vivian says she and Jeffrey are going to the theatre and won't be back 'til midnight. Daniel stays in his room and I don't see him. Poppy has a test tomorrow on a science project and I sit at the kitchen table and ask her questions about ants. Apparently there can be twenty million ants in a single colony. You think ants are tiny and insignificant, but if you fall over injured, a colony of army ants can eat an entire person in a couple of hours. It makes me think about how I feel sometimes, small and insignificant.

I was with one family when I was about nine, and there was a whole cloud of flying ants in the garden, and Terry, whose house it was, made a few of us into a production line, bringing out saucepans of boiling water and putting the kettle on and stuff, to pour boiling water down an ant hole. What kind of sicko gets a load of kids to pour boiling water on a family of ants? Some people are deranged. You learn stuff as a kid and you think it's normal. But it isn't normal.

When Poppy goes to bed I go into the living room and sit on the massive sofa and put the telly on. I wonder what it would be like if I lived here all the time. I find a load of old episodes of *Friends* and watch about ten of them back to back. When it gets to eleven thirty I go upstairs to the loo in case Vivian comes back early. It's quite a way back to Shaniqua's and I need a wee before the walk.

As I go back down the stairs I notice my jacket on the peg in the hall. It looks like it's moving. I stare at it hard. If it was moving, it's stopped now. It's probably just a trick of the shadows. Maybe it was never moving at all.

Then I think I hear a door close upstairs. I go up the stairs again really slowly so I don't make a noise. About five stairs from the top, I stop. From here I can see along the floor of the landing and below the doors. Poppy's light is off, but there's a light coming from under Daniel's door. I think about knocking and asking him if he's been messing with my jacket. I don't like the idea of anyone going through my things. But I'll feel stupid if he's asleep and I wake him up. I decide to leave it.

Vivian and Jeffrey come back at quarter past midnight. Jeffrey just disappears upstairs. Vivian gets my money and an extra ten pounds because they were late, and she won't take it back when I say she doesn't need to.

I walk home, looking at the posh houses. Some of them are split into flats but most of them are just one house. A whole big house like this just for one family. I guess some people are lucky and get born into a rich family like Poppy and Daniel. Other people like me are born into something else and just have to get on with it. I don't like to think badly about my mum, but she never really gave me a chance. Her mum never really gave her a chance either, from what she said. But it's shitty all the same.

I see a night bus behind me, and I run to the stop to get it, but I'm too far away and don't get there in time. As it goes past me, the lights are orangey inside and it looks all warm and cosy. Once it's gone round the corner the night seems darker and colder than before. I pull my jacket tighter around me.

That's when I feel it. Something hard in my pocket. Only I know my pockets were empty when I set out from Shaniqua's.

Carefully, I put my hand in my pocket and feel what's in there. It's firm and cold and kind of crinkly. I know what it is even before I take it out and look at it.

A Twix.

. . .

I HAVE a bowl of cornflakes for breakfast. It's one of Shaniqua's beauty college days, so she's rushing round in a tizzy coz she's on a final warning if she's late in again. Liam's on the sofa with his top off as usual, eating toast and watching *Cash in the Attic*. Shaniqua leaves and I go for a shower.

When I come out, Liam's still sitting on the sofa.

But now he has my bag.

He has some of my things out on the sofa beside him. I stand in the doorway, frozen, not knowing what to do. He looks up at me and I think he'll jump because I've caught him, but then he looks back down and just keeps going through my things. I've only got Shaniqua's dressing gown on, and I'm in bare feet. Because I'm not properly dressed I feel more vulnerable.

"Tracey Jones," he says. He's reading it off my ID. Not the fake one he got me. My real one.

He looks me up and down. I pull the dressing gown tightly round me. I try to stare him back and not look like I'm scared, even though I am.

"Be a shame if that bloke found out you were here, Tracey Jones."

Even though I don't think that's my name anymore, I don't like him saying it. I watch as he leafs through the money Vivian gave me last night. He peels notes off one by one. He puts a single tenner back in my bag, like he's doing me a favour, then puts the rest in his pocket. He gets up and walks towards me and I wonder if he's going to hit me. I step back slightly until I'm pressed against the door jamb. He keeps going past me, and brushes against me as he goes through the doorway. I can smell his sweat. He's smiling, like he knows he's beaten me. Even though he's barely touched me, it makes me feel dirty, like I need another shower.

When Shaniqua comes back later I don't tell her. I need to get away from here now. I need to get away from Liam. Bullies don't stop, ever. But with no money I can't get away. And if I do earn any more money, I know Liam will take it.

A COUPLE of days later I get another message from Vivian asking me to sit for the kids. I say yes. The only thing I think is that Liam doesn't know what hours I'll be doing and how much I'll get paid. If I leave most of the money I earn in my bag, I can hide ten pounds of it in my shoe. It'll take me longer to save up but at least I won't lose everything. This time when I get there, Vivian tells me Poppy is at some kind of sleepover and it'll just be Daniel in the house.

About twenty minutes after Vivian and Jeffrey leave, I'm in the kitchen when I hear the noise of a door upstairs. Soon after, a dark-haired boy is in the kitchen doorway. He just stands there, looking at me. He has a kind of blank expression on his face, like he doesn't want to give anything away.

"Alright?" I say. "Are you Daniel?"

He just nods.

"Your mum left a shepherd's pie for you," I say. "I was going to eat it all, but now you're down I guess I'll have to give some of it to you."

I say it in a way that sounds grumpy, but I'm joking. I can't tell if he gets it, but his face changes a bit. The worst thing you can do to someone who doesn't trust you is be too nice to them. It's a waste of time. If you give someone a bit of cheek, it gives them something to come back at.

I get up and go to the fridge, take out the shepherd's pie

and put it in the oven. Out the corner of my eye, I see Daniel
move over to sit at the kitchen table. I go back and sit opposite him. We don't say anything for a bit. Then he talks.

"Thanks for the Twix," he says, quietly, looking down at
the table.

"That's okay," I say. "Oh, and thanks for the Twix."

He almost smiles. He still doesn't look at me.

"Was it just the same Twix you gave back to me?" I ask.
"Or a different one?"

"A different one," he says. Then he looks up. "I ate
yours."

"Good," I say. "And I ate yours on the walk home for a
bit of energy. It was fucking freezing."

He lets himself smile then. I know people won't
normally swear like that around him, but I do it deliberately.
I want him to know I'm on his side.

We eat our shepherd's pie. Then Daniel asks if I want to
see his snakes. I'm not really into snakes, to be honest. They
scare the shit out of me. But I figure it's a big thing for him to
let someone into his bedroom and show them his stuff, so
I go.

The truth is, there's been something about Daniel right
from the start that reminds me of me, or at least makes me
think about how I felt as a kid, that I was on my own and
didn't have anyone. I guess I've always felt the lowest of
the low, like a human ant, and it gives me a warm fuzzy
feeling thinking I could do something nice for this boy and
look after him a bit, not just because I'm being paid to
do it.

The snakes are creepy. He also has spiders. He loves
them – like, really loves them. He lets one of the spiders walk
across his hand, a great big furry one. He says I can touch

them, but there's no way I'm doing that. Watching it on his hand makes my insides go all shivery.

We go downstairs again, with Daniel following close behind me like a little puppy.

"The other thing," I say, "is that your mum asked if I'd help with your English homework. I don't think she thought you'd come down, but you have, so maybe we could do that. I know it's boring, but you'd be doing me a massive favour."

"Okay," says Daniel with a smile. He thunders upstairs, then comes back down with a book.

"What do we need to do?" I ask. I'm actually useless at doing homework.

"I've already done it," he says. Blimey, he's keen. I had him down as someone who wouldn't join in with anything, but maybe not.

"Oh yeah?" I say. "What was it?"

"We had to write a poem."

"Yeah?" My heart sinks. I hate poetry. Most of it doesn't make sense and half the time it doesn't even rhyme. But I pretend to be interested. "What about?"

"Anything, really. We just had a title. *You.*"

"Right. Want me to read it?"

He pushes his exercise book across the table to me. "It's about my parents," he says. He's only twelve but his writing is much neater than mine. I can see where he's pressed the pen into the paper really hard. The title at the top says *YOU* and it's been underlined with a ruler.

YOU
Father's anger, mother's shame,
Two vile monsters, both the same,

Trap me here, in shadows thin,
Smile and sneer, let darkness win.

Your hands and words, they bruise and burn,
For your respect, I'll never yearn,
My mind's a hot and endless fire,
Fed by your lies and black desire.

You think you've won, you think I'm beat,
But in my mind, your end's complete.
One day, I'll rise, I'll break these chains,
And dance upon your cold remains.

I finish reading. I don't know what all of it means, but I get a weird feeling inside, the same as I did when I watched that big black spider crawling across Daniel's hand. No twelve-year-old I've ever met before could write that. He's watching me carefully as I read it, and when I'm done I don't know what to say.

"Did you really write that?" I ask.

He nods. All he says is, "Don't tell my mum."

"I won't," I say.

NEXT MORNING, as soon as Shaniqua leaves, Liam grabs my bag and takes most of my money. I notice a disgusting vein on the back of his hand as he counts out the notes. He doesn't even bother to look at me, just throws the bag back down on the sofa and goes out. I manage to keep ten pounds back. I want to work out how long it'll take me to save up enough to get away, and as I'm trying to do the maths, my phone rings. It's Vivian.

"I'm not sure how you've done it," she says, "but Daniel came down for breakfast today. I can't remember the last time he did that. He said *good morning*. It's a minor miracle. I see all the shepherd's pie got eaten."

"Yeah," I say. "He came down for some of that too. He showed me his snakes." I don't mention the poem.

"He let you in his room?" She sounds amazed. There's a long pause.

"Listen, Ariana, Jeffrey and I are busy with work. We don't have the time to deal with... we don't have the time to give Daniel what he needs. And Poppy too, of course. Would you consider coming to stay with us, to live with us, as an au pair? We can discuss terms and responsibilities and all that sort of thing. But is it something you might be able to do? Would you consider it?"

I only sort of half hear what she's saying after the bit about asking if I'll go and live with them. I wait 'til Shaniqua's out at work and Liam is out somewhere. I shove my things in my bag. I write Shaniqua a note on the back of an envelope thanking her for letting me stay. I let myself out of the door and into the street.

I practically run all the way until I get to Vivian's.

As I come up the drive, the door opens and there he is.

Daniel.

11

NOW

The door opens and there he is. Daniel.

A week has passed since the funeral. I've been going into the gallery every day, working with Cassandra to see if I can keep this shitshow of a business afloat. We've been phoning round the artists, setting up meetings, ready to put Cassandra's plan of a charm offensive into action. It's a last, desperate measure.

Every now and then, in pauses between calls, I think of Daniel, wondering if he'll show up again. He must have read about the funeral through the gallery. I half hope he'll turn up here. Though it's a sad way to find me again, I'm so glad he's tracked me down.

I keep having dreams about Henry. Henry coming home from work. Henry lying in the bed next to me. Henry standing exactly where Daniel was standing at his own funeral. Or nightmares. Nightmares about Henry, and the sound of that car and his body at the side of the road. I'm anxious about everything, about Henry and money trouble, and somehow in my dreams Daniel's reappearance gets wrapped into that. The brain's such an odd thing, and my nightmares seem to muddle Henry's injuries and Daniel's scars into one entity.

Henry's absence and Daniel's absence start to feel the same. As the days pass and there's no sign of him I begin to feel increasingly uneasy. Why show up at the funeral and then just disappear? Why reappear after all this time? What does he want? Is he pissed off because I let him down? Because I abandoned him? Does he want some kind of payback? Revenge even?

Melodrama isn't in my nature, and I know what I'm thinking is ridiculous. I know this is all about Henry, but knowing and feeling are two different things. I can't seem to shake the feeling of nervous anticipation, like there's something not right with the world. Every time the gallery door opens I look up, hoping it will be Henry, and then thrown back into grief when it isn't, even though I know it can't be. I dread the sound of the door, and who will come through it when it opens. The unbearable thump of reality when it isn't Henry standing there. I know it's crazy, but I can't get past it.

And today, of all days, Cassandra is on her day off and I'm here, entirely on my own, when the door opens.

And it's him.

"Daniel," I say. I've pictured his burns in my head since the funeral, but it does nothing to ease the shock of the reality. I'm not remotely prepared for how disfigured he looks and how startling that is.

He walks towards me and I stand up. I wonder what's going to happen next.

But then he smiles, and pulls me into a hug. We hold each other, not talking. Now I can't see his altered face, I just hold him and remember who he really is. Daniel. We stand like that for a long time. Time stands still. The hug is full of all sorts of things, Henry, and the fire, and a connection reaching across ten years and looping around and bringing us back together. The bond we forged. The secrets we shared.

My anxiety melts away and I feel something I haven't felt for days. Happy. "I'm sorry I lost you," I say. "Now we've found each other, I'll never let you go."

"We're like two planets," he says softly into my ear as we hug, "both with their own distinct orbits, but destined to pass each other again."

He releases me and takes a tiny step back. We both laugh a little. We don't need to say it. We know.

"I'm sorry about Henry," he says at last. The way he says it, so directly, seems to cut through all the unspoken nightmares I've been having. It makes it feel more real, and it helps.

He looks at me with real sympathy. I stare into his eyes and notice his right eye is cloudy. I wonder whether the fire which burnt that side of his face so badly also affected his sight. I'm afraid to ask about it.

"Do you want a coffee?" I ask. "We've probably got a bit of catching up to do."

"Yeah." He laughs at the understatement. "Sure."

"Well," I say, as I put two mugs on the table, "you kind of know my big news. Tell me what's been happening with you."

He puffs out a kind of *where to start* sigh as he sits down.

"I was in the hospital for three months initially," he says. "The biggest fear was infection. I'd inhaled a lot of smoke and there was lung damage too, so that meant everything took longer. Once I was discharged there was a lot of surgery. The burns were pretty bad."

I don't know how to look at him. I don't want to avoid looking at him, but I worry if I look at him he'll think I'm looking at the scars.

It's as if he can read my mind. "I know it's a lot to take in, how I look. I still get days when I'm taken aback by what I see in the mirror. Startled, like it's not me. But it *is* me. This is who I am now. Please don't feel embarrassed about looking at my scars. They're me as well. They're who I am."

Maybe he *can* read my mind. Or maybe he just saw something in how I looked at him. The awkwardness.

"There was all the other stuff as well," he continues. "Finding out Mum and Poppy had died. Dad too, of course, though I was less concerned about him, obviously. Though therapy taught me you can't just ignore the death of your dad, especially when he's a dad who's killed your family and tried to kill you."

I notice he has a rectangular locket on a chain around his neck. I recognise it as one I saw his mother wearing once. I'm glad he's managed to find some positive way of hanging onto her memory.

"Where did you go when you came out of hospital?"

"I didn't have any other relatives," he says. "Mum and Dad were both only children, and I didn't have any living grandparents. I went into care. I know people have all sorts of ideas about what that word *care* means. Some of it was more caring than other bits. But it was okay."

I never told Daniel about my own past, and I don't tell him now. It's something I don't think about if I can help it. But as Daniel tells his story I'm struck by how similar it is to my own. Two damaged orphans, kicked around the system.

For months after I left hospital I told Henry we should take Daniel in to live with us. Henry told me he followed up with the authorities, who insisted Daniel was best off in the care system. The feeling was that Daniel needed to progress with his new life, and it wouldn't be good for him to be reminded of the trauma by seeing me. I don't trust anything those people say, but Henry did. After a few times of asking, it was obvious he wasn't going to let Daniel come. It made me sad, but I went along with it. I guess I felt lucky Henry had rescued me from that system and I didn't want to blow it.

Seeing Daniel now, hearing his terrible story, I'm horribly aware how selfish I was. "I made a mistake," I tell him. "I should have done more."

"You were only really a kid yourself," he says.

He's right. But it's still not an excuse.

"It's not that," I say. "I was too selfish, too carried away in my relationship with Henry. I put myself first. I abandoned you, Daniel. I'm sorry."

"It's okay," he says.

He reaches across the table and takes my hand in his. I see the back of his hand is covered in burns as well, the skin pulled thin and tight like my own. Our hands look like they're two hands belonging to one person.

"Henry was right. It would have been too much for me, seeing you then. I needed to draw a line and look forward, not backwards. And it would have been too much for you too. I'd have just reminded you of all that bad stuff. I'd have pulled you backwards."

He's amazingly generous in how forgiving he is. But there's a weight of guilt I've carried around inside me like a cold, hard stone. It's sent its roots deep inside me, like plant roots spreading into the ground. It can't be pulled out so easily.

"You know," he says, "you were the only person who ever listened to me as a kid. I never had any friends. My family never listened, not really. The only attention I got from them was toxic. You were the only one who ever seemed interested in me."

"I get that," I say. And I do. The truth is, Daniel was the only person who ever seemed interested in *me*.

"There was lots of talking after," he goes on, "therapy and stuff. But that isn't the same. They didn't care like you cared, authentically. You got me to come out of my room and you got me to come out of myself."

It's like he could be talking about me, not himself, all the things I've felt about myself for years, isolated and different from everyone else. Everyone except Daniel. We're like two halves of one thing.

The phone rings, and I assume it'll be another one of the artists getting back to me. "I'm sorry," I say, "I'm on my own today. I'll have to get back to things." I'd much rather talk to Daniel, but I have to make this gallery stuff work.

"That's fine," says Daniel, standing and picking up his jacket from where he'd thrown it over the back of the chair. "I just dropped in on the off-chance."

"Can I get your number?" I ask. "We need to catch up properly, go for a drink, have some dinner maybe. It's been far too long."

"Sure, that would be nice."

I walk him to the door and we hug again, more briefly this time. He opens the door to step into the street, but pauses in the doorway and turns back to me. He looks at me intently.

"You saved me," he says. "As much as I saved you from the fire, you saved me."

12

TEN YEARS AGO

"You saved me. You literally saved my life."

"It's just a pasta bake," I say.

"No, really," says Vivian, "you've saved my bacon. This is great. This is perfect."

Christ. She's going on about it like I just cured cancer. It's not even a good one. It's just a tin of tuna and grated cheese, and I've left it too long in the oven, so some of the packet pasta pokes out of the sauce like crispy brown fingers. Still, it's nice to be told I'm doing a good job. I always wonder what someone wants when they're nice to me. But maybe Vivian really does think my pasta bake is some kind of Jamie Oliver banquet.

It goes on like this for a few days, with me doing bits of housework and feeding the kids while Vivian and Jeffrey get on with work and stuff. I don't see much of Jeffrey. He's at work or playing golf. When he's here, he always seems in a bad mood. It makes me think about that poem Daniel showed me, about his dad's anger and the fact that he's a monster. You'd be amazed at the shit that goes on in the nicest of houses. It'd make your eyes water.

Daniel comes out of his room more than Vivian is used to. He doesn't talk to anyone, but he does talk to me when no one else is around. He bunks off school a lot but he even starts going on a few days, if I walk him. He's got a bike he likes to ride and he rides it up and down the road while I walk along the pavement. He could ride off on his own, but he doesn't. He produces a weird-looking pen and writes something on the frame of his bike. He says it's his postcode and house number, but it's invisible. He tells me it has ink that shows up in a special light, in case someone steals it. It feels like he's showing off to me a bit. I like that he likes me.

Sometimes when I pick him up from school he gets off his bike and pushes it along the pavement and talks to me about lessons or books he's read. He knows everything about everything and I don't understand a lot of what he says about science and history and stuff, but I like it that he talks to me. It makes me feel special that he bothers with me.

Vivian and Jeffrey don't pay me much in wages, but they pay for all my food, so I save everything I earn, and that piece of shit Liam can't rob it off me. For a couple of days I worry he'll show up, but he doesn't. I hope Vivian doesn't tell Shaniqua I'm living here when she gets her hair done. I think about saying something to Vivian, but I don't want her to think I hang out with the wrong sort of people, so I don't say anything.

I get on okay with Poppy. She's a pretty average kind of girl. Nothing like Daniel. Sometimes Vivian asks me to help Poppy with her homework, and we sit in her room staring at her books like a pair of right idiots, with no idea what we're looking at. Poppy doesn't care. We dump the homework and she chats to me about boys and stuff, like I'm some woman of the world or something, which I'm not.

After a week, Vivian asks me if I can stay here permanently. I say yes without even thinking. It's weird, but I already get a sense I belong here. I've been looking for somewhere safe to go, and this is it. Though it's not my family, they want me here. No one is getting paid to have me here. They're paying me!

It's Tuesday afternoon. Vivian and Jeffrey are at work and Poppy is at school. Daniel's in his room – it's one of his bunking-off days. I've been doing a deep clean behind the fridge and it's knackered me, pulling the great big metal coffin of a thing in and out. I'm sweating like a pig. I'm getting my puff back and drinking a glass of water when Daniel comes in.

"Hi," I say, peeling a sweaty strand of hair off my forehead. I must look a fright.

"Hello," he says. He goes to the fridge and takes out some milk.

"I've just cleaned behind there." Seeing Daniel take the milk out, it occurs to me it would have been a lot easier moving the fridge if I'd taken the stuff out first. Idiot.

"You wouldn't believe the crap that ends up behind a fridge," I say. I gesture to a heap of dust and food crumbs and bits of broken glass that must have pinged under there over the years. Daniel wanders over and looks at a pile of scrappy papers I've put on the kitchen table. "Those were under there too," I say. It's mainly rubbish, old Post-it notes with shopping lists and empty envelopes and ancient bills and things.

"It's inevitable," says Daniel as he leafs through the papers. "People stick things to the front of fridges because they want to keep them. But the fridge door is the thing that moves about most in a kitchen, so of course they fall off."

He doesn't sound like a kid. Most of the time he sounds like a grown-up. If he didn't look like a kid I'd think he was proper old, like forty or something.

"It's the gap underneath," I say, not really following him but wanting to join in. "They should get rid of that stupid gap."

"It's so heat from the condenser coils can circulate," he says, whatever the hell condenser coils are.

"You're so clever, Daniel," I say. "How do you know all this stuff? I mean, you plug it in, it gets cold – that's all I know. God, you must think I'm a right thicko."

"No I don't," he says defensively. "You're amazing."

No one's ever said anything like that to me before. A warm feeling washes down my body, like a blush that turns into a funny feeling in my stomach, like when you get hunger pangs.

Daniel is looking down, leafing through the bits of paper. He stops at a page I noticed before, a coloured pencil drawing of a mum and dad and boy and girl, in front of a house with criss-cross windows and a yellow sun with sunbeam lines coming off it, and a garden with flowers.

"Who drew that," I ask, "you or Poppy?"

"My dad hates me," says Daniel quietly.

"I'm sure he doesn't," I say. But what the hell do I know? Maybe he does. Daniel just keeps looking at the drawing of the happy family.

"He does," he says. "He hates me. He's up to no good. He keeps secrets. He was meeting another woman from his work. I heard him on his phone. I know what was going on and he hates me for it."

"Does your mum know?" I ask.

"Not about the other woman," he says. "She knows Dad hates me. He locks me in my room. He hits me. Now you're here he can't get away with it. He's too much of a coward to do it in the open. Mum pretends it isn't happening. She's weak. That's as bad as doing it, don't you think? Knowing about it and just letting it happen?"

I don't know what to say. Kids have a shit time and no one stands up for them.

"They tell lies about me," he says. "They make stuff up with the school so no one will believe me about what they're like. The school are on their side. Poppy's their favourite. They never wanted me. Look!"

He waves the drawing at me.

"Poppy has no idea. Look how she's drawn me smiling!" He throws the drawing on the table in a tired sort of way, like he's a little old man who's given up.

I'm out of my depth. I don't understand why he's telling me all this. Why he's telling *me*. Maybe he can tell what I'm really like, who I really am. Tracey. He's right about kids not being believed. No one would believe me about Rob taking my money or Craig looking at my tits. No one cares. It's easier to just say nothing.

But Daniel *has* said something. And he's chosen me. That feels important. I want to help him like no one ever helped me. But what can I do about it? He says I'm amazing, but I'm not. I'm nothing special. I'm nothing at all.

I sip my glass of water, trying to get my head round what Daniel just told me.

"Daniel, I want to help you. I do. But I don't think I know how to."

Daniel looks at me with his stormy eyes. "I told you," he says, "you're amazing."

"I'm not," I say. "I'm just... ordinary."

"You're not ordinary. You're extraordinary."

I shake my head. The more he says it, the more I feel pathetic and hopeless. He's chosen the wrong person.

"You think you're ordinary," Daniel says, "like that water." He points to the glass. "But you're not. Water isn't ordinary. It's two invisible gasses combined to make something you can hold in a glass. That water you're drinking has been part of oceans, it's drifted through the sky as clouds, it's fallen as rain. It's been drunk by dinosaurs and cried by Egyptian pharaohs, and bathed in by Roman emperors. It's travelled across the universe. It's been here since the beginning of time. It's existed for 13.8 billion years. And it will be here for another 13.8 billion after we've gone. Don't be fooled just because something looks ordinary."

I can't describe what I'm feeling. What he's saying sucks all the air out of the room. I feel dizzy.

"You're made of the same stuff," Daniel goes on. "You're made of stuff from the Big Bang that was born in the hearts of stars. Every atom in your body was created in the fiery death of a star. You're literally stardust. You're part of everything that ever was and everything that ever will be."

I feel my stomach tighten, like hunger or nerves. I never felt like I was anything before, but Daniel makes me feel different. Like I'm connected to something. Connected to everything.

"I told you because you're special, Ariana. You're important. You matter."

My breath catches in my throat. No one has ever made me feel like this before.

Loved.

For the first time I feel like I can be someone who makes a difference. I can be someone who matters. And I know I won't ever, ever let Daniel down.

Finally I manage to speak. My voice is barely a whisper. "What do you want me to do?"

PART 2

13

NOW

"What do you want me to do?"

Cassandra and I are working away at our laptops when the door opens and Daniel appears. He stands in the gallery office, jacket over his shoulder and shirt sleeves rolled up, like he's ready for anything. We went for coffee yesterday, and he said he had a lot of spare time on his hands and was up for helping in any way he could.

And here he is.

I see Cassandra staring at him. I understand why, but it's embarrassing. Even though I'm anticipating the burns on his face, they still shock me, so I get why Cassandra can't look away. I feel I should stop her somehow.

"Cassandra," I say, "this is Daniel, an old friend of mine. He's going to help out around here for a few days. General admin, art handling, that sort of thing."

Daniel smiles. "Hi, Cassandra."

"Okay, great," says Cassandra, then looks away.

"Hey, Cassandra," says Daniel. "You can look at me."

Cassandra smiles. "Thanks." She goes back to her computer.

"No," says Daniel to her, "I mean, *really* look at me. It's okay. You don't have to pretend I don't look different. I know I do."

Cassandra meets Daniel's eyes. She doesn't look away. Something happens in the room. It's electric. She just looks at him and he looks back. I don't know how long they stay like that. His confidence and bravery are extraordinary. He's amazing.

"Listen," I say, "I've got to go for a meeting. I'll leave you with Cassandra. She can point you in the right direction."

"No worries," says Daniel.

I leave them to it, happy to have Daniel back in my life again. I get the car out of the world's most expensive car park and drive home. I'm meeting Phillip Tench, the little baldy guy who accosted me at the funeral. He's left several voice-mails offering to help and suggesting we should talk, and though I'm finding him pushy and annoying, I figure he knows a lot about gallery stuff, and if he knew Henry then maybe he can be helpful to me.

When I get to the house he's already there, parked up in his black Range Rover.

"Mrs Clough," he says as I get out, marching over to meet me with his arm extended for yet another handshake.

"Sorry I'm late," I say, even though I'm not late. He's early by about fifteen minutes. "And it's Ariana, please. Come on in."

Tench scampers up the drive behind me and we go into the house. I see him scan the artwork in the hall on the way through. I make us a coffee and we sit at the kitchen table. He's wearing the same pinstripe suit he had on the other day, but now he's got a silk bow tie with blue and white polka dots. As he sits, the legs of his trousers ride up and I notice his socks in bright-coloured stripes. He looks like a circus clown on a tea break.

"So, Ariana, how is it going?"

He meshes his fingers together and gives me a syrupy smile like a second-hand car salesman. I tell him about the show that's just finished, the challenges of the art market as I see it, and my plans for the future, including Cassandra's idea of meeting with all the artists.

"Well," he says at last, "it sounds like you *have* been a busy bee." He sits back in his chair and purses his lips, then heaves a thoughtful sigh, like he's weighing it all up. "Ariana. Can I be candid with you?"

"Please do."

"The art market isn't what it was, all puffed out with city boys on big bonuses, filling their Canary Wharf apartments with big shiny sculptures and hoovering up hot painters as fast as the art schools could churn them out. There's recession. There's trade wars. Brexit. Covid. These things cast a very long shadow. Now we have to work for a living!"

He laughs at his own joke, which feels painfully rehearsed.

"I admire Henry, and what he tried. He took an East End gallery and gave it a good shot on Cork Street. Very brave. But, with one or two exceptions, he brought artists with him who were more East End than West End, if you follow my drift. By all means have your coffees and cakes with them, but I fear you'll be holding on to the millstones that pulled Henry under."

Pompous little fucker. I feel like picking my coffee cup up and hurling it at his grotesque shiny head.

"You said you might be able to help, Phillip," I say, managing to keep a lid on it.

He puffs out his cheeks. "As I say, I'm underwhelmed on the whole with the roster of artists you have, but there's a possibility of doing something interesting with one or two of them under the right circumstances. I wondered if you might allow me to take the burden of the artists and the gallery lease off your hands."

I wasn't expecting that. I try to get my head round the idea. Maybe this could be a way out of things. Henry's work can carry on in a way. And I might be able to salvage something. Save this house.

"Thanks, Phillip," I say at last. "Did you have a sum in mind?"

"Hmmmm..." There's a very long pause. "Let me have a think about that, Ariana. I'll give it my most serious consideration."

He takes a notebook out of his jacket pocket and jots some figures, thinks, sips his coffee, scribbles some more. It's all very theatrical. Finally he writes a number down and draws a line under it.

"The filthy business of commerce," he says. "But alas, there is sometimes no other way. Might this suffice?"

He turns the pad around so I can see the number he's written. I don't know what I was expecting, but what he's offered is a tiny fraction of what I need. He's lucky I don't jam his wanky fountain pen in his piggy little eye. But I don't have many options, so I bite my tongue.

"It's a big decision. I'll need to think about it."

"Tick tock tick tock," says Tench with an oily smile. He tears out the page with the insultingly small number from his little notebook and leaves it on the table, then puts the book away.

I walk him to the door. He pauses in the hallway to look at a painting by the stairs.

"Oh, is that a James Balentine?" he asks casually. I know he knows it is, because I saw him clock it on the way in. James Balentine is the artist Henry represented the longest. A bit of a star back in the day, by all accounts.

"Yes, I think so," I say.

"Don't suppose you'd consider selling it, would you?" asks Tench. "I think I know someone who might be interested in one from this period. We could go fifty-fifty on it."

"I don't think so," I say. "It was one of Henry's favourites. Not for sale, I'm afraid."

"Pity," says Tench. He peers at the painting more closely. "Actually, now I look at it, there's a bit of damage to the canvas, see? Some wear around the frame. Probably not what someone would be after in its current condition. Ah well."

I watch him waddle off down the path in his horrible suit, like a toad late for a court appointment.

"I'll email you!" he calls as he speeds off.

In the hall, I look at the James Balentine painting. It's galling the little bastard is right about the damage. In a fit of pique I take the picture down and stomp into the street, loading it in the back of my car. I'll take it to an art restorer later. I should have used gloves and wrapped it properly, but I was too pissed off. Some gallerist I am! Too late now. I'll just have to drive round corners slowly so it doesn't rattle about.

Back at the gallery, Daniel and Cassandra are carefully wrapping artwork, making me feel doubly guilty about the painting I've just dumped unceremoniously in the boot of my car.

"Careful with those drawings," I say, rather snappily. "That non-reflective glass is a pain to clean if you touch it."

"Don't worry," says Daniel. He holds up his scarred hands and wiggles his fingers. "One plus of getting these babies burnt. No fingerprints."

I'm not in the mood for jokes. I collapse at my desk and stare into space.

"Are you okay?" asks Daniel. My temper must be obvious.

No. I'm not okay. I'd set my hopes on Tench helping me dig myself out of this hole, but now the hole feels like a grave and Tench is standing on the edge of it, kicking soil down on my head. This might be the end. I think I'm finished.

"I was just going for a sandwich," says Cassandra. "Anyone want anything?" She takes our orders and makes a tactful retreat into the street.

"What's up?" asks Daniel. And I tell him – everything I've been holding inside me for days, all about the financial worries, Henry's debts, the house, and the offer from Tench. I unscrew the crumpled scrap of paper I'm holding in my fist and toss it onto the table so Daniel can see the pitiful number Tench offered.

"It's hopeless," I say to him. "It's over." Even though I feel utterly deflated, it's a relief to have someone to talk to.

"Ariana, listen," says Daniel. His voice is low and calm. "If you didn't know everything that was going on, I'm sure it was because Henry loved you and wanted to protect you. He was an amazing man who came along at an extremely tough time in your life and rescued you."

And Daniel doesn't know the half of it, my crap childhood and years in foster homes.

"Now you're at a tough time in your life again," Daniel continues, "and you were hoping Phillip Tench might rescue you. But you don't need anyone to rescue you. You can do your own rescuing. You're amazing."

It's sweet of him to say it, but I don't feel amazing.

"I'm not," I say. "I feel like a fraud. I feel like a straw man. Not solid, like Henry was, or you, or like this table. I feel like people can see right through me."

"Listen. This table," says Daniel, rapping his knuckles on it, "it looks solid, but it isn't. It's just a cloud of molecules jiggling about, neutrons held together by electrons. It's the same with us. We're just a cloud of atoms, we're mostly empty space. The wrong kind of energy can split us apart, but the right kind of energy keeps us solid. You're as solid and substantial and capable as anyone I've ever met."

Daniel's brilliant. I can never follow it entirely but somehow he makes sense of everything.

"Tench is nothing," he continues. "He's just a maggot hungry for what he can get for himself. He only wants to serve himself. He's nothing compared to you. He's all empty space. Don't entertain his offer. Don't even give it a second thought."

I loved Henry. I did, with all my heart. But if I'm honest, I never felt he really understood me. He rescued me from my bad life. But he never made me feel like this, like Daniel does now. There's a bond between us I can't fully explain. There's a force that ties us together. What we've shared, who we are, what we've done together and never told another soul. Henry rescued me in one way, but Daniel walked into fire for me. He makes me feel invincible.

Before I know it, I pick up my phone.

"Hello, Phillip," I say. "I've given our conversation careful consideration and I've come to the decision you can shove your offer up your arse, you slimy little prick."

I hang up. I feel elated. I could dance around the gallery screaming.

I feel I could do anything.

I *can* do anything.

Daniel's back.

14

TEN YEARS AGO

"Daniel's back."

It's half past nine at night when the front door slams and we hear feet thundering up the stairs.

"Jeffrey, Daniel's back!" Vivian yells into the back of the house, where Jeffrey hides himself away in his study, when he's around at all. He makes the odd appearance, like an angry ghost, clanking his golf clubs in and out of the house. But otherwise, you wouldn't know he lived here at all.

There's been a right commotion for the last few hours. Daniel went out this morning on his bike. Everyone figured he'd gone to school, though I don't know why. It's completely hit-and-miss whether he goes to school or not. Anyway, there was no sign of him when school finished. Still no sign an hour later. Poppy hadn't seen him between classes or at lunchtime. Vivian spoke to the school, who said he hadn't been there all day. Since then Vivian's been on her phone for hours, calling people. I don't know who she'd call. Daniel doesn't have any friends. Apparently he's never disappeared like this before.

Jeffrey storms out of his office and we listen to the thump of his feet up the stairs, then hammering on Daniel's door. There's shouting – *let me in* – *get out* – *get away from the door* – *get out of my room* – that sort of thing. Then from the sound of it, Jeffrey gets into Daniel's room and the door shuts. There's more shouting and protesting from both of them. It's all muffled and I can't make any of it out.

Vivian flops down at the kitchen table and refills her enormous glass of wine. She's been hitting the booze hard between phone calls, and she's onto her second solo bottle.

"He'll be the death of me, that boy," she mutters, either to me or to herself, chucking her head back and swilling down a mouthful of wine like she's taking a pill. She starts to tell me things about Daniel, how he was difficult even when he was a baby, how he doesn't love her whatever she does for him, how there was some trouble with violence towards another pupil at school, which Daniel denied and they could never prove was him. She's not even telling me, really, just getting it off her chest, I reckon.

Lots of what she says sounds familiar. She doesn't know what kids are like. It sounds like most of the kids I've known in care, and I've done all of it myself. I think she's telling me all this so I'll be on her side. But it just makes me believe the stuff Daniel told me about them. They don't get him. He's a kid just like I was. Like I still am, maybe.

There's a door slam. Jeffrey thumps down the stairs and into the kitchen.

"He won't say where he's been, or what he's been up to. Well, he's missed dinner so he'll bloody well have to go without. Sod him."

I think of the plate of dinner Vivian put out for him

hours ago, getting cold on the table, then getting covered in foil and put in the fridge.

Jeffrey disappears back into his office with another door slam. Vivian picks up her glass and bottle of wine and goes into the other room. After a minute I hear the TV go on.

I sit there, wondering what to do.

I don't want to make any noise, so I half fill a saucepan with water and put it on the gas, then take the covered plate from the fridge and put it over the saucepan. It'll take longer to heat like this, but I can't risk the ping of the microwave. After ten minutes I put the plate and a fork on a tray and tiptoe upstairs.

"Daniel," I whisper. Nothing. "Daniel? It's me, Ariana."

After a moment, the door opens a chink. I push it and go into the half-light of the heat lamps from his snake tanks. Daniel's over the other side of the room, curled up on the duvet with his face buried in a pillow.

"I brought you some cottage pie," I say, and put the tray on the floor. I sit on the edge of his bed. He doesn't move and I don't think he's crying, but he might be. I reach out and put my hand on his shoulder. As I sit there with my hand resting on his shoulder, it doesn't feel weird or anything. It feels like he might be my little brother, and I like it.

Daniel looks up at me and I see he isn't crying. His face looks blank. One of his eyes is red and bruised, and there's blood on his cheek.

"My dad did it," is all he says.

I feel a lot of stuff go through me. I'm angry and sad and I don't know what to do. I still have my hand on his shoulder and he leans against me, and my hand slips round his back, so I have my arm round him. We sit there for a long time while the cottage pie goes cold. We're facing the window.

The curtains are open and it's a clear, dark sky. The window is a big square of black.

"I'm sorry," is all I can say to him. I want him to know someone cares.

"It's okay," he says, staring at the window. "It doesn't matter."

"I know it feels shit now," I say, "but one day all this will feel better."

"The universe is 13.8 billion years old," he says. "One black eye won't make any difference."

I don't know what he means, but we just sit there looking at the black square of night. We look at the stars, and how big and empty the night is, and I find it scary how small and unimportant I feel. But also it makes it okay at the same time. Whatever I do it doesn't really matter, so why bother worrying about it?

Eventually the rest of the house goes dark and I get up and wish him goodnight. I take the tray out and go back to my room. I lie awake, thinking about Daniel and Jeffrey and what I'm going to do about it all. Then I fall asleep.

IN THE MORNING when I wake up I'm lying on my bed still with all my clothes on. My shoes are by the side of the bed and I don't remember taking them off but I must have. At the end of my bed there's a bit of paper, and when I lean down and pick it up it's a folded paper star. It's beautiful. I can see there's writing on it, and I don't want to unfold it because it's so pretty, but I can't read it as it is. I recognise the writing as Daniel's from his homework the other evening. I open it carefully, trying to remember the moves so I'll be able to fold it up again, but I soon get lost. I flatten out the paper and see it's another poem.

Before the Spark
The world was dead and cold, before the spark,
A vacant, silent, endless, empty space.
No stars, no light, no joy, no hope, all dark,
Just nothingness, a sad and lonely place.
A vacuum, missing warmth or gleaming glow,
A universe empty of love or laughter.
No comfort comes, no hope for light to grow,
Just endless dark, no happy ever after.
Then came the flash and burst of fire's light,
Exploding through the dark and empty skies.
A surge of heat, a force that shone so bright,
A dawn that made new worlds before my eyes.
From lonely cold to blazing light above,
Creation's fire, lighting my life with love.

I sit there looking down at the crumpled paper on my lap. The poem Daniel has written for me. There's a faint tap on the paper and I notice a patch of the ink has run. It's wet. My cheek is wet too. A teardrop has fallen from my face onto the paper.

Daniel's twelve, and he's the cleverest person I've ever met. He's twelve, and he's written me a love poem, and it's the most wonderful, amazing thing anyone has ever done in my life.

Deep down, I've always felt useless. No one wanted me. But for the first time, there might be a reason I'm here.

I have to save him. I'll do anything to save him. Anything.

15

NOW

"Anything?" I ask.

"Well no, not *anything*," says Cassandra. "I mean, don't offer to have sex with them swinging from the light fittings. Not unless you want to. But basically, promise anything to keep the artists with the gallery for now and we can worry about what you've promised later on."

I've been working through the list Cassandra wrote a couple of weeks back, all the artists and their contact details. It's in two columns. The first is the 'good' list, the artists who are nice, understanding, or who'll be desperate to stay with the gallery no matter what. The second column is the 'bad' list – artists Cassandra says are difficult, or downright unpleasant, or who are actually good and might look to jump ship to another gallery.

I'm working my way through the bad list. I've spent a pretty humiliating week courting them over a series of expensive dinners, my face frozen in a forced grin, listening to all their whinging anxieties and absurd demands. It's like being trapped in a nightmare of speed dating where your date is vile but the bell to switch tables never rings.

Cassandra is fabulous at filling me in on all I need to know. Her capacity for being charming to their faces and scathing about them behind their backs is the only enjoyable thing about the whole miserable experience. I'd like to chuck my spaghetti carbonara into some of their smug faces, but instead I just have to grin and suck it up.

I have two more artists to see. The first is a woman called Samantha Dodds who makes sculptures like a sofa half-buried in cement, or a desk disappearing into the floor. Cassandra says they *symbolise the overwhelming nature of modern life.* All I know is they're big ugly cement things no one has room for in their house. I'm dreading the painful lunch I've arranged with her this afternoon.

The last one on the list is James Balentine, the artist whose painting I still have sitting in the boot of my car. I've left several cheery voicemails to which he hasn't replied. After the third call, I'm ready to give up. But Cassandra won't let me. Balentine, or 'JB' as he cringingly nicknames himself, is the gallery's best-known artist. She says we can't afford to lose him. If he goes, everything will come down like a house of cards.

I'm staring into space when my mobile rings and JB's number flashes up. I answer, with as much fake joviality as I can muster. "Hello. Ariana Clough."

"Oh, hello," says a woman's voice, completely throwing me. "This is Elspeth Balentine."

"Oh, hello, Elspeth," I say. There's an awkward pause, and I can't work out whether she's going to say any more, or I'm supposed to say something. Finally she speaks.

"JB doesn't like the phone, but he got your messages.

He'd be happy to meet with you. When were you thinking of coming?"

Cassandra pushes a pad towards me. She's scribbled *North Yorkshire*.

"Ah," I say, "I was rather hoping we could meet in London. Does JB have any plans to be down at all any time soon?"

"Oh no," the woman says. She has a wobbly voice, like an old lady. I've been assuming it's his wife, as I know he's sixty or so, but maybe it's his mother. "JB doesn't like London, but he'll see you here if you like. He has some time at the end of this week."

So that's it. No option. I have to suffer a demeaning lunch with the sort of man who gives himself a nickname, and I have to travel all the way to the backwoods of Yorkshire to do it.

That's the whole list spoken to. It's one ordeal of sorts over, but it hasn't solved anything, in spite of the encouraging pep talk Cassandra gives me. Nothing's changed yet. The bills keep coming in.

Cassandra points at the clock and reminds me I'm due at Andrew Edmunds in ten minutes for my lunch with Samantha Dodds. I don't know where Daniel is. He said he'd be in this morning, but there's no sign of him. I'll have to leave Cassandra holding the fort on her own. I grab my jacket and hurry out across Soho, walking faster than I'd like to in these heels. I arrive a minute late, feeling sweaty. Annoyingly, Samantha is there and I'm already on the back foot.

I make small talk as we order. Samantha goes for a salad with ox tongue and a roast boar chop. Even her food choices feel confrontational, like she could rip wild animals apart with her bare hands.

Talk moves to Henry and how they met, fifteen years ago when she'd just done her MA. Her anecdotes make me warm up to her a bit. She talks about Henry fondly and it feels like he's in the room. For the first time I begin to feel I might make this work, might find a way of continuing Henry's project in a way I could enjoy.

The waitress clears the starters and I nip to the loo. I find myself in a queue for the toilet behind a couple of women in smart tailored suits. I lean against the wall and feel slightly lightheaded from the lunchtime drinking even though I've only had a couple of glasses. The women in front of me seem to take ages. I'm aware I've left Samantha waiting and I don't want the rapport between us to seep away while I'm gone. Finally I get in and pee.

As I head back to the table I see a man standing next to Samantha, chatting to her. I immediately recognise the shiny pinhead of Phillip Tench. He's leaning over, close to her. He has his hand resting on the heavy material of the tablecloth. They're both laughing about something. I stop in the doorway to watch their easy conversation, and any positivity I feel drains away. Tench spots me and, without breaking his laugh, he takes a step backwards and retreats towards his table.

I come over and sit down.

"I must say," says Samantha, "this wine is absolutely delicious."

Neither of us makes any mention of Tench. We carry on talking about art, Samantha's plans for future work, about anything but Tench. Our main courses arrive and we eat. Tench is in my eyeline, gobbling away at a table of people I don't recognise, a smart-looking couple who might be collectors and a pretty young girl who could be their daughter or Tench's gallery assistant. At one point Tench catches my eye and gives me a little smile.

The prick. I know his game. He's trying to move in on my artists, anyone he thinks might be profitable for him. Samantha or anyone else. The oily little shit is trying to destroy me because I turned his offer down. He'll probably win as well. He doesn't even need to pay me the tiny sum he offered. If I go bust, he'll just pick up the pieces for nothing.

I stare at him, grinning away.

Samantha chews on her chop. I'm so pissed off I can't think of anything to say. We just eat in awkward silence. Five minutes ago I was feeling like things might work out. But the good mood has seeped away.

It's gone.

16

TEN YEARS AGO

It's gone.

I've looked everywhere but I can't find it.

My ID, the fake one Liam got for me, with my new name on it. It's gone. I've hunted through my bag and in the drawers in my room and under my bed. It's not here. I don't understand it. I haven't taken it anywhere. I can't have lost it. That can only mean one thing. Someone has been in my room.

Then I have an idea.

"Hi, Poppy," I say, knocking on her door.

Poppy's in her bedroom, listening to music while she does her homework, some Jess Glynne song I don't know the name of.

"Oh hi," she says, looking up and smiling.

"How's it going?" I ask a bit too cheerfully and looking like an idiot, I bet. I go in and sit on her bed. I make stupid idle conversation about her friends and what she's been up to. I'm wondering if Poppy has taken my ID to sneak into a club or to buy alcohol or cigarettes. I don't want to make it obvious I suspect her, and I can't ask her directly, but it turns out I'm useless at asking the right questions and my fishing expedition gets me nowhere. She must wonder what the hell I want. I feel stupid and embarrassed, so I make something up on the spot, grab a pile of her dirty clothes and say I'm putting a wash on. I go out.

I haven't found anything out, but Poppy didn't seem at all guilty. If anything, I was the one acting all guilty. Anyway, Poppy's not the sort to sneak around and break rules. She's a bit of a goody-goody if I'm honest. Drinking cider and smoking fags in the park isn't her style.

I wonder if Daniel took it. He couldn't use it for anything, as it's got my picture on it. But I know he likes me. I wonder whether he wants my photograph. Even as I think that, I feel stupid. A twelve-year-old isn't going to want some naff photo of me that's about the size of a postage stamp.

I wait until everyone else is out of the house. I stand outside Daniel's bedroom and knock. I still don't know how I'm going to ask him. "Daniel, it's me, Ariana," I say in a whisper, my face pressed close to the door.

"Come in," he says.

As usual, the curtains are closed and the only light is the yellow glow of the heat lamps from the tanks. Daniel is sitting on the bed with something black cradled in his hands. At first I think it's a mobile phone.

But then I see it's one of his big spiders.

My stomach tightens, and I can feel my heart thudding in my chest. I've never been good with spiders. They terrify me, those quick, jerky movements, the long legs that seem to move in every direction at once. That horrible way you spot them just as they disappear under the sofa.

But Daniel's different with them. He's so gentle. He

turns his hands like a dancer, and the spider keeps walking to stay balanced on top.

Daniel looks up at me. "Come closer," he says softly.

His voice is like the lights from the tanks, like a warm blanket wrapping around me. I want to shake my head to say no. I want to turn and leave. But something in the way he's looking at me makes it impossible to go. I watch his hand move and the spider move and it's like I'm hypnotised.

"It's okay," Daniel says. "She won't hurt you."

I glance at the spider with its body so close to his fingers. I feel a rush of fear, the kind that sits in the pit of my stomach and spreads like ice through my veins. It's not just the spider – it's everything I've ever been afraid of.

"Come on," Daniel says again. It's like he can see straight through my fear, past the surface stuff to all the darker things underneath. "You can do this," he says.

I force my feet to move, step by step, until I'm standing right in front of him. My chest is tight.

"Hold out your hand," he tells me.

My hand is trembling as I reach it out. The spider's legs brush against my skin and I almost pull back, but Daniel's voice catches me.

"Just breathe," he says. "It's okay. You're safe."

Slowly, the spider walks onto my hand. It's so light it's like a whisper against my skin. It feels strange and unsettling, but not as terrifying as I thought it would be. It's almost gentle.

"You're doing it," Daniel says, and something sounds like pride in his voice. "See? You're stronger than you think."

I look at the spider, at the way it moves across my hand, and I can't believe I'm doing this. Ten minutes ago, I would have said it was impossible, that I could never, ever do this. But here I am. I'm doing it.

Daniel reaches out his hand towards mine, and our fingers touch, making a bridge. The spider walks from my hand to his. I drop my arm and I realise I'm grinning like an idiot as Daniel smiles at me.

My stomach feels like the spider felt on my hand, nervous, but excited as well. If I can do this, maybe I can do other things too. Maybe I can do anything.

Daniel puts the spider back in its tank. I realise I got distracted and remember why I came in here.

"Daniel," I say, as casually as I can, "you haven't seen my ID kicking around, have you? I've lost it."

I watch him for any kind of reaction, to see if I've caught him out, but he doesn't flinch.

"Where did you lose it?" he asks.

"That's the stupid thing," I say, "I thought it was in my room. I don't remember moving it."

He looks at me for a moment, thinking.

"Dad," he says. "My dad must have taken it."

That makes no sense.

"I know he's horrible to you," I say, "but why would he take my ID?"

Daniel laughs. "He doesn't like people knowing stuff. I found out about him and look what he did to me. He didn't ask you here, did he? Mum did."

That's true.

"You're a stranger. He doesn't know you. He wants to know who you are. He can see you and I are friends. He must wonder what I'm telling you about him. He won't like you knowing."

I don't shiver, but I feel a kind of cold go up me, like

someone has walked over my grave. I want to protect Daniel, but I never thought about me. I didn't think I'd have to protect myself.

We go downstairs and Daniel says he'll keep watch in the hall. I'm scared, but I sneak into Jeffrey's study. It's a big room. He's got a big wooden desk with papers in neat piles and a computer with an enormous screen, more like a TV than a computer. There's a grey sofa against the wall, and bookshelves next to it. I'm scared to touch anything in case he knows someone's been in here, but I look around and I can't see my ID. Of course, he wouldn't leave it lying around where anyone could see it.

I make a mental note of where his chair is, a swivel chair on wheels. I sit on the chair and look at the drawers in his desk. I half hope they'll be locked, so I can stop this and go out, but when I pull one, it opens.

There's a pile of papers. I don't read anything as it all looks boring. I scroll through them carefully, like a deck of cards, seeing if my ID is in between. But it isn't. I push the drawer back closed again. I start to panic I'm making it obvious I've been here. My heart is thumping away and I feel shaky.

I open another drawer and this one has loads of bits and pieces in it, business cards and dozens of old cables for phone chargers and whatever. I'll never be able to move any of this and get it back as it is, so I decide not to scrabble about in here. But as I'm closing the drawer the light catches on something and I stop. There's something plastic in with the business cards. I carefully reach my hand past the cables, like I'm playing that stupid Operation game and trying not to set off the buzzer. I pick up a business card. And there it is, lying next thing up.

My ID.

A million thoughts go through my head all at once. Why has he got this? Does he know it's a fake and I'm not who I say I am? Does he know I'm Tracey Jones?

I carefully put my ID back where it was and slide the door shut.

"It's in his desk," I tell Daniel.

He isn't at all surprised. "Did you leave it?" he asks.

"Yes," I say. "What do we do?"

"Nothing," says Daniel. "He doesn't know we're on to him. We wait."

So that's what we do. We carry on as normal.

It goes on for a couple of days, and every time Jeffrey comes into a room I feel my heart speed up about a billion miles an hour. I don't look at him. I feel I'm acting so weirdly everyone must know what's going on, but no one notices or says anything.

Then a few days later I'm in my room looking for some makeup and there it is in my bag. My ID. Like it was there all the time. Except it wasn't.

I hurry to show Daniel as soon as I get a chance.

"He's covering his tracks," he says. "Now there's no evidence. Except, we know."

Later that day, I'm in my room when Daniel knocks on the door.

"Come with me," he says.

He leads the way and I follow him down the stairs and through the hall. He's holding a torch. I realise with dread he's leading me towards Jeffrey's study. I stop walking.

"Everyone's out," he says.

"What are we doing?"

"He's not the only one who can keep secrets," Daniel

says with a kind of weird smile. He takes my hand and pulls me after him to the study door. He turns the handle and pushes it open. The Venetian blinds are tilted half-closed, and it's gloomy in here, but not so dark we need a torch. Daniel reaches into his pocket and pulls something out. It's his security pen, the one he used to write on his bike in invisible ink. He waves the torch at me. "Ultraviolet light," he says.

He switches on the torch. The study walls explode into life with marks that were invisible until now.

Monster. Bastard. Tyrant. Hypocrite. Betrayer. Liar. Child-beater. Adulterer. Coward. Manipulator. Deceiver. Home-Wrecker. Soul-Killer. Destroyer of Dreams. False Idol.

"Imagine him sitting in here," says Daniel, "doing his work, on his calls, showing off to people, and all the while he has no idea this is staring down at him, telling him who he really is."

Every wall is covered, floor to ceiling, in a wild, glowing scrawl.

"It gives me power over him," says Daniel, smiling.

It's mad. But it's brilliant. It's full of rage and hatred, but I understand. It's easy to be a victim and not fight back.

A serious look clouds over Daniel's face. "A person doesn't have to know you're getting revenge for you to get revenge."

Then he turns to me and grins. He grins like he's just had the best idea ever.

17

NOW

"Best idea ever, this," says Daniel.

I've been looking forward to properly catching up with Daniel. But we've been on the road now for nearly six hours. Six bloody hours. And JB, as I'm obliged to call him, is at the end of it. Like a pot of shit at the end of a motorway rainbow.

Daniel met me at six this morning and we took the gallery van, stopping briefly in Camden to drop that painting in at the restorer's before it gets any more bashed about in the boot of my car. Then up to the M1 and out of London, depressing miles of motorway all feeling the same, like you haven't gone anywhere.

I look at Daniel behind the wheel. I think about the scar damage across his face. I still can't get over how extensive it is. It's shocking. But sitting here on his left, as he faces the road, he barely looks scarred at all. Sure, I can see the change in his hairline, the peculiar profile of his nose where it's been reconstructed. But the less injured side of his face shows what he might have looked like without the fire. A normal, ordinary, attractive twenty-two-year-old man. It makes me sad, thinking about the other life he could have lived, the ordinary life without the fire.

Not that there was ever anything ordinary about Daniel.

We chat happily for a while. But after an hour or so I sink into a miserable fug, staring out of the window. The journey isn't good for me. Too much time to think about bills and expenses and bloody Phillip Tench.

After an eternity we hit the edge of the North York Moors and JB's little village, Glaisdale. It's all grey stone buildings and incredible views. In the abstract it's beautiful. But after six hours in a van I couldn't give a shit what it looks like. All I think is that it's too bloody far from London. Have we really said we'll do this round trip in a day? Madness.

It's noon when we drive out of the village and find ourselves on a rise where we pull into where JB lives. It's a dilapidated old farmhouse, with crumbling dry stone walls and a rusting caravan with ruptured tyres that can't have been used for twenty years. As we park and get out, a woman opens the front door and greets us.

"JB's out for his walk. He won't be long."

This must be the Mrs JB I spoke to on the phone. I'm pissed off he isn't here, but Daniel is upbeat and smiling. He walks over and shakes her hand. I see her react in horror to Daniel's scars and almost leap back in shock before she plasters a smile on again. But Daniel doesn't flinch at all. He just keeps chatting. Is this what it's like for him, fifty times a day? How strong do you have to be to take that in your stride and not sink into a hole?

We go in. The kitchen has dark stone flags on the floor and a black slate worktop with dark wooden cabinets. Whatever the opposite of welcoming is, it's this. We have tea.

Then more tea. There's a weird cuckoo clock on the wall, ticking loudly in the echoey room.

"Can we call him maybe?" I ask hopefully.

"Oh no," says Mrs JB as if the idea is absurd. "He never takes his phone on walks. He hates to be disturbed."

Of course he does.

It's another hour before JB finally comes in, wax jacket and knackered walking boots, long grey hair all thrown about in a tangle. He looks like a scarecrow that's been tipped over in a gale and blown in through the front door.

"Ah, there you are," he blusters in a gruff tone that suggests it's us who are late and he's the one who's been waiting. I can feel the anger bubbling under my skin, but I push it down.

He sits heavily at the table and starts unlacing his boots.

"Henry was a good man," he says. "I'm sorry he's gone. We didn't always see eye to eye, but then I don't see eye to eye with most people."

He's a cantankerous old shit and he knows it. He wears it as a badge of honour. I know his game, laying down the battle lines. I need him to stay with the gallery and he knows it too. That gives him carte blanche to say anything.

"How do you plan to run that gallery now?" he asks. "Big shoes to fill, wouldn't you say?"

I force a smile, though it feels like my face might crack. "I've got plans I'd love to share with you, JB."

"Plans," he mutters, with a look on his face like I've just taken a shit on his kitchen table. I've already said the wrong thing. An old relic like him doesn't want plans. He won't want change. Bugger.

JB takes out a metal box and rolls himself the skinniest cigarette I've ever seen. He looks up and glances at Daniel briefly while he lights it, but doesn't react to his scars. He spits a tiny flake of tobacco from his lip and tilts back in his chair, balancing on the back legs in a way that gets you told off at school.

"Henry knew how to do things," he chunters on, "sometimes right, sometimes wrong. But he had vision. That's what the gallery needs, not some half-baked ideas. You've got to keep that vision alive."

I clench my fists under the table, digging my nails into my palms. I want to lash out, to punch him in his ugly yellow teeth and tell him to go fuck himself, but I can't. Not if I want to keep this gallery afloat.

"Look, JB, I'm not Henry. I wish he was still here too, God knows. But he isn't. However, I share the respect he had for you and your work and hope we'll be able to continue to support you."

I don't tell him I've had one of his lousy paintings bashing away in the boot of my car for days. I'd love to. That'd wipe the smug look off his craggy face.

I glance at JB's wife, busying herself with the teacups. She moves around like a ghost, utterly silent, always smiling, like she's been doing this for so long she's forgotten how to be anything else. I wonder what it's like living with a man like JB. To have your spirit slowly eroded until all that's left is this polite, nodding shell. She puts a mug down and JB leans towards it and drags it across the table. His fingernails are almost black with years of oil paint trapped under them. He stirs his tea slowly. His eyes narrow slightly as if he's sizing me up.

Stalemate.

Daniel sits in the corner, nursing his tea, staring at his feet as he chews thoughtfully on a biscuit. "I guess we could talk this round in circles," he says, "but there's only one way to find out." He sounds confident and authoritative. "You've got a show coming up and it's up to us to push it. Full-on production, no half-arsed stuff. Big and bold. Like Ariana plans. Like Henry would've done."

Daniel's got the measure of JB in an instant and seen what he wants. That straight-talking man-to-man directness. Plus a bit of blowing smoke up his arse to massage his ego. It's not Daniel at all. It's an act. But it's an act JB falls for. His expression shifts slightly, losing some of that hard edge.

"Let the dog see the rabbit, right?" says Daniel. "It's all blah blah blah until then."

"We'll make sure it's the best show the gallery's ever produced," I add, redundantly.

"Good," says JB, leaning forward again and landing the front legs of his chair on the floor. He stands. "Let's go to the studio," he says.

We go out, seen off in the doorway by his wife, still smiling silently like a halfwit. We cross the patch of ground in front of the house, Daniel beside JB, chatting away, with JB giving the occasional chuckle. I follow after. I hate all this macho bullshit, but it's working, so I leave Daniel to it. We come to a big old stone barn and JB unpadlocks a huge wooden door and swings it open.

The room is vast. Maybe it was an old cowshed or something. The concrete floor has chips and cracks, and the roof has a few missing tiles where I can see daylight, and bird shit on the rafters where the pigeons have got in. It must be freezing in winter.

JB leads us to one side where some repairs have been undertaken and a tarpaulin sail of a roof has been stretched across the ceiling to keep the weather out. There are several big canvasses turned to the wall up on bricks. Maybe thirty or so. Each one taller than me.

"Someone's been busy," I say, trying to lighten the tone.

Big fat nothing in reply from JB. Instead, he takes hold of the wooden batten on the back of one canvas and turns it round, then sets it down and steps back for us to admire it.

I'm not sure what I expected, but it wasn't this.

The painting is almost overwhelming, a storm of colours and bold, sweeping gestures. The brushstrokes are wild, almost chaotic, but there's a raw power that pulses through the thick layers of paint. Somehow it forms something coherent. It's like the landscape we've just driven through, the wild, sweeping smudges of paint like the rolling hills and ominous skies up here. It's dangerous and abandoned, as if the moors themselves have been forced into this canvas.

It's more than that even. There's something personal in it, something that feels like JB himself. Unwelcoming and angry and passionate. It's wild and beautiful too. Romantic in a way that I would never have imagined coming from him. I find myself irresistibly drawn to it.

And if I'm this captivated, others will be too.

"I have more," JB says gruffly. One after another, he reveals the paintings, each one infused with the same raw energy and connection to the landscape. Now I understand what Henry saw in all this stuff, and why he'd put up with a miserable old shit like JB. The results are worth the pain.

I don't need to play-act now. I just tell JB what I honestly think. That they're brilliant. That I know, without a doubt, I have to have these paintings for the gallery. I tell him it's not just about keeping the business afloat anymore – I want to be part of showing these paintings to an audience. That they're going to sell, and not because of Henry's reputation, or a gallery's 'vision', but because they're powerful, beautiful works of art that people won't be able to ignore.

"Alright then," is all JB says. And like that, we've agreed to do a show.

We settle back in the van at about 3 p.m. and buckle in for the long drive back. It won't be until about 10 p.m. before we get home. It's been a stupidly long haul, but I feel elated. I really might have a chance to save the gallery and prove something to that oily toad Phillip Tench while I'm at it.

"Well!" I say to Daniel, as we pull out of the farmyard. It's the first time we've been alone since we arrived.

"I know," says Daniel. "What an insufferable cunt. And those awful paintings!"

"You didn't like them?" I ask in surprise.

"God no. Like some half-baked school exhibition." He stops himself. "You did?"

"Yes," I say, beginning to doubt myself, "yes, I did."

"Oh," says Daniel, "I thought you were bullshitting."

We sit in awkward silence as I drive too fast on the bendy roads, braking too hard, grinding the gears.

Then I feel Daniel's hand on mine, on the gear leaver as I make another reckless turn. "Maybe you're right," he says at last. "But that's the funny thing about art. There's no right answer. You love it, I hate it, who's to say whether it's good or not? There's no way of knowing."

He gives my hand a squeeze.

"Really," he says. "I'm sure you're right."

18

TEN YEARS AGO

"I'm sure you're right."

I'm on the landing, taking clean laundry up to the ironing room when I hear Jeffrey's voice from his and Vivian's bedroom. Whenever he's in the house it gives me the creeps. I stop dead where I'm standing, holding the plastic washing basket. I'm not prying on purpose, but just where I've stopped lets me see into their room through a chink of the open door. I see them reflected in their wardrobe door mirror. Jeffrey's dressed up in a suit, and Vivian's holding a tie against his neck. She has about ten other ties over her arm.

"Of *course* I'm right," she says. "You can't wear a stripe with a check suit."

I only see flashes of what they're doing. Jeffrey's buttoning his shirt, and Vivian's fussing over him like a mum getting a schoolboy ready. She's tying his tie. I realise I've stood here too long now, holding the heavy washing basket. The plastic handle is digging into my fingers. But I can't move, in case they hear me creaking on the landing. They'll know I've been eavesdropping. So I stay still.

Vivian finishes the knot. Then she leans in and kisses Jeffrey. It's not the quick peck I'd expect from married people. The kiss goes on too long, and something about it makes my stomach twist.

It's as Vivian moves away that Jeffrey sees me in the mirror. It's not long, just a second, but it's enough to make me feel guilty. Jeffrey knows I was watching. I feel like I've seen something I shouldn't have. I look away quickly, then rush off, pretending I wasn't looking. But he knows I was. I feel caught out, like he knows something about me that even I don't know.

They're getting dressed up for a dinner party. I'm supposed to be helping out, like some kind of glorified maid. Vivian's all dolled up in a swanky black dress with some dangly silver earrings and a silver locket round her neck. She looks posh. Vivian asks me what I've got that's smart to wear, but I haven't got anything smart, unless the pair of jeans without ripped knees counts as smart. Vivian tries one of her dresses on me, but it's too big. I look like a little kid playing dress-up. Then she has the idea of going to Poppy's room to find something. Poppy's out at the cinema and Daniel hasn't come out of his room for hours. We won't see him tonight.

Poppy has loads of nice clothes. I'm older, but I'm small for my age and Poppy is about the same size as me. Vivian picks an outfit. I feel pathetic knowing a thirteen-year-old has nicer clothes than I have. I'm self-conscious about it, but I don't have a choice. I'm just a prop in their perfect little evening.

My hair isn't so easy to fix. I've tried everything – combing, brushing, even wetting it down – but it's still a mess. I've been cutting my own hair because I can't afford the hairdresser's. I'm rubbish at it. I hacked away with the scissors, but I think I overdid it. I don't remember doing it this badly, but there's a chunk missing, and no matter how I try to style it, it's obvious.

I wish I could just disappear.

The doorbell rings, and I scamper downstairs to pour champagne and take coats to help Vivian with the dinner party. I'm supposed to dress nice, act polite and pour champagne. But really, I'm supposed to be invisible.

The first couple are John and Linda. John's too loud and obviously thinks he's a big something. Even how he smiles at me when I open the door makes me feel small. Linda's quieter, but she smiles at me like she doesn't mean it, all fake-capped teeth and thick lipstick. They're the kind of people who make you feel like you're doing something wrong, even when you're just standing still. She has some red lipstick on one of her teeth, but I don't tell her. Soon after there's James and Catherine. He's no better than the first bloke. Catherine's friendly enough, I guess. But they all make me feel like I'm a piece of furniture, something that doesn't matter.

Vivian gets me to take their coats, which I'm supposed to put in her and Jeffrey's bedroom. I feel weird walking into that room since Jeffrey saw me watching from outside. I put the coats on the bed. They must do it in that bed, but I try not to think about it. I wonder if Vivian knows what Daniel told me, that Jeffrey's been shagging around. I get the same feeling I had when I snuck into Jeffrey's office. I don't like the sense I'm doing something wrong, so I come out and close the door.

They've set up a fancy table in the living room. I've helped Vivian in with the starters about ten minutes ago and while they're all busy chomping away I take the chance of a loo break. I'm just heading to the loo when there's a ring at the front door.

It's a scruffy-looking bloke in a tatty coat that looks more like a sack than a mac, soaking wet because it's started lashing it down. He looks in a right state. He says he's called Henry and he's late for the dinner. I feel a bit sorry for him actually, and I grab him a towel as he comes in so he can rub his hair dry and not look so much like a drowned rat.

Maybe it's because he's in such a mess, but he doesn't seem snobby. He thanks me for the towel and when he gives it back to me he says sorry and sounds like he means it. He's got a nice smile.

Later, when I'm in the kitchen, clearing dishes, Henry comes in to help. I tell him he doesn't have to, but he carries on scraping food into a bin and loading the dishwasher. He asks me about myself, and I have to make up some stupid story about taking a year off before university. I know I've got to lie that I'm older, but even so, it makes me feel sad, pretending to be something I'm not.

I glimpse my reflection in a glass cabinet and notice my hair, the missing chunk I'd forgotten. I try to smooth it down, embarrassed by the way I must look. Henry doesn't seem to notice, or if he does, he's too polite to say anything. He just keeps talking, telling me about the gallery he runs, and how Vivian does bookkeeping work for him. There's something about him – maybe the way he looks at me like I'm a person and not just a waitress or a cloakroom attendant. It feels good to have him there.

Then, out of the corner of my eye, I see Daniel in the hallway, watching us through the open doorway like I was watching Vivian and Jeffrey earlier. It makes me jump and feel guilty, even though I'm not doing anything.

"Daniel!" I call out to him, but he doesn't answer. Instead, he turns and runs upstairs, leaving me with a strange feeling in the pit of my stomach, like nerves or something.

Henry doesn't seem to notice anything weird. He just keeps talking.

But I can't shake the feeling something's changed. Something I don't understand.

19

NOW

"I don't understand."

I'm staring at an email from JB, in which he confirms we're going to transport forty of his canvasses to London. Forty!

"Look at this place!" I can feel myself getting angry. "Has he been here? Those paintings are enormous. We'll be lucky if we can fit four in here, let alone forty."

Cassandra's leaning over my shoulder, staring at the email too. She hasn't said anything, but she looks worried.

"Did you agree this?" I ask her. I hear how snappy I am.

"No, I didn't," she says. I can see she's about to tear up, which takes me by surprise. She always seems so confident.

"Erm, that might have been me, actually," says Daniel. He's over the other side of the room, painting the gallery walls. He puts his brush on the rim of the paint pot and comes over.

"You said we'd transport forty paintings?" I half think he must have misheard me, it's such a blatantly stupid thing to agree to.

"He called last week," says Daniel. "He said he couldn't narrow down the choice of paintings until he saw how they looked together in the gallery. He didn't think the show would work with only four or five paintings. He was saying we might have to cancel."

I can smell the paint on Daniel's hands while he waves them about as he talks. "He was all blustery about it," he says. "You know what he gets like when he's on one. So to calm him down I said we'd bring them all down here and make a choice in the space."

I look around the gallery again. It's like some kind of impossible maths problem.

"But where are we going to put them all?" I say, a bit too high-pitched.

"Look," says Daniel firmly, "he was having a hissy fit and was about to walk. I did what I needed to keep him on board. It's better to have too many paintings than none at all, right?"

The firmness of his tone takes me aback. But he's right. I've got creditors breathing down my neck. We need to keep this show alive.

Maybe because he knows he's been too shouty, Daniel calms it down.

"Listen, I'm sorry if I overstepped the mark. If you want, I can call him back and say I made a mistake. Or, I'm happy to drive up there and get the paintings. I'll do two trips if the van isn't big enough."

What's the point in arguing now? It's done. We'll only be able to fit seven or eight of the paintings in here, maximum. Christ knows what we'll do with the others. Drive them back up the day after we open, I guess. Or store them somewhere. Christ, this is going to cost a fortune. I'm haemorrhaging money I don't have. If I sink any lower, I'll have to crawl back to Tench with my tail between my legs and beg him to make his offer again. I'm not sleeping at night as it is. Everything feels like it's held together by a thread.

Still, as Daniel says, he's saved us from the show being cancelled altogether. "It's fine," I say. "Sorry I lost my rag. You did the right thing." The gallery van isn't going to be anywhere near big enough, so I jump online and hire a lorry. Cassandra and I switch to wall painting duties and Daniel goes and picks up the lorry. The following day, as good as his word, Daniel sets off on the drive to Yorkshire. It's a week until the show opens.

"WHY IS DANIEL DOING ALL THIS?" asks Cassandra.

I'm crouched down trying to get a neat line of white paint that doesn't go on the concrete floor. Cassandra's up a ladder going hell for leather at the walls with a roller.

"What do you mean?" I ask. "We're friends. Old friends."

"I know," she says, "I get that, obviously. That's great. He's great."

"So?"

I get up and stretch my back. What am I missing?

"I mean, the drive to Yorkshire," she says, "the donkey work here, volunteering to go up there again and deal with JB. That's fine if you're me, and you're hoping to work your way up in the art world. But what's in it for Daniel? How does he have the time? Doesn't he have a job, or a girlfriend or something? Doesn't he need to be somewhere? Somewhere else? I mean, it's a lot."

Cassandra goes back to her painting. I can hear the sticky rasp of the wet roller against the wall. I consider what she's said. I've been so wrapped up in my own life I haven't stopped to think about Daniel's. We've spoken about the fire, his recovery, his time in care. But all of that was a long time ago. I don't know what he's been up to since, or what his life looks like now. I have no idea how he has so much spare time to devote unpaid to me and the gallery. What else does he have going on?

He knows pretty much everything about me, and I realise I know hardly anything about him. Nothing really.

I stoop back down and carry on with my painting. The mindlessness of the labour leaves space for my thoughts to chunter on.

Daniel. He's a mystery.

Does he have a job? *Does* he have a girlfriend? *Does* he have a somewhere else?

She's right. It's a lot.

20

TEN YEARS AGO

"It's a lot."

"I don't mind," Daniel says. "I'll get it for you."

He ignores the five-pound note I'm holding. He lays his bike down on the grass and runs off towards the ice cream van over by the pond. There are scratches on the side of his bike I don't remember seeing before. Maybe he fell off it but was too embarrassed to say anything.

There are loads of other kids swarming around the ice cream van. I put my money back in my bag and when I look up I panic when I can't see Daniel. Then I notice him. He was there all along. He's just another kid in the crowd, the same as the others. It feels odd, because I never really think of him as a kid. Most of the time he feels older than me, not twelve. He's cleverer, and more grown up. But right now he looks just like an ordinary kid, out at the park playing on his bike and getting ice cream.

Poppy's come with us too, though she hasn't hung out with us much. She's a nice girl, but she's a bit dim, I reckon, and we don't have anything in common. Once we got to the park she headed off to her group of mates over by the play-ground. I hear the girls screeching with laughter and the boys taking turns to see how high they can go on the swings. They're harmless.

I got a text from Shaniqua this morning asking to meet up. I feel bad just disappearing, so it's nice she's got in touch. I don't want her to know where I'm living, so I thought the park was a good place to meet. I check the time on my phone and look over to the football posts but there's no sign of her yet.

Daniel comes back with the biggest ice cream I've ever seen. It's a massive swirl of vanilla in a jumbo cone, with three flakes, chocolate sauce, red sauce, nuts and sprinkles. He laughs as I take it. I wonder if this is the first time I've ever seen Daniel laugh. I hand him my phone and get him to take a photo of me while I try to eat it. He puts his coat down by his bike so he can take the picture, and I see he only got himself a lolly, still in the wrapper.

I lick the cone a couple of times while he takes photos. It's not a hot day, but the squidgy mountain of ice cream is already starting to melt. I'm gonna have to wolf it down or I'll end up wearing most of it. I look towards the football posts again to see if Shaniqua's there.

But it's not Shaniqua.

It's Liam.

Shit.

Shaniqua must have told him where I was. Or he got hold of her phone and tricked me. He starts coming over.

I don't want him to see I'm with Daniel, or Daniel to see me talking to him.

"Go for a ride on your bike," I say.

"Why?"

"Coz we're in the park and that's what people do. Ride round the path and stuff. Go on."

"I don't want to," he says. "I want to stay here with you."

"Just do it, Daniel, for fuck's sake!" I've never spoken to him like that before.

Daniel picks up his bike. He stares at me. He gets on it and pedals off fast. He chucks his unopened lolly into a bin on the way past.

"Alright?" I say when Liam gets up to me. "Is Shaniqua with you?" I'm hoping I've got the wrong idea and he's just tagged along.

"No," he says. "Just me."

"Oh, right." I want it to sound casual, but I know my voice sounds weird. I'm scared.

"You left without saying goodbye," he says.

"Yeah," I say. "I didn't want to make a fuss." What does that even mean? I'm just making shit up now.

"You're living with that posh family? The one with them kids."

He must have been watching. "Yeah," I say. "Just for a bit." He was probably waiting here when we arrived. He must have seen me with Daniel and Poppy. I try not to show I'm worried. I can feel a trickle of sticky ice cream running over the back of my knuckles. There's a little puddle of it on the grass by my feet.

"You got a key to their house?"

Oh God. I want to say no, but I'm terrified. What if he searches me and finds it and knows I've lied? "Yeah," I say.

"Give it me," he says. I can hear he means it.

I can't open my bag with one hand, so I throw the ice cream in the bin and wipe my hand on the grass. I take out the key. Liam reaches out and takes it. He puts it in his track-suit pocket.

"I'll be round tonight, and every night 'til I get in," he says. "Put something in the window so I know everyone's out."

"What sort of thing?"

He looks irritated, like I should understand how all this works.

"Something that shouldn't be there. Fruit."

"Right."

He comes over to me and grabs a handful of my hair in his hand. He clenches it so tight I think he's going to rip it right out of my head. I picture that vein on the back of his hand, throbbing with the effort of squeezing my hair in his fist. He leans his face in close to mine. If anyone's watching it'll look like he's kissing me. His breath stinks.

"You'd better fucking do it," he says. He lets go of my hair and walks off.

I'm terrified. I've just helped someone plan to rob a house. This isn't just shoplifting. I could go to prison for this. He walks off past the football posts and keeps going. I watch him as far as I can until he disappears round some trees. I want to know he's a long way away.

My legs feel wobbly. I turn to look for a bench to sit down. That's when I see Daniel. He's not moving, straddling his bike, on a path about a hundred metres away, looking this way. Shit. It's too far for him to have heard anything, but I wonder whether he's seen. What does he know?

I give him a wave and he rides over.

"Sorry I shouted at you earlier. I've got a bit of a headache," I lie.

"That's okay," he says.

I leave a pause to see if he mentions anything about Liam. But he doesn't say anything.

"Thanks for the ice cream," I say. "It was lovely."

"That's okay."

I try to act normal on the way home, but I feel terrible I keep thinking about Liam coming to rob the house. I feel so scared I think I might be sick. Poppy gabbles away about her friends from the park, then calls in at a house where someone from her school lives. Daniel wheels his bike on the pavement but he doesn't talk. Even when Poppy goes and it's just him and me, he doesn't say anything. I can't help wondering what he's seen. I feel so guilty and nervous I'm sure he must be able to see it on me.

When we get home everyone's out and we can't get in the house. Daniel doesn't have a key. Poppy has one but I don't know when she'll be back. I make a show of looking in my bag to get my key out. I do it slowly, trying to work out what I'm going to do next, but my head's too muddled to think clearly. Maybe I can pretend I *lost* my key.

While I'm thinking, Daniel walks up to a tree in the front garden and picks up a rock. I think he must know I don't have my key and he's going to smash a window. But then he turns the rock over and opens a flap. It's a fake plastic rock. He shakes it and a key falls out into his hand.

"They have no idea about security," he says. "It's like they're asking to be robbed."

He opens the front door, then puts the spare key back in the rock and puts it by the tree. Still, he doesn't say anything about what happened at the park.

"Tell them you lost it," he says and goes into the house.

21

NOW

"You lost it?" asks Cassandra, laughing.

"Too right," says Daniel. "As I picked the tray up the lid came off and steaming hot latte went all across the counter and dripped down my trousers."

He waves his damp trouser leg around for emphasis.

"I look like I've pissed myself. I told them the last thing I need is to get burnt." He points to his scarred face. "And what do you know, they gave us these for free." He throws a big bag of pastries onto the table.

I reach for a croissant and notice the puckered skin on the back of my hand. I tug my sleeve down out of habit, trying to hide the damage. I don't know how Daniel makes jokes about it. There's something unbelievably attractive about his approach to adversity. A kind of magnetism that has nothing to do with looks.

It's 11 a.m. and we're on our third coffee. Daniel got back late yesterday, having driven JB and his forty paintings from Yorkshire to London. Imagine doing that journey all the way with JB. Daniel must be some kind of saint. JB insisted on being put up in a boutique hotel in Soho. More bloody expense. We were due to meet at ten this morning to look at his work. But he's late, of course.

Daniel's been unloading since nine. Now the canvasses are spread around the room, facing the wall. They look vast, bigger than they did in JB's studio, in the way a sofa looks bigger at home than it did in the showroom. Forty of them in here is bloody ridiculous.

At half past eleven JB swans in.

"Morning," he says in his gruff accent. No hint of an apology for being late, the graceless twat. He grabs a croissant and shovels half of it into his mouth. He goes straight over to the paintings and starts turning them around to see the fronts. We've been using white gloves, but JB hauls them around with his rough hands, throwing the protective cladding across the room, not worrying whether he touches the surface of the canvas or not. Daniel, Cassandra and I stand back and watch him work.

"It's smaller than I remember it," he says, looking around the gallery disapprovingly, like someone revisiting their tiny childhood bedroom. "I suppose it'll have to do."

He works fast, sorting the paintings into different piles, pairing a few together, leaning them against different walls, and going to the window to peer at the amount of light coming in. It's physical labour, and he puffs and mutters as he does it, but he's energetic and strong for a man of his age, and he clearly knows what he's after. He surveys his work and pauses.

"Where's the storm? The black storm? The big one?"

"Yes," says Daniel, standing up. "The big one? It's still on the lorry. It doesn't fit through the door, I'm afraid."

I watch as JB's face clouds over.

"Unacceptable," he says.

What follows is frankly farcical. We look between us in silence. We all traipse out to the lorry. We measure the painting. We get out of the lorry and measure the doorway. We get back on the lorry and measure the painting again. It's too big and won't fit.

JB stands with his hands on his hips, halfway between the lorry and the gallery door. "It has to fit," he says. He turns towards us, with Cassandra first in his eyeline. "Why the fuck didn't anybody tell me this?" He's almost shouting now. "The entire show falls apart without it."

What the bloody hell does he want us to do? Alter the rules of physics?

Cassandra takes me inside and pulls me into the office. "I sent him all this," she whispers. "I was very clear about the maximum size any painting could be. I can show you the email." She looks stressed. Her eyes are sparkling with rage and maybe tears on the verge of coming. She wipes hair away from her forehead and I can see her hand is shaking.

"I'm sure you did," I say. "Don't let that miserable old shit upset you. He'll just have to leave it in the van. He's got enough bloody paintings."

That's when I hear an almighty thump. It sounds like the building has been bombed. My first thought is that JB's driven the van into the front of the gallery. Cassandra and I fly across the room.

It's not much better than I imagined. But instead of JB destroying the gallery, it's Daniel. He's hefting something that looks like a tyre iron and smashing away at the brickwork above the door. He looks up at me, grinning, his hair and face covered in plaster and brick dust.

"We decided the painting *does* fit," he says and goes back

to ripping the doorway down. I'm livid, but what the hell can I do now?

"Right," I say, just about holding it together. "I'm going to post something. Back in a minute."

I step over the pile of rubble and walk outside. I march up the road and round the corner onto Clifford Street. There is no letter to post. I just need to get out of there before I lose my shit. I'm not even sure where I'm walking, but I find myself outside The Coach & Horses and go in. I order a gin and tonic, a double, and sit in the corner fuming. What the hell is Daniel doing? JB's insufferable and he's keeping the obstinate old git happy, but even so, he just starts smashing the gallery down without even discussing it with me? There's helping out, and there's taking over. This feels like it has crossed the line.

I sip my drink. I'm glad I came in here to let off steam. No point in losing my shit in front of everyone. I'll need to get a plasterer in. More expense. That's if they haven't knocked the entire building down by the time I get back. This is my life. Mine. I keep drinking my gin and thinking about the conversation I need to have with Daniel. I'm dreading it.

I give it half an hour and head back to the gallery. The doorway is now enlarged, and there's a three-foot-high open gap above it. Thank Christ it's not raining. The pile of bricks and plaster have been cleared away somewhere.

Cassandra's in the office, staying out of what's happening. Daniel and JB are both covered in dust. They're laughing together and admiring a large painting which is leaning against one of the walls.

"JB was right," calls Daniel. "It pulls the whole show together."

"You've got a good eye," says JB.

"Yeah, the left one," says Daniel, winking with his cloudy right eye. JB roars with laughter.

"Yes," I say. "That's great. Daniel, can I have a quick word?"

We leave JB moving the other paintings around and head to the office. Cassandra's already got her coat on and is heading towards the door.

"Thought I'd do a coffee run," she says and escapes before anything kicks off.

I sit down wearily in my chair, dreading what's coming. Daniel stands in front of me, like a schoolboy called to the Head Teacher's office. I want to tear into him, but I'm suddenly struck by how he looks. The dust has covered his scars completely. He looks how he'd have looked if he hadn't gone into the fire for me. The shock of it takes my breath away.

"I know that mess out there is bad," he says in a hushed voice, so JB won't hear him, I guess. "I would have spoken to you, but he was all for getting back in the lorry and buggering off. Even if we're right, a man like him won't budge. He wants to win the argument. It's pointless talking to that sort of person. You just have to act. So I got his big ugly painting in and he's happy. The rest is a mess but it's fixable. It's just a wall. I'll get some bricks and plaster. Two days from now you won't even remember it happened."

I half hear what he's saying. I'm still mesmerised by how beautiful and perfect he looks, pale, like a ghost. Like the ghost of the person he could have been. I'm overwhelmed by sadness and guilt.

Christ, if Daniel can live with the damage he did to himself saving me, I can live with a bit of bloody plaster dust.

And once again, he's managed to save the show from imminent cancelation.

And yet something about what he's done still unsettles me. The speed with which that wall collapsed brings home how fragile this gallery is. The house, the gallery, Henry. This whole plan is hanging together by a thread anyway. It doesn't need a crowbar to have it on the verge of collapse.

Just get this show done and see what happens. Sink or swim.

It's all I can think about for the next few days.

22

TEN YEARS AGO

It's all I can think about for the next few days.

Liam.

Liam scaring me in the park. Liam taking my key. Liam saying he's going to rob the house. He's waiting for me to give him a signal to come in, when everyone's out. At breakfast Vivian cuts a banana up on her cereal and all I can think about is Liam telling me to put some fruit in the window. Liam. Fucking Liam. I don't know what to do.

On Saturday Vivian says they're going away for the weekend, some friend's wedding or something. I get a sick feeling in my stomach. Until now, it hasn't been up to me. But now the house is going to be empty. Vivian and Jeffrey are going to a hotel somewhere, and Poppy has some birthday sleepover with a friend. Even Daniel is on a school trip to York for something about Vikings. Who knows why. Maybe he just really likes Vikings.

Daniel disappears before anyone's up for breakfast. I'm lying awake when I hear the front door go, and the click of his bike chain fading as he pedals down the road. The school coach must be leaving early. I get up and walk past his door, half-hoping I might have got it wrong and he's still here. I knock on his door and say his name, but there's just silence.

Vivian and Jeffrey are hurrying round the house. Jeffrey comes down the stairs with a couple of small suitcases and takes them out to the car. I eat some cornflakes quickly so I can get finished and out of the kitchen in case Jeffrey comes in and wants breakfast. Poppy comes down with a canvas bag. It's only nine in the morning, but she's got glittery eye shadow and sparkly lip gloss on. She asks if she can borrow my denim jacket. She's never been interested in my clothes before. I say she can and she hugs me. Vivian slurps some coffee and takes Poppy's bag into the hall. They're going to drop her at her friend's on the way to their hotel.

Eventually they all leave and I sit listening to their car as it drives off. Then silence.

What am I going to do? I don't want to let Liam in here. But what will he do to me if I don't? I know nothing about him. But he gets fake IDs, joyrides from the police, and he threatened me. I'm sure he's not messing about.

I wonder what would happen if I don't do anything. If he just keeps looking for the signal but it never comes. But then I have a thought. If he's watching the house for a signal, maybe he's already seen Vivian and Jeffrey go. Maybe he knows the house is empty. If he knows that, he'll know I haven't done what he wants me to. Then I'll really be in the shit.

Lunchtime comes and goes, but I'm too nervous to eat. I just stare at the fruit in the fruit bowl.

I go upstairs and sit in my room. I listen to cars coming and going outside. I wonder if Liam will get bored waiting for my signal and just come in. I lie on the bed, listening out for the sound of a key in the lock. But I don't hear anything. It's too obvious now anyway, in broad daylight. Even with a key, he wouldn't risk letting himself in when the neighbours might see him. I kneel on the bed and pull back my curtains a bit so I can peek out without being seen. Some kids are playing football over the road. There's a man two doors down washing his car, and another man over the other way mowing his lawn. No. If you were going to rob a house you'd do it in the dark, when you could slip in without anyone noticing.

I could just go out. But I'm too scared to go out in case I run into Liam. So I stay where I am.

I must have fallen asleep at some point, because I suddenly jerk awake thinking I've heard the front door close. I sit up on the bed and listen. My eyes are straining wide open but I can't see much because it's got dark. My heart is thumping in my chest with panic. But I can't hear anything. It was just a dream. A nightmare.

The traffic noises are quieter. People must have gone home for the evening. The streetlamp outside is lighting my room up with an orange glow, like the heat lamps in Daniel's room. It feels creepy. I don't know whether to put the lights on in the house or not.

I tiptoe down the stairs as if someone might hear me. But there's no one to hear me. I'm on my own. The curtains are all open and light comes in from outside. It's not quite a full moon, but nearly, and there aren't many clouds about. I've been lying in the dark so long my eyes have adjusted to it. I can see everything. I have a funny feeling in my stomach. It's fear, but maybe hunger too. I didn't have lunch and now I haven't had dinner. I go into the kitchen and pick up an apple from the bowl.

But I don't eat it.

I put it on the window sill in the living room.

I close the curtains in the living room so I can't see it. I go back into the kitchen. I twist the blinds so they close and sit at the kitchen table. I can see up the hallway and to the front door from here.

I keep thinking about the apple in the living room window.

I sit and wait. It's at least a couple of hours by the kitchen clock. The longer goes by, the more I hope Liam isn't coming. But also the more tense I get.

Just after midnight I think about going back upstairs when I see a shadow move on the kitchen blinds. Someone's at the side of the house. It's windy outside, and I wonder if one of the trees in the garden is blowing and making the shadow. But this shadow isn't moving. I hold my breath and watch it. Then it goes.

It's completely silent, and my heart is banging away at a million miles an hour. Then I hear something in the hallway. It's a key going into the door lock. The door begins to open. I hope it's Daniel, sent home from his trip, or Poppy having fallen out with her friends. I hope the groom has stood the bride up and Vivian has come home early. I even hope it's Jeffrey.

But it isn't.

It's Liam.

I can't see his face properly. It's in shadow, but I know it's him. He walks slowly up the hallway. He keeps walking straight ahead and then he freezes. He's seen me. Neither of us moves an inch. He knows there's someone here, but he doesn't know who it is.

I don't know what he'll do if he thinks he's been caught, so I whisper, "It's me. It's Ariana. Tracey."

He starts walking towards me. He comes into the kitchen and comes right up to me. I can see his face now and he looks pissed off.

"The place is supposed to be empty. Who else is here?"

"No one," I say. "Just me. Sorry."

"Get out the way then," he says. He grabs me roughly by the arm and hauls me off my chair. He does it fast and I lose my balance as he pulls me sideways and the chair tips over. I lurch forward and my head hits the corner of the work surface. They're fancy stone counters and my head hits the edge incredibly hard. Liam keeps hold of my arm and his fingers dig into me. The pain in my arm is agony, but then that stops hurting as much as my head. It feels sharp and hot, and the hotness begins to spread across my forehead and round my face. I think it might be blood, but when I reach up with my other hand and feel my face, there's no blood there. It's just the shock of the bump.

Liam drags me sideways. I'm not sure where he's taking me or why. I try to stand up properly but I can't get my feet to grip on the floor as he's racing me along. There's a clatter of the chair on the floor as he drags me past it and then there's a bang on the door.

Then suddenly there's a shout and someone else is in the room. Liam yells and lets go of my arm and I drop to the floor. I can't see what's going on in this light, but Liam moves and there's a flash of something, and suddenly I realise Daniel's here. Then Liam's rushing out of the kitchen and up the hallway, out through the front door into the night. Daniel's standing there, puffing, and he's holding one of the big kitchen knives, shining in the light, and I can't tell if the shininess is the metal or blood.

"What are you doing here?" I say. "You're on your trip."

It's a stupid thing to say. Of course he isn't on his trip. He's here in the kitchen holding a knife covered in blood.

I switch the light on. There's blood on the kitchen floor and all up the tiles in the hall to the open front door. Daniel has blood on his front, and on his face. All up his arm. I grab him.

"Are you okay?" I check him to see if he's hurt.

"I got him," he says. His eyes look mad, and he's kind of grinning, but he also looks like he might cry. "Twice, I think. On his arm. I slashed him. Look at all that blood. Maybe I got an artery."

The place looks like a murder scene. I hurry up the corridor and nearly slip over on blood as I go. I close the front door. I look back at the mess.

"What should we do?"

I know we should call the police, but I don't want to. I'm seventeen. They'll send me back. And I gave Liam the key. I'm in all sorts of trouble. I can't think straight.

Daniel takes the knife to the sink. He puts it in the sink and turns the tap on. He rinses the knife under the water, then washes some of the blood off his hands and arm. He pulls his bloody school jumper over his head and puts it in the washing machine. He kneels down and opens the cupboard under the sink, and pulls out various cleaners and cloths, rubber gloves and a bucket. He stands and takes a roll of paper towel off its wooden holder.

"Clean everything. Clothes and any kitchen equipment go in the washing machine and the dishwasher. We never, ever tell anyone about this. Right?"

He stares at me in deadly seriousness.

"Right," I say. I start to head off to the hall holding kitchen roll and a thing of Mr Muscle.

"And Ariana," says Daniel, stopping me in the doorway.

"Yes?"

"Don't forget the apple."

So we're going to sort this out ourselves. This is going to be our secret.

I look around the room and wonder, what have I done? What have I become a part of?

What now?

23

NOW

I look around the room and wonder, what the hell have I done? What now?

JB's paintings are finally hung to his satisfaction. Seven of them in the end, including the big one that meant half the doorway getting knocked down and rebuilt. I've had to put the other thirty-odd paintings in storage while the show goes on, as JB says he might want to 'refresh the hang' if the weather shifts and the light in the gallery changes. Christ, he's an insufferable twat. What with the transportation, storage and insurance for them, it's costing a small fortune.

The show opens tomorrow. It's been such a frantic dash to get everything sorted. But now we're ready and I don't have the practical tasks to distract me, my mind is racing. Was this whole thing a terrible idea? Am I just throwing good money after bad? If this doesn't work, that's it. I'll have to sell the gallery and almost certainly the house. Maybe I've just been in stupid denial for these last few weeks. I can't believe I've let my entire future rest on that miserable shit of a painter. How the hell did Henry ever put up with him?

Henry.

Poor Henry, who loved this gallery. Who was so lovely to me and helped me when I was lost and in trouble, and whose legacy I think I might be destroying. Still no news from the police on who killed him. The longer goes by, the more I feel I'm losing my connection to him and Henry is becoming something from the past.

As I'm thinking all this over, the door bursts open and Daniel appears, after another of his occasional mysterious absences. He drags his bike into the back of the gallery. He looks flustered.

"What's up?" I say. "Did you fall off your bike or something?"

He sits down at the table opposite me. He looks serious. "Listen, I haven't been entirely honest with you. I need a favour." He toys nervously with the locket around his neck.

"Okay..." Daniel has never asked me for anything. He's always the one helping *me* out.

"The fact is," he says, "I did something stupid a while back and got in trouble. There's a guy I knew in care. I was holding some dope for him. Not much, but enough so they couldn't let it go. I got a short suspended sentence. The annoying thing is, I've got a probation officer, a guy called Robin. He's alright, but he has to check up on me – where I live, where I work, who I associate with."

"Right."

"So, is it okay if I tell him I've been working here?"

I know the sort of people you get caught up with in care. I think about Shaniqua, and Liam, who we don't ever mention.

"That's fine," I say. "I mean, you *have* been working here."

"Thanks," he says. "He's coming here this afternoon. I hope that's okay."

"Sure, no problem," I say.

"Oh, one more thing," he says as an afterthought. "Robin says my 'rehabilitation' is about making new contacts. I'm not supposed to associate with people from the past. So is it okay if we tell Robin we've just met? You advertised for an assistant or something, and I interviewed and got the job?"

"Yes. Okay."

It feels good to be doing something for Daniel, even if it's just this tiny white lie. I've felt so obligated to him across the years, and then so guilty about abandoning him after I promised I'd look out for him forever. I'm happy I have the chance to repay some of that.

"Thanks," he says. He reaches across the table and puts his scarred hand on mine.

Later that afternoon, probation officer Robin comes in and is polite and pleasant and very discreet. He's wearing jeans and a t-shirt and is maybe a couple of years younger than me. You'd never in a million years guess what he did for a living.

Daniel's in the office, updating some software on the laptop, giving it a good old clean-up. My guess is he wants to look busy on an essential task for Robin's sake.

Robin goes into the office and chats with Daniel for a while and then asks to talk to me, alone. He asks if I know why he's here, and I explain what Daniel told me – that he's on probation for a drug offence. I tell the lie about advertising for an intern and make up some bullshit about having a policy of supporting people with criminal records and giving them a second chance.

It all comes out pretty smoothly because, deep down, I

believe it. I know how easily a bad start can doom you to a lousy life, and how incredible it is when someone comes along and rescues you, like Daniel did for me. He was only twelve, but he believed in me in a way no one ever had before.

Robin buys it all. He has another quiet word with Daniel and then he leaves.

"Thanks," says Daniel when Robin's gone. "I owe you."

"You don't, Daniel," I say. "I can't imagine how I'll repay everything I owe you. I'm glad to do this little bit."

"You don't owe me anything," says Daniel. "Really, you don't." He looks at me intensely and the atmosphere in the room changes. He gestures to his scarred face. "You mean this, don't you?"

I feel suddenly awkward and embarrassed. I look at him and take in what I've tried to get used to over the past few weeks, what I've tried to ignore and pretend isn't there. The terrible damage. I feel a hot flash of shame.

"Yes," I say. "I mean that. Your face. Your poor face. I'm so sorry you had to go through all that for me."

"I'm not," he says. "I'm not at all sorry. I'm glad."

"Glad?" The idea shocks me.

"Yes," he says, grabbing my hand. "Really, I am. I'm glad. Look at us," he says, and he takes my hand in his and splices his fingers through mine so our two hands are intertwined, palms down, with the scarred skin facing upwards. I try not to look at my hands. I don't want to think about that night. I'd rather forget it. But Daniel stares at our hands and I look at them too.

"Look," he says. "They're the same. We were both there. It's a part of us. The fire. It won't ever go away. We can't ever forget. It ties us together. A bond forged in the fire. Forever."

And he looks at me. He smiles. The pull of the muscles in his jaw stretches the puckered skin taut across the ravaged side of his face.

He smiles, like it's the most wonderful thing he could possibly imagine.

PART 3

24

TEN YEARS AGO

He smiles, like it's the most wonderful thing he could possibly imagine.

"Great," says Henry. "It's a date then. No, I don't mean a date, but..." He starts stuttering, all embarrassed.

"It's fine," I say, "it's just a walk in the park. You haven't asked me to marry you or anything."

Then it's my turn to get embarrassed. I don't know why I said that. Shit. I hope he doesn't think I'm after him like that. Oh God. We're a right couple of idiots.

Henry's come to the house a couple of times since the dinner party. Even though he must be thirty or something, I always try to hang around in the kitchen more when he comes, hoping I'll bump into him. And he seems to go in and out of rooms a lot as if he's trying to bump into me.

It's nice to have something to look forward to. But as soon as Henry goes, my mind drifts back to what I've been thinking about.

Liam.

It's been two nights since he let himself in the house and

Daniel cut him with that knife. We scrubbed it all down until it was spotless. Daniel made me stand on a bin bag and change out of my clothes and put them in the washing machine. Underwear too. He went into the hall while I did it. I felt weird standing in the kitchen with nothing on. He knocked on the kitchen door and passed a bathrobe through the gap. Then he came in, and I went into the hall, and he stripped off the same as me and put his clothes in the washing machine.

I don't think I had much blood on me, but he did. A lot.

It was three in the morning by the time our clothes were washed and clean and we'd dried them in the tumble dryer. We agreed we'd never say anything about what happened that night. Not even to each other.

I haven't asked Daniel what he was doing there and not on his school trip. I wonder what he saw at the park. He knew about the apple in the window. Was he there deliberately? I hope he's okay. He was weirdly calm when we were cleaning up. Maybe he's in shock. A kid called Raheem fell down the stairs once at Rob and Julie's. He had a bit of bone sticking out of his leg, like a snapped bone when you're eating chicken. I was really calm while we waited for the ambulance. But later that night I had a proper panic attack, like the whole thing was happening right then. Now I wonder if Daniel being so calm is shock. I need to keep an eye on him. He's only a kid.

I went to bed once we cleared everything up, but I couldn't sleep. When I closed my eyes all I saw was Liam's shadow coming up the hallway, and the flash of the knife in Daniel's hand. The shine of the metal and the blood.

Liam still has my key. Does he think I double-crossed him? He must hate me now. Is he gonna come back and get me? I keep thinking that, over and over, all Saturday night, and Sunday in the day, and Sunday night.

But now it's Monday, and Poppy, Vivian and Jeffrey have all come back. There's been no more sign of Liam. Not yet.

We're having dinner. Vivian, Jeffrey, Poppy, Daniel and me sat at the table. I don't think we've all been like this before. I guess Daniel's trying to act normal after the Liam stuff. Though if he really wanted to act normal he'd lock himself in his bedroom like usual.

"Thanks for lending me your jacket," says Poppy. "I put it back in your room."

"Okay, thanks," I say, trying to be chatty and natural. "How was the party?"

Poppy goes into a long story about some catty falling out between two friends. I'm not interested, to be honest, and I don't hear most of it because I'm watching Daniel out of the corner of my eye. He's not eating. He's just staring at his plate, pushing a meatball around with his fork like a bored snooker player.

I see Jeffrey watching him too.

"How was your weekend, Ariana?" asks Vivian. "Did you get up to anything interesting with the house to yourself?"

"Boring," I say, probably a bit too quickly. "I didn't do anything."

Daniel's still prodding the meatball with his fork. It's kind of coming apart, like mince on his plate from all that poking. As far as I can tell he hasn't eaten anything.

"And how about you, Daniel?" asks Vivian. "How was York? Did you learn much about the Vikings?"

He doesn't say anything. He doesn't look up. He can't

answer, because it'll give away that he never went on the trip. He can't let anyone know he was here. So he just sits there, staring at his spaghetti.

"Daniel," barks Jeffrey, "your mother asked you a question."

I dread what's coming next. Are we going to get found out?

"Oh, sorry," says Daniel cheerfully. "I was miles away thinking about this delicious dinner. York was great, thanks."

I hold my breath, gripping my fork tight. I'd like to keep eating so I look normal, but my mouth is dry and I can't swallow.

Daniel wipes his mouth with his napkin. "The Jorvik Centre was amazing. They've got this full Viking village, and you can even smell the woodsmoke from the hearths. There were blacksmiths making tools, and they told us about how Vikings used to make swords using iron from bogs. This stuff called bog iron, just sitting in the marshes, and they dug it up and turned it into weapons. Isn't that incredible?"

Vivian smiles. "That sounds fascinating, Daniel."

I nod along, trying not to seem too interested, but my heart is pounding. Where's he got all this from? He must have learned it off the website or something.

"The best thing was they have an actual, restored long-boat – well, parts of it. They explained how Vikings used their ships for raids but also for exploring, like when they discovered Iceland and Greenland. I mean, imagine rowing across an ocean with just the stars to guide you."

"Sounds like you got a lot out of it," Jeffrey says, twirling a fat twist of pasta on his fork and shovelling it in his mouth.

Daniel shrugs. "I guess I did. It was hard not to. On the coach ride up, I sat with Tom and Haruki, and they were moaning about how boring the trip was going to be. But I knew it wouldn't be. It was brilliant."

"And how was the hotel?" asks Vivian.

"Alright," he says casually, stabbing his fork into his food. "The usual boring stuff – tiny beds, awful breakfast. The cereal was basically cardboard. But at least there was Wi-Fi, so no complaints."

"I'm really glad you went, Daniel," says Vivian. "I'm proud of you." She's smiling, but she looks like she might cry.

He finally takes a bite, like he hasn't just spun an entire story on the spot. I can't believe it. I *know* he wasn't there, and even I believe him. He smiles at me while he chews, then goes back to looking at his plate.

We finish dinner and everyone leaves while I clear the plates and load the dishwasher. I can't get over how convincing Daniel was. It's like he honestly believed what he was saying. I feel like I'm living in a different universe, where the stuff at the weekend never happened. Daniel *did* go to York with the school. He wasn't here when Liam came round. He didn't cut Liam with a knife. Liam was never here.

I go upstairs to my room. Poppy's left my jacket on the bed and as I'm hanging it up in the wardrobe I notice the left sleeve is coming away from the body. It's bad. It wasn't like this before. I'm pissed off. It's not a great jacket, but it's the only one I've got and now it's ruined.

I knock on the door quite hard. It's not locked and it swings open. Poppy's on her bed reading a magazine.

"Hey," she says.

"Listen, Poppy, I don't mind you borrowing my stuff, but if you damage it can you tell me, please?"

"What d'you mean?" she says. She sits bolt upright and she's immediately serious.

"This," I say, waving the jacket I'm holding. "The sleeve wasn't like this when you took it."

She gets off the bed and comes over. She takes the jacket and stares at the sleeve like she's confused, like it's a hard maths sum she doesn't understand.

"It wasn't like that when I had it," she says. "I swear."

She looks genuinely upset. But there's no way she couldn't have noticed. The sleeve's practically hanging off.

"Okay, whatever," I say. I can't get into a blazing row with the boss's daughter.

Poppy stares at me, and then she stares over my shoulder.

"Him," she says. "He did it."

I turn round and look where she's looking. Daniel's door. It's closed, as always.

"He's done it. He can't stand that you lent me something. He's pathetic. He's sick! Happy now, sicko?!"

She yells across the corridor, then throws the jacket my way and slams the door. I'm used to this sort of stuff from places I've lived before. But not here. Poppy's never said anything bad about Daniel. And he's never said anything about her. But now I think about it, I don't think I've seen them say a single thing to each other. Ever.

As I'm going back to my room, Daniel's door opens a chink. I go in.

"She's in with them," he says. "She wants to turn you against me. Why would I damage your jacket? What reason would I have?"

He's upset. He almost looks like he might cry.

"You're my friend," he says. "I would never do that. I haven't even had your jacket. She's just a spoilt brat who doesn't care about anyone else and wants to blame anyone except herself."

I don't know what to think. I know Daniel likes me. So why would he do anything to upset me?

"Do you want to help me feed the snakes?" he asks.

But I don't. That stuff holding the spider. The graffiti in Jeffrey's room. The stuff with Liam. It's all getting too much. I'm tired, and I just want to be on my own to clear my head.

"I'm tired," I say. "I think I'm just gonna go to bed."

"Okay. Maybe tomorrow. Goodnight, Ariana." He gives me the most beautiful smile.

"Yeah, maybe tomorrow," I say. "Night, Daniel."

I go out and shut the door.

I don't know why, but for some reason I don't tell him about Henry.

25

NOW

I don't know why, but for some reason I don't tell him about Henry. I'm so tired of dealing with sympathetic strangers. That pitying look they get on their faces and the embarrassment of not knowing what to say next. It's easier just not to mention it.

"Out, is he? Not like him on the day of an opening!" He's a nice, smiley guy about my age. He's standing in the doorway, holding a box with a label stuck on the side – *Red Bus Printing*. "Will Henry be back to check these over or can someone else do it?"

He looks speculatively over my shoulder into the gallery, and I wonder whether he's looking for Cassandra. I wouldn't be surprised if he was. She's cute. But instead he sees Daniel in the back room of the office. I see the guy freeze in shock. It's a look I've got used to over these past weeks. People notice the scars and they feel compelled to stare, in the way people driving past a terrible accident feel compelled to look. The guy just stands there, flustered, holding his cardboard box.

"I can look at those," I say. "Pop them down here."

I pull out a sheet, a double-sided piece of paper with images of JB's paintings and a statement about the show, which JB and Daniel wrote together. They're best buddies now, thick as thieves. We could have bashed these out on the gallery printer, but Daniel suggested we go for something more luxurious. The paper's indulgently thick, and the reproductions are rich and intense. It shouts quality. What difference is another couple of hundred pounds going to make in the face of total financial ruin?

"These are great," I say. "Thanks."

"No worries," says the guy, smiling as he heads to the door. "Say hi to Henry for me." And he's gone.

"Told you," says Daniel, coming up behind me and taking the flyer out of my hand. He puts it to his face and sniffs it deeply, like someone checking wine in a restaurant. "Mmmm, I can smell the money now."

Right. The money I haven't got and can't afford.

"Can you man the fort?" I ask. "I have to help Cassandra move in."

"Sure. You go. I've got it."

I head out to the car, then drive back to the house. As if there wasn't enough going on, the friend Cassandra lives with is moving to Australia and Cassandra can't find anywhere else she can afford. I don't want to lose her from the gallery, so I said she could move in with me for a bit. I give her a hand hauling her luggage inside. She looks like she's packed for a year in Australia herself.

"Jesus, Ariana, this place is gorgeous."

We drag the cases up the stairs to the spare room on the second floor. It's got big skylight windows and its own ensuite bathroom. It's a nice day and the room is bright and sunny.

"You'll be comfy up here, I hope." I hand her a set of keys. "Come and go as you please."

"Oh God, Ariana, thanks so much. I really do appreciate this."

Truth is, she's helping me in more ways than just at the gallery. I've been so bound up in work my days look after themselves. But at night, coming back here on my own, I can't help but think about Henry. Moving through rooms full of his art. Watching the TV on my own next to the funny little bronze sculpture of his face. Trying to ignore the wardrobe of his clothes I know at some point I'll need to clear. I feel sad, and angry, and lonely. It's nice to think about someone friendly putting a key in the lock and coming through the door.

"I'll unpack my shit later," says Cassandra, "otherwise we'll miss the fucking opening entirely."

We look at her mountain of suitcases and laugh, then thunder back down the stairs, into the car and back to the gallery. It feels fun to be doing something young and silly for once.

When we get back, Daniel's there, overseeing a large delivery of boxes. Cases of wine. About twenty of them.

"What's this?" I ask.

"Can't have an opening without booze," he says.

I open one of the cases. It's champagne. It's got to be thirty quid a bottle.

"What was wrong with the other wine?" I ask. We had cases of the stuff out back, from the opening that never happened on the night Henry was killed.

"They picked it up when they dropped this off. I thought

we could do better. We want to make an impression, and we don't want that impression to be–"

He pulls a face, like someone sucking a lemon. His distorted expression is made even more grotesque by the way his skin pulls with the scarring. I'm not sure if that's what he intends. But anyway, the unpleasantness of his appearance makes his point.

Christ, though. How much must this have cost? I look at the number of cases and try to do the maths in my head. Twelve multiplied by thirty, multiplied by however many boxes there are. I can't work it out. But it's a lot. It's as if Daniel's working for Phillip Tench, not me, actively trying to ruin me.

I wait until Cassandra goes into the office, then pull Daniel to one side. "Look, I'm grateful for your help, Daniel, but–"

"I know what you're going to say. This cost a fortune, right? Money you haven't got."

"Yes. Exactly." I hate being interrupted. "I'm on the verge of sinking here, and you're standing there with a bucket bailing water *into* the boat."

"Listen," he says, taking my hand. I wonder if Cassandra can see. "It's all just numbers in a computer. This wine was just numbers on a computer in the off-licence that turn into fewer numbers in your bank. People come in here and they seem rich, but they just have more numbers in their account and they give those numbers to you. You need to stop thinking about money. It's not real."

"Yeah, but those numbers ARE money!" I say. I can feel myself getting angry. I don't understand why he's coming out with this hippy-dippy horseshit.

"No," he says, "it's not money. It's about more than

money." He points to the painting nearest to us. "What's that painting worth? I know what we're selling it for, but what is it *worth*? Is it worth the cost of the canvas and the paint and the wooden frame? Is it worth the time JB took to paint it? Or is it worth whatever anyone is prepared to pay for it?"

He grabs a bottle of champagne and waves it in my face.

"They know the cost of this," he says. "If you're giving them this champagne for nothing, then what must that *painting* be worth?" He points at the painting. "It's worth more *because* of the champagne."

Somehow it makes sense. If we want to sell the art for a decent price, we need to look like we understand quality. "We're not a four-ninety-nine-a-bottle organisation," I say. "We're a champagne organisation."

Daniel smiles. "Now you've got it."

"Sod it then," I say. "In for a penny, in for a pound."

At some point in all this, Cassandra has drifted in from the office. She's standing in the open doorway, leaning against the wall, staring at Daniel. Staring at him like she's mesmerised, like he's the most brilliant, charismatic person on Earth. Which he maybe is.

It's all about confidence. Daniel has it in bucket-loads. Maybe he got that from the fire. Maybe if you've walked through fire and survived it, it makes you invincible. That's how he comes across anyway. Like he can do absolutely anything.

Perhaps that's why he doesn't seem to mind the scars. They're like a badge of honour. His force field. His armour. His scars are his membership to the club of *Fuck You To Everything*.

26

TEN YEARS AGO

"...Fuck You!"

I only hear the end of the shouting as I come through the door, but I immediately recognise Henry's voice.

"No, fuck *you!*" It's Jeffrey, shouting back at him.

I freeze in the hallway. They're somewhere in the back of the house. It's embarrassing and I don't want to hear it. I'm about to make a dash for my room when a door bangs open and Henry comes charging at me down the corridor. Jeffrey's behind him.

"That's right, fuck off." Jeffrey's standing in the kitchen doorway, red in the face. He's scary. He looks like if he got hold of Henry he'd do something violent.

"Sorry," mutters Henry to me as he passes. He's white as a sheet. I don't know if it's because he's angry or because he's frightened. He opens the front door and disappears onto the street. Jeffrey stares at me for a moment, but I'm not even sure if he's looking at me or through me to where Henry's just gone. Either way, I feel like I've heard something I shouldn't have. Thankfully, Jeffrey spins round and heads back to his study. I hear the door slam.

I creep up to my room, and as I'm on the landing I think I can hear Vivian crying in her bedroom. I tiptoe across the landing as quietly as I can and go into my room. I close the door and lie on my bed. What the hell is going on?

There's an envelope on my bed and a Mars bar. I open the envelope. It's a card from Daniel. He's done an amazing drawing of a rocket in space, with Earth in the distance behind it. There's a round window on the side of the rocket and he's drawn two faces, me and him, looking out of the window. The faces are pushed close together and we're smiling.

It makes me feel weird. I want to help Daniel, but I worry he's getting too attached to me. But maybe it's just me who isn't used to being close to anyone. I wonder if the picture of us in the rocket is about us running away together. He's mentioned that before and I ignored it. He doesn't know I'm a runaway already.

I open the Mars bar and take a bite, but I'm not hungry. I have a wobbly feeling in my stomach. I think about Daniel and Henry, Jeffrey and Liam. I feel like I'm in a muddle, but I don't even know what the muddle is so I don't know how to fix it.

My phone buzzes and it's a message from Henry asking if I can meet him.

I sneak out of my room and across the landing. I can't hear anything from Vivian's room now. I go past Daniel's room and wonder if he's in, but I can't talk to him right now. I walk as quietly as I can down the stairs and outside.

I get to the coffee shop where Henry said he'd be. He's got a coffee, but he asks me what I want and goes off to get me a latte. He comes back with the drink and a slice of carrot cake and two forks.

"I'm sorry about that back there," he says.

"What was it all about?" I ask. Then I wonder whether I'm being too nosey. But I guess he wouldn't have asked me to meet him if he didn't want to talk about it.

"I knew it was a mistake, talking to Jeffrey. I should have trusted my instincts." He sips his coffee and shakes his head. "I'm moving the gallery I run from the East End to a place in central London. On Cork Street, where a lot of big galleries are. Vivian said Jeffrey might be up for investing. She did bookkeeping for me back in the day."

He pokes the carrot cake with his fork but doesn't eat any.

"But as the meetings have gone on, it's obvious he isn't going to cough up any serious money. He started asking for discounts on artwork. He's not interested in art, he just wants to flip a few paintings on the cheap. I challenged him on it today and he just blew up. Jesus, he's got a filthy temper."

Henry looks sad. I guess he must really need that money.

"I reckon you're better off anyway," I say. "I can't say too much, but from what I know he's a proper arsehole. You're better off out of it."

"Yeah," says Henry. But he doesn't sound like he means it. He pokes the cake about a bit more. I jump in with my fork and spear the big icing carrot on the top. I shove it in my mouth and grin at him. He grins back. I thought it might cheer him up, and it does.

Once we've finished our coffee we go for a walk in the park. We talk about all sorts. Henry's lovely and easy to talk to, and even though he's a lot older than me I do kind of fancy him. I can't tell if he fancies me. If he does, he doesn't do anything about it. He's too much of a gentleman, I reckon. When we come to the end of our walk I thank him for the coffee and cake and I reach up and give him a kiss on the cheek. He gets all flustered about it and goes a bit red. He's sweet.

It's only as I'm walking back home on my own that I remember Liam, and whether he's going to be coming back to get me. Shit. I must really like Henry if he made me forget that.

When I get back to the house I'm glad that Jeffrey's car isn't in the drive. I let myself in with the new key I got cut from the spare in that fake rock. The house sounds completely quiet. As I go upstairs I see Daniel's door is open a crack. He swings it open when he sees me. "Did you hear all that shouting?" he asks.

"Yeah," I say. "What was that about?" I don't want to let on I've spoken to Henry, or even that I know Henry was here.

"It was Dad and Mr Clough," says Daniel. "They were arguing over Mum. I think Mum is seeing Mr Clough to get back at Dad about going on dates with that woman."

"Wow," I say. I can't let on I know what the argument was really about.

"And look at this," he says. He's holding sheets of paper. I can see they have emails printed on them. "It's conversations between Dad and that woman from his work. They look like work emails, but there's a kind of code in them. They're about having a *follow-up meeting* and *let's schedule a review* and *let's touch base tomorrow*. He thinks he's being clever but it's so bloody obvious."

They sound innocent to me, just work stuff, but I guess

that's the point. Anyway, Daniel's the smart one, and the more I hear about Jeffrey and see what he's like, I wouldn't put anything past him.

"Where d'you get these?" I ask.

"From his study. It took me a few tries to work out his password, but I got it in the end. D'you know he uses the same password for everything, the idiot."

"Daniel! You need to be more careful!" I remember how angry Jeffrey sounded shouting at Henry, and Henry's worried look in the cafe, and Vivian crying. Plus I can't forget the mark on Daniel's face where Jeffrey hit him that time. Then I think about Daniel and me going into Jeffrey's study and Daniel showing me the graffiti he's done in that invisible ink. It's dangerous. Jeffrey's dangerous.

As if he can read my thoughts, Daniel looks at me intensely.

"He'd kill me if he found out," he says, waving the pieces of paper at me. "I'm going to take them to the park tonight, to burn them. Do you want to come?"

"I can't," I say. "I have to cook dinner." I've just made up the first lame excuse I can think of. I feel like I'm getting in waaaay over my head.

"You've read these now," says Daniel. "You know too. It's our secret. Like Liam."

It's the first time Daniel's mentioned Liam since that night. How does he know he's called Liam anyway? I guess I must have said his name when it all happened. And wasn't Daniel the one who said we should never speak about it, even to each other? It's weird having all these secrets. There's a bit of me that likes it. I've never felt a connection with anyone before like I do with Daniel. Even if it's over something bad, it still feels important.

But at the same time, it scares me. I thought I was helping him because he was in trouble. But now I feel like I'm in trouble too. Oh God, I have no idea what terrible trouble I've got myself into.

"I'm sorry you're involved," says Daniel. "I know you don't want to be, but you are. Remember, Dad had your ID. The moment you came into this house you were involved."

Daniel grabs my hand. He looks up at me and there's real fear in his eyes.

"We should make a run for it," says Daniel. "Before anything bad happens. We should get away, while we still can."

27

NOW

"We should make a run for it," says Daniel. "Get away while we still can."

We're in the back office of the gallery, watching people arrive for the opening of JB's show.

"Good idea," I say. "You cause a diversion and we'll sneak out."

"Right. I'll set fire to one of the paintings. As soon as the sprinklers start, you get the car. See you out back in five minutes."

"It's a deal."

But of course, neither of us moves.

More people come through the door, and Cassandra greets them with a smile, an absurdly expensive leaflet and a glass of vintage champagne. She's dressed in a cute, baby pink bouclé mini dress, and looks bubbly and fun, like the champagne.

Daniel watches her. His expression gives nothing away. Daniel's in a suit and looks dashing. What might his life have been like if he hadn't been so badly burned? Jesus. What kind of father does that to his own child? It's an awful thing to think, and I feel guilty and ashamed that I'm still noticing. I know I should be able to see past it by now. But I can't.

I realise I'm pulling at the sleeve of my dress instinctively, trying to hide my scars.

"Shall we?" asks Daniel, tilting his head towards the gallery space.

I reach out towards him and take hold of his tie. I adjust the knot so it sits tidily in the centre of his collar. The scarred knuckle of my right hand brushes lightly on the taut skin that pulls across this throat.

"You look handsome," I say.

We drift out into the crowd. It's already getting busy. Daniel approaches a woman looking at one of the paintings and she almost jumps back at the sight of him before plastering on an awkward smile. Daniel carries on as if he hasn't noticed, but I find it too painful to watch.

I look away and scan the room. I recognise a few faces. Some of the other gallery artists are hovering around Cassandra and the free booze. No sign of JB, the feckless prick. Probably propping up the bar in a shitty pub somewhere, on his third pint. I'm surprised he's not here, lording it. He's just the sort who loves to be the centre of attention. Still, it's a relief I'm not having to stop him offending buyers, or wrestling champagne bottles out of his hand.

"Hello."

Someone taps me on the shoulder. It's a short woman in her fifties, wearing a flowing dress in swirls of orange and green and a huge pair of bright blue glasses. Her grey hair is cut in a clean Vidal Sassoon bob with an asymmetric fringe. It's a look you'd only ever see at a bloody art gallery.

"Ariana, isn't it?" she asks. "I have to leave for another

opening, but I just wanted to say hello before I go. I rather lost touch with James Balentine's work a few years back, and I don't think I'd have come to this show if it wasn't for your email. So thank you very much for inviting me."

"No problem. My pleasure." I have absolutely no idea who this woman is. I certainly didn't invite her. Maybe it's someone on Cassandra's mailing list. As soon as big glasses woman goes, I head across to where Cassandra is pouring champagne. I spot the mountain of empty bottles gathering in the corner and stop myself from guessing how much money I've thrown away on those.

"Who's that?" I ask, pointing to Glasses as she walks up the pavement.

"Elizabeth Arnold. She's a journalist at *Frieze*. It's amazing she came."

"Did you invite her?" I ask.

"No," says Cassandra. "I assumed you did."

"*I* did," says Daniel, joining us. "Your laptop was in the office and I noticed the mailing list. I added a few names. I hope you don't mind."

I don't like the idea of him going on my computer. Yet again, he's just taken over. But what can I say? If he hadn't done it, we wouldn't have a critic here from *Frieze*. If I complain I'll just look an idiot.

"Of course not," I say. "It's fine."

Cassandra heads off again to chuck more champagne down people's throats. Daniel stands looking at me. He can see right through me.

"You're not okay about the laptop," he says. "I get it. The reason I didn't tell you is because you don't believe in yourself. You wouldn't invite someone from *Frieze* because deep down you don't believe you deserve it."

"What is this, therapy?" I laugh. "Do you want me to lie on the couch?"

"I mean it," says Daniel. "You doubt yourself too much. You don't trust what I know is true. How brilliant you are."

"Okay..." I say, trying to brush off the compliment. He's right. I don't trust myself, doing all this. I feel like a fraud.

"Don't do that," he says. "Don't sell yourself short. Look." He gestures to the crowded room of engaged, chattering people. "You did this. *You.*"

It's true. I did. Against all odds, we've got the exhibition open, and the gallery is crowded with people. I don't know what will happen next, but it's a start. We haven't drowned. We're still here.

"I want to show you something," he says. He takes my hand and leads me across the gallery, back to the painting where he frightened that woman. On the wall at the bottom is a little red dot. "We sold one."

I feel a rush of excitement. Daniel's right. I haven't allowed myself to feel positive about things, to really believe I could do it. But I have. This is the turning point. This is the beginning of something new and exciting. Instinctively, I hug him and feel like I did that first day he showed up in the gallery. Happy and full of hope.

But the positive feeling doesn't last long.

Over Daniel's shoulder, I see the door open and JB comes crashing through it, loud and drunk. And worse, Phillip Tench is with him. The whole room seems to turn and notice them. The two of them are laughing together like naughty children.

Phillip bloody Tench.

Why the hell is he here? What does he want? Whatever it is, it means trouble.

28

TEN YEARS AGO

What does he want? Whatever it is, it means trouble.

I'm kneeling on my bed and peeking through the window, careful he can't see me if he looks up.

Liam.

I was making my bed and opened the curtains and saw him. He could have been there ages. All night maybe. He's dressed in black and he's hanging about in front of a garden opposite, leaning against a tree and smoking. His other arm is in a sling. That must be where Daniel cut him.

I stand as still as I can and watch to see what he does next. After about ten minutes he wanders off. I wonder if he's walking round the block and will come back, but after quarter of an hour I figure I can't sit here forever watching for him, so I go downstairs.

I pour myself a bit of cereal but I'm not hungry. I keep thinking about Liam. He still has my key. Is he waiting for me to put another bit of fruit in the window? Or is he here for something else? Revenge for his arm, against me and Daniel?

Jeffrey heads out with his gold clubs and Vivian goes out too, taking Poppy to drop her at school. Daniel hasn't come down yet. This must be one of his bunking-off days. The school psychologist has agreed he can have days off if he doesn't feel like going in. That's what he says to Vivian anyway. But Daniel's told me he doesn't trust the psychologist, that she's reporting back to his parents, and he's 'playing her at her own game'. That's how he describes it. Sometimes he talks like an old man.

I knock on Daniel's door. "Daniel?"

After a bit he opens it. He's wearing school uniform.

"I saw *him* outside this morning." I don't need to say a name. Daniel knows who I mean.

"He won't do anything," says Daniel. "He knows we're on to him."

"He must be angry. What if he's come to get us? For revenge or something."

"He won't. That's why he took your key. He's too scared to even break in. He wants it easy. He's not going to make trouble for himself."

Like always, it feels like Daniel's the grown-up and I'm the kid. But he sounds so sure that I trust him.

"I've got to go," he says. "Another meeting with the psychologist."

I follow him downstairs and watch him put his coat on and get ready to go out the back door where he keeps his bike. He stops in the doorway.

"He's not going to come back and bother you. I promise."

Then he goes. I listen to the sound of the back gate and then hear the click of his chain as he rides off. I'm still nervous, so I double-lock the front door, then go up to my room to look out of the window again. There's no sign of

Liam. I sit there for ages but he doesn't come. Eventually I go
to do some chores, washing and stuff. Every now and then I
check out of my bedroom window. But Daniel's right. Liam
doesn't come.

The whole day goes by without anything happening.
When it gets near 4 p.m. I unlock the front door. Poppy and
Daniel will be home from school soon, and I don't want
Poppy asking why I had the door locked.

Eventually, everyone comes back. I sit down with them
and eat. Vivian's been asking me to cook more and I'm
getting quite good on simple things. I've made lasagne with
some mince and tinned tomatoes, and I even made a cheese
sauce. It sits on the table, golden and bubbling at the edges.
Daniel even comes down and eats with us.

It all seems quite normal. But because I know all these
secrets about Jeffrey, it's weird. Like everyone's trying too
hard to make it feel normal when it isn't. It's like a thick kind
of lump that hangs in the air. I'm nervous, sharing these
secrets with Daniel. I feel like if someone looks at me, they'll
know. I serve myself some lasagne and try not to look at
anyone. Daniel scrapes his fork across his plate, watching the
food more than eating it.

"So, how was school today?" Vivian asks Poppy while
she gets up and fusses away at the kitchen counter, emptying
a plastic bag of salad into a bowl.

"Okay," Poppy says. "In history, we're doing the
Romans, but Mr. Denby's so boring. He went on and on
about aqueducts or something, and half the class fell asleep.
At lunch, Mia slipped on a slice of pizza in front of everyone, and got up and acted like she'd meant to do it. It was
hilarious."

God, what a lame story. I try to eat my lasagne faster so I

can get out of here, but the cheese sauce is too hot to wolf it down – my bad luck.

Vivian comes over with the salad. We all chew in silence.

"I had another meeting with the psychologist," says Daniel, out of nowhere.

"Oh yes?" says Vivian. She's trying to sound casual, but you can tell she's surprised.

Jeffrey leans back, holding a forkful of lasagne he was about to eat. His eyes are fixed on Daniel.

"What does a psychologist even do, anyway?" Poppy pipes up. "Sounds boring." She's utterly dense about the atmosphere in the room. Or maybe there isn't an atmosphere. Maybe it's just me thinking there must be, because of all the stuff I know about how Jeffrey treats Daniel.

Vivian looks uncomfortable, like someone trying to stop a sneeze from coming out. "They help, sweetheart," she murmurs. "It's important."

"Help?" Jeffrey's voice cuts through the room. "Help with what, exactly?"

Oh God. This feels bad. I sit staring at the table, frozen, like that bit in Jurassic Park where they say if you don't move, the T-Rex can't see you. I wish I was anywhere else but here.

Daniel looks up. "They did this exercise..." he says to Jeffrey, looking directly at him. "She asked me to write down three things I was scared of." He sounds completely relaxed and calm.

"Like monsters under the bed?" Poppy mocks him. She makes a stupid monster face.

Daniel almost smiles but not quite. "Not exactly. Not all monsters live under the bed." He's not talking about Jeffrey directly, but everyone knows the truth, and what monster he means.

Jeffrey's hands rest on the table. He doesn't move. Vivian holds her fork over her dinner, but she doesn't eat.

"So what did you say?" asks Jeffrey. "What scares you?"

"Oh," says Daniel brightly, "I'm not allowed to tell you, or it won't work."

Jeffrey stares at him, then goes back to his lasagne without pushing it further.

"She told me to imagine a place I feel safe," says Daniel, "where no one can hurt me." He looks over at me. I can feel his eyes on me. "I'm not allowed to tell you what that is either," he says.

But I know what he means.

Me. I'm his safe space.

It makes me feel really special that he thinks that.

After dinner, Daniel stops me on the landing and whispers. "Did you see his face? He thinks I'm afraid of him, but I'm not." He means Jeffrey. I believe him.

"Was that thing about the psychologist true? The three things you're afraid of?" I ask.

"Yes."

"What did you say?"

"Spiders, snakes and the dark," says Daniel. He smiles. Then he goes back into his dark room, with his spiders and snakes.

I go into my room and lie on my bed. It's getting really bad between Daniel and Jeffrey. Daniel thinks he's got it under control, but it feels like something bad could happen. I think about telling Henry what's going on, but I don't know what he could do.

Just then my phone buzzes. Someone's calling. I reach over to see who it is.

It's Shaniqua's number. I never get calls, only texts.

Of course, I know it isn't Shaniqua. This is Liam, just like it was when he used Shaniqua's phone to trick me to the park. What does he want?

I let it ring until it goes to answerphone. But after a couple of seconds it starts ringing again. And again. It's obvious he's not going to leave me alone. On the fifth time, I decide to answer it. I tap the button but stay silent. I hear breathing and sniffing. Then a voice.

"Tracey?" It's Shaniqua.

"Yeah," I say. "It's me. It's Ariana."

She's crying. She can't get the words out.

"It's Liam," she says. "Liam's dead."

I don't know what to say. I just sit there, holding the phone.

29

NOW

I don't know what to say. I just sit there, holding the phone.

My desk is set up with a bottle of champagne and a bunch of *congratulations* helium balloons bobbing about on coloured ribbons.

Cassandra stands behind me, reading the review from *Frieze* on my mobile.

"*Clough's on Cork Street plays host to the resurrection of James Balentine, whose impact has erupted back into view with the raw and electrifying energy of a long-lost comet returning to orbit. His new exhibition, The Black Storm, is nothing short of a revelation, confirming that Balentine is not just a forgotten talent but one of the most vital and arresting voices in contemporary art.*"

Cassandra looks across the room at Daniel. "Jesus Christ." She goes back to reading.

"*There is something uniquely visceral in his work. Balentine is no longer the great overlooked painter of his generation. He is its defining one.*" She squeezes my shoulder. "It's amazing. You're amazing."

Daniel comes over and stands so he can read the screen as well. He rests his hand lightly on my other shoulder. We read it all again, over and over. We pop the champagne. We toast the success of the show. Then the phone starts ringing. It's buyers, calling to ask which works are still available. A distinguished-looking man in a beautifully cut suit comes in to ask about a painting and Daniel goes to talk to him. After fifteen minutes, the man leaves and Daniel comes into the office and hands me a business card.

"He's asked to put a painting on hold. He'll call by the end of today."

"Oh my God," I say. "That's fantastic."

"I told him it was eighteen thousand."

"What?" I assume he must have made a mistake. "We're selling them for *eight* thousand."

"I know," says Daniel. "But that was before the review. It only came out this morning and look how many calls we've had."

"We can't do that," I say, "just make it up on the hoof."

"Of course we can," says Daniel. "Demand dictates price. Eight thousand's a figure we plucked out of the air, so eighteen thousand is no more absurd. It's all dictated by what people will pay. I told him eighteen, we'll do it for sixteen, and everyone's happy."

It feels wrong. It feels like just playing fast and loose with everything. It's reckless.

But weirdly, it seems like it's a turn-on for people. They assume because we're asking so much, what they're getting must be that good. For the rest of the afternoon I watch Daniel in action around the gallery. He's better at it than I am, the schmoozing stuff. Cassandra nearly wets herself laughing when she hears what price Daniel's asking for the paintings. But once she calms down, she backs him on the audacity. By the end of the afternoon we've sold three of the paintings and have another one on reserve.

The gallery closes for the day. Cassandra heads off to meet some friends. It's dark outside and has started to drizzle. The large glass window at the front is a massive black rectangle streaked by white and red light from passing cars.

I think of Henry. I wonder why I felt he was drifting away from me, too busy with other things. In contrast, Daniel seems to have all the time in the world for me. Even so, part of me feels not completely in control. Daniel smashing part of the gallery down. Ordering all that champagne. Going onto my laptop to email that critic. Everything has worked out okay... but things are spinning too fast for me to hold on to.

"Thanks for today," I say to Daniel as he comes over and starts getting his cycling stuff ready, his helmet and lights. "Will you be okay in this rain? You could leave your bike here. I could give you a lift?"

"No, I'm good," he says. "I've always liked cycling. Nipping in and out of the traffic. I'll be fine."

"I can't believe you're here again," I say. "We shouldn't have left it so long. Ten years ago, everything that happened back then, your dad and everything. It feels like a completely different universe. I'm so glad you're back."

"There's a theory about universes," he says.

He reaches across my desk and takes two of the helium balloons by their strings.

He leans in very close to me. The room is silent.

"People think our universe is like a balloon, expanding in all directions, containing everything that's ever existed and ever will exist. But maybe there isn't just one universe.

Maybe, outside our balloon, there are lots of other balloons, lots of other universes all doing the same thing. And so there's this big space full of billions of different universes."

He looks at me intently. There's an awestruck tone in his voice. He speaks very softly, almost in a whisper, and I have to lean forward to make sure I catch what he's saying.

"And sometimes," he whispers, "the universes bump into each other."

He moves the two balloons and they bump gently together with the faintest of noise in the silent room.

"Maybe you and I were in different universes for the last ten years, moving in different directions. But now those universes have touched and we've come together again."

Bump. The balloons lightly touch each other.

"We were always going to be together. And now we are, I'll never let you go."

His face is so close to mine I can feel his breath on my lips. I see the strange, stretched skin of his own damaged face, alien and otherworldly. He's dazzling, and brilliant, and charismatic. And what he says is the most romantic thing anyone has ever said to me.

I'll never let you go.

But the intensity of it scares me.

I don't know why.

Maybe there's something wrong with me.

But something about it terrifies me to the core.

PART 4

30

TEN YEARS AGO

Something about it terrifies me to the core.

Liam's dead.

I should be happy. I know he's not coming after me. But something feels wrong. He was outside here this morning and now he's dead. Is that really just a coincidence?

I knock on Daniel's door. When I go in, he's playing with Lego. Sometimes I forget he's just a kid, but that's exactly what he looks like now. A twelve-year-old kid.

"He's dead," I say.

Daniel looks up from his half-complete model. It looks like it's going to be a space shuttle or something. "Who?"

"*Him!*" I say, with real emphasis.

"Oh," says Daniel. "Him. What happened?"

"I got a call from his girlfriend. He got stabbed. She reckons it's some drug deal gone wrong."

"Sounds about right," Daniel says. He's got a Lego block in his hand and I can tell he's itching to attach it to the model. Maybe what I've told him hasn't registered. He seems so calm about it.

"Do you think it was a drug deal?" I ask. "Seems a bit weird he came here and got injured, and now he's been stabbed."

Daniel puts the Lego on his desk. He looks thoughtful. "Maybe my dad did it," he says.

"Jeffrey? Why?" I don't understand at all.

"Think about it," says Daniel. "Dad's got all these secrets. Who knows what else he's up to? Maybe the robber knew something. Maybe that's why he wanted to rob the house. If you saw him hanging about outside, chances are Dad saw him too. You know how violent my dad is. He'd totally be capable of killing someone."

I've been wary of Jeffrey, but this thought makes me terrified of him. Could Jeffrey be a murderer? The more I find out about him, the more I think it's possible.

"Did they find your door key on the body?" asks Daniel.

"I don't know. Shaniqua didn't say much."

"What if he had the key on him when Dad killed him? Dad will know you let Liam into the house. He'll think you're part of it."

I don't know what to think. But Daniel could be right. Maybe we do need to run away from here.

When I leave Daniel's room, I go back to mine and check my savings. I haven't got enough to go anywhere else. And I can't leave Daniel here. I have to take him with me. But a twelve-year-old can't live rough on the streets.

I go down into the kitchen. Vivian is drinking wine at the kitchen table. She looks miserable. All the dirty plates from dinner are still there, so I begin to scrape stuff into the bin and load the dishwasher. I look at the knife block. Two knives are missing from it. As I load the dishwasher, I find one of the knives in there. But there's no sign of the other one. I try to think whether the block has always had a knife missing or whether it's only just disappeared, but I can't remember. The lasagne tray has a black crust around the edge where cheese has burnt onto it like charcoal. I go to the sink to put it in to soak.

That's when I see something in the garden. It's dark outside, and there's a bonfire. As I'm looking I see it flare up, and realise Jeffrey is there. He's just thrown something onto the fire, paper maybe.

"Ignore him," says Vivian behind me. I spin round and realise she's watching me stare out of the window. I feel my face go hot, like I've been caught doing something I shouldn't be. "It's letters," she says in a flat voice as she tops up her wine glass. Her speech is slurry and I reckon she's pretty sloshed. "They're from Henry. We dated for a while at university. He wrote to me when he was studying in America. Jeffrey said it was fine, that it was all a long time ago. But it appears he isn't fine." She laughs, but it's one of those laughs people do when they don't find something funny.

Later I'm lying in my bed. I can't sleep. Thoughts are going round and round in my head.

I think about Vivian and Henry. Did they really date? Henry didn't say anything about it.

Why would Vivian tell me such a personal story?

Maybe they *were* letters from Henry on that bonfire.

Or maybe they were something else.

I must tell Daniel in the morning.

But I already know what Daniel will say. That the bonfire wasn't letters from Henry at all. It was something to do with Liam's murder. And Vivian was lying. And the fire was Jeffrey, destroying the evidence.

31

NOW

"The fire destroyed the evidence, so they've got no leads on Henry's murder."

The policeman who came to the house before is here at the gallery, with some woman. Another detective maybe.

"That's terrible," says Daniel. "It must feel so unresolved. I'll give you some space." He grabs his jacket and heads out onto the street.

I sit down in the office with the policeman and the woman, who explains she's from Victim Support. I guess if you consider sitting in silence with a fake smile on your face 'support' then she's doing a fantastic job. Other than that, she's useless.

"As I explained when we last spoke, Mrs Clough, the vehicle which we believe struck your husband didn't give us any useful forensic evidence. And after reviewing all the CCTV footage, we aren't able to develop any leads on the driver. We've had an increased presence on the lookout for joyriders, but there haven't been any other incidents. They probably know they've messed up and are keeping their heads down. I want to be clear we're certainly not closing the case. Often leads come to light when a witness emerges for some reason. But until someone comes forward with more information, I'm afraid the trail has gone cold."

"So, you're not closing the case. You're just not doing anything else about it?"

He shifts awkwardly. "I'm sorry."

"If there's anything else you need, you can contact us on this number," says Victim Support woman. She passes me a leaflet. It's got pictures of actors holding telephones, pretending to talk to a helpline. Bizarrely, most of them are smiling.

The two of them leave. I shove the leaflet straight in the bin.

That's it then. Henry's dead and we're all just supposed to carry on as if nothing has happened. Business as usual. But Daniel's right, it's all unresolved, and I feel like I'm drifting in limbo. I know I have to get on with things and move forward, but I feel stuck.

I throw myself into work. The gallery's been busy in the last couple of days, with enquiries from collectors in Germany and China. We've sold four paintings. After the third one sold, Daniel pushed me to put the prices up again, to twenty-four thousand this time. He said it sounded like a more real number than twenty-five thousand. It was only once I agreed he told me he'd already sold the fourth painting for that amount.

I have the same feeling I had before, that I'm not in control of things, that they're spinning too fast for me to hold on to.

There's a Post-it note on the corner of the desk with a message that Cassandra's taken: *Phillip Tench called at 3.30 p.m.* And a phone number. It gives me great pleasure to throw the Post-it in the bin with the victim support leaflet. With the money that's come in so far I've been able to pay off a chunk of the mortgage arrears, and I won't need to sell the gallery to that smarmy little shit any time soon.

I go into the laptop to look up some of the other enquiry emails about JB's exhibition. I search *Balentine*. An email chain pops up between Cassandra and Henry. Of course Henry and Cassandra will have discussed all the gallery artists.

But what I start reading isn't what I'm expecting at all.

Henry,
I know why you need to be with her this weekend. But whatever you do with her, imagine it's me instead. Whatever you do to her, picture me there instead. God, the thought of you and what you do to me. The way you make me feel... I can't stop thinking about it. I can't wait until we're together again. Cassie xxx

I look at the search box and realise I've accidentally hit V instead of B and searched *Valentine*. I think of the Valentine's weekend Henry and I had in the Cotswolds last year. That lovely hotel. The spa. I remember how distracted Henry was, and how I thought he was stressed with work. How sorry I felt for him.

All the way as I drive home I play things over in my mind. How busy Henry was at the gallery. How absent he seemed. And even after he died, my certainty his behaviour was to hide the finances from me. That he was protecting me.

I feel like an idiot. The liar. How am I supposed to grieve him and hate him at the same time?

I park outside the house and go in and up to the guest room. I shove all Cassandra's things into her suitcases, and take all her stuff out of the bathroom and chuck it into a plastic bag. I haul the heavy suitcases down the stairs, journey after journey. I drag them out onto the front drive. I pause briefly to get my thoughts straight enough to write her a text.

> *I know about you and Henry. Don't come back to the*
> *gallery. Your things are outside the house. I don't*
> *want to see you again.*

I double-lock the front door.

I sit in the bedroom, my thoughts spinning in an unfocussed muddle. After five minutes the phone rings. It's Cassandra. I let it ring until it cuts off. It rings again. And again. And again. There's a long pause, then a ping to tell me I have a voicemail. After half an hour it rings another three times. Then another ping, another voicemail.

I lie on the bed, staring out through the window up at the sky, watching clouds move in different abstract shapes. It gets darker. After an hour or so I hear a car stop outside, and there's a knock at the door. My phone rings again and I let it ring until it stops. The engine keeps running and I hear voices I can't identify. After five minutes the car drives off.

The phone doesn't ring again.

After half an hour I delete the voicemails without listening to them.

I go downstairs. Cassandra's keys are on the mat where

they've been pushed through the letterbox. I open the front door. It's twilight. All the bags have gone.

It seems like something's been dealt with, but it hasn't really. I've dealt with a symptom but the root cause is still there. Henry. Henry's paintings in the hallway. Henry's furniture. Henry's taste in decorations. Henry's coffee maker on the kitchen counter.

I have to get out of this house.

32

TEN YEARS AGO

I have to get out of this house.

I'm scared.

At least with Liam I knew he was after me. But I've no idea whether Jeffrey is after me or not. But Daniel's sure he is, and he should know. I close my eyes and picture that bruise on his face where Jeffrey hit him. And he's just a little kid.

I don't know what to do. I can't relax. It's crazy I could be living in the same house as someone who wants to hurt me. I'm already a runaway and now I might have to run away from the place I've run away to. I'd laugh if it wasn't so deadly serious.

Henry's meeting me for lunch. It's a restaurant with a weird name called Andrew Edmunds. I wrote the name and address in my phone so I wouldn't forget. When I look up how to get there, it isn't too hard to find. I get the tube to Tottenham Court Road and come out by a theatre with a massive sign for *We Will Rock You*. I'm stupidly early, so I wander up Oxford Street and look in shop windows before I cut down a side street and follow the map on my phone.

There's a pile of boxes in a shop doorway with an old sleeping bag shoved inside, but when I look closer there's a person inside it. Will that be me? Am I going to have to run away and end up on the streets?

Henry's waiting outside the restaurant when I arrive. He kisses me on the cheek. We go in. He's sweet and talkative and I think he's a bit nervous. We've been for quite a few walks in the park, but this is our first proper date. He looks around the room as if he's looking for people he knows. The waitress brings us handwritten menus. Lots of the food sounds weird and I don't know what to order, but Henry's been here before and tells me things he's had which are nice and I order some of that. He orders a bottle of wine. While we wait for our food Henry looks around the room again and then holds my hand across the table.

All the time this is happening I'm wondering about whether I should tell Henry what's going on at Vivian's. But if I tell him what Jeffrey was up to, burning that stuff, then I have to say about him dating Vivian and writing her letters, and I don't want to look like a soppy, jealous teenager. Even worse, I'll have to tell him about Liam, and then everything about me being in care and running away, and I don't want him to know any of that.

I don't say anything.

After lunch Henry says he wants to take me somewhere, and we walk for about ten minutes 'til we come to a street with a load of galleries on it. We stop outside one that's shut. It has big glass windows the whole length of the shop, but it's all white and empty inside.

"This is it," says Henry. "Where the new gallery is going to be. What do you think?"

I don't know what to say. It looks like all the other galleries along here, and all I can think to say is "Yeah, it's great."

We press our faces against the glass and cup our hands against our cheeks so we can see inside. Henry talks about changes he's going to make and I can hear how excited he is. He's really lovely and I like the way he talks to me like a real person, not some kid who's younger than him. I know there's an age gap but it doesn't feel like there is unless I think about it.

He keeps talking, all excited, and then he holds my hand, and then he kisses me. It's lovely. Tender. Not like all that fumbling boys have done in the past. He doesn't grab at me or anything, but he puts his hand behind my neck and under my hair while we kiss. He asks me when I have to be back and I tell him I'm free until I have to cook dinner. He asks if I'd like to come for a coffee at his, and I say yes.

His house is lovely. It seems really big for just one person and I wonder how he doesn't get lonely. As soon as we go in, we kiss in the hallway. While he's making the coffee I go upstairs to the loo. I can't resist peeking into the rooms and see one of them must be his bedroom. It's got a big bed with a puffy grey duvet and an orange blanket at the end. It looks really smart and masculine, like something out of a magazine. I tiptoe in and slip my shoes off and lie on the bed. It's probably the comfiest bed I've ever been on. I pick up one of the grey pillows and for some reason I put it over my face so it all goes dark. It smells like Henry. I close my eyes and lie there wrapped in the darkness and imagine what it would be like if I lived here.

I take the pillow off my face and open my eyes and see Henry's in the doorway, smiling at me. I'm embarrassed he's caught me in here. "Sorry," I say, but he keeps smiling and comes over and lies down on the bed next to me. He puts his arms round me and kisses me again. We kiss for a long time. It's nice. It's slow and it feels more gentle than passionate. He keeps asking me if I'm okay and if I like it. And I do. I feel even more that I like him. We lie there cuddling and kissing for ages.

"I could move in here," I say, "if you wanted."

I feel him go tense in the bed and realise I've made a mistake asking. I've been thinking it all through lunch and on the trip back here, but I haven't said anything to him and I've blurted it completely out of the blue. Oh shit. It's a bad idea and I know I've messed up.

"Or not," I say, as casual as I can manage. "It's just an idea."

"Oh," he says. Then there's a long pause when I want the bed to open up like in *Nightmare on Elm Street* and just swallow me so I won't be so embarrassed. "That's very sudden."

"That's fine, no worries," I say, getting out of the bed. I'm trying to act like I don't care, but I know I look stupid. The more I pretend I don't care the more obvious it is that I do.

"Ariana," says Henry. He sits up and puts his arm round me as I'm sitting on the edge of the bed putting my shoes on. "Wait. You took me by surprise, that's all. I like you. I like you a lot. But it's very sudden. And you're only nineteen. I feel, I don't know... It's a big gap and I'm not sure how I feel about it. For you, I mean. I don't want to take advantage. I think we should take it a bit slow, that's all."

He strokes my hair.

"I hope I haven't upset you. I don't want to mess this up."

I can't tell him now. I can't tell him I'm only seventeen. Or about care. Or about running away.

"It's okay," I say. "Really. But I have to go."

"Shall we have that coffee?"

"No, I really do have to go now," I say. He knows I'm hurt. He comes downstairs with me and sees me out. He kisses me goodbye but he looks sad.

As I walk back to the tube I feel sad too. I like Henry but I've got this big secret I can't tell him. It feels like a lump in my stomach. I'm going to spoil things and I don't know what to do about it.

When I get back to the house, Vivian's in the hallway as I come through the door. "Ariana, can I have a quick word?" She sounds serious. It's that sort of voice people use when you've done something you shouldn't have, and I try to think what it is I've done as I follow her into the kitchen.

Jeffrey's sitting at the table. The way he looks at me makes the lump in my stomach knot up. I feel sick. Vivian sits down as well, but I just stand there.

"This is awkward," says Vivian. She sounds nervous. She's picking away at one of her fingernails, and there are tiny flakes of nail varnish on the table in front of her. "Are you dating Henry Clough?"

"What if I am?" I've said it before I think. I'm pissed off. I don't like being told what I can or can't do. But now I've basically admitted that I'm seeing Henry.

"Your private life is your lookout," says Jeffrey angrily, "but if you're involved with that man it doesn't work, you being here." He stands up. "Pack your stuff. You need to go."

He walks out of the room. I stand there, not knowing

what to do. Vivian looks at me side-on. She can't even look me in the eye properly.

"I'm sorry," she says. "It just makes it too difficult. Anyway, the plan was always for you to be here for just a couple of months." I don't know who she's trying to convince, me or herself. "We'll pay you until the end of the month, obviously."

"Thanks," I say quietly, though I don't mean it. I don't know what to say. I feel numb. I wanted to get away from here, but not like this. I've got nowhere and no one. And what about Daniel? I've got away, but what about him? I can't just abandon him here.

Vivian gets up. As she passes me, she looks at me properly for the first time. "It's good you're going," she says, in a quiet voice. "It really is. It's for the best."

Then she looks off towards the hallway, where Jeffrey's just left. She whispers.

"Get away while you can. You've had a lucky escape. He's dangerous."

33

NOW

"It's good she's going," says Daniel. "It's for the best. You've had a lucky escape."

It doesn't feel like that. I feel like I'm trying to get back on my feet in the middle of a bloody earthquake.

"You don't need someone toxic like that in your life."

"I know," I say.

But in spite of everything, I'm really worried. Cassandra was so good on all the gallery stuff. I'm out of my depth on my own. I feel like I'm going to drown without her.

"There's something else," says Daniel. "I didn't want to show you this before." He pulls out a piece of paper. It's a copy of an email from Cassandra to JB. "She messed up the measurements for the doorway. It was *her* fault we had to knock half that wall down. She was a liability."

God, is my judgement so bad I couldn't see what she was like? "It all feels like it's spinning so fast I don't know what to hold on to."

"I understand. But you've had more than your fair share of disruption, and you've hung on fine so far."

"I keep waiting for things to settle down, but they don't."

"They never do," says Daniel. "Where we're standing right now, the Earth is spinning on its axis at a thousand miles an hour." He makes a show of holding onto the edge of the table, as if he'll fall over if he doesn't. "And the Earth's orbiting round the sun at seventy thousand miles an hour. And the sun's swinging round the Milky Way at four hundred thousand miles an hour. And the Milky Way's flying outwards from the Big Bang at two million miles an hour."

He lets go of the table and stands there steadily, like he's performed some amazing superhuman feat.

"And look at you," he says. "You haven't fallen over yet."

He gives me a twinkly smile. The skin on his neck pulls tight. His left eye glints with a cheeky sparkle. His cloudy right eye remains grey and cold and I wonder how much, if anything, he can see out of it. I hate myself for still thinking these things, for noticing.

"Anyway," he says, coming over and putting his arm around my shoulder in a friendly hug, "if you feel yourself wobbling, I've got you."

"Thanks," I say. And I really do feel better, knowing Daniel has my back.

"Would you like me to stay on?" he says. "At the gallery, I mean. I know we were pretending I work here to keep Robin happy, but maybe I could work here for real until you find someone permanent?"

"If you can stay and help, that would be absolutely brilliant." I give his arm a squeeze. It feels thin and bony, and it takes me by surprise. I'm slowly getting used to the scarred parts of him I can see, but I've forgotten that the rest of him must be damaged too. The parts I can't see. I can't even begin to imagine what other damage might have been done – inside.

So Daniel comes into the gallery most days. Every now and then he disappears unexpectedly. He must have other things going on, I guess, away from here. I want to ask him about the rest of his life, but whenever I do he makes a joke and changes the subject, so I drop it.

Once or twice Robin the probation officer pops in but doesn't say much. Occasionally he asks if everything is okay, by which I assume he means everything with Daniel. "Fabulous," I say, with as sweet a smile as I can muster. I have an inherent dislike of people who work for the system. I want to make things as easy for Daniel as I can.

Daniel refuses any kind of payment, but I finally get him to work on commission. He has an incredible instinct for sales. I watch him with people considering buying. They're not confident, but he's confident, and his confidence seems to infect them. By the end of the week, we've sold all seven of JB's paintings, including the big one we couldn't get through the door. Daniel has three collectors interested and plays them off against each other in a bidding war. He pushes the final price to forty-eight thousand.

I do the maths. It's eye-watering. In just over a week, I've made enough to pay off all the most pressing debts. I feel a wave of relief wash over me. For the first time in as long as I remember I feel something I barely remember feeling. Happy.

"Let's go to dinner," I say to Daniel. "My treat. JB's coming in for a chat. Now we've sold all the work, he probably wants to remind me how brilliant he is. Once he's gone I'll lock up, and we can go somewhere, have some nice wine and celebrate. What d'you say?"

"Sounds great," says Daniel. "I have to pick my bike up from the repair shop, so I'll meet you somewhere."

I think for a moment. "Have you been to Andrew Edmunds?"

I don't know why, but it feels right to go there. Maybe so it stops being Henry's place and starts being mine. I decide not to overthink it and make a reservation.

Fifteen minutes after Daniel leaves, JB arrives. He strides through the gallery and looks around the show briefly, making the odd approving grunt, as if they aren't his own paintings he's admiring, the arrogant twat. He saunters into the office.

"Just you, is it?" he asks. "The burnt fella not here? He's a good chap. Or the girl?"

I bite my tongue. "Nope. Just me."

"Well," he says, sitting down with his legs splayed in some kind of power stance, "that's probably best."

"Congratulations, JB. We've only been open for a week and we've sold out the entire show. You must be pleased." I push a bottle of champagne towards him across the table. I've tied a ribbon round the neck and attached a couple of my *congratulations* balloons and I've written him a card in an envelope. Now he's sitting here it's obvious he's not a ribbons and balloons sort of person and I feel like an idiot. He doesn't pick them up.

"I'll come to the point," he says. "I'm grateful for the show, and for the shows Henry gave me before. Some things went well this time round, some not so well. That stupid mistake with the door size." He lets the thought hang there, disapprovingly.

"But good we could sort it so quickly," I say. He's going to make me eat shit for this. Even with a sold-out show, he has to act like he's the genius and the rest of us haven't got a clue what we're doing.

"Anyway," he says, "having thought it through, it's time for a change. My new work will be on a larger scale and it's not going to fit here. I've been talking to another gallery and I'm going to give it a go with them for a while."

I'm completely wrong-footed. My mouth opens to talk, but nothing comes out.

"So, that's that," he says.

Finally, I manage to speak. "If it's a question of scale, we shouldn't just think of gallery shows. We can place larger works in institutions–"

"No," he interrupts. "You're too small. My mind's made up."

We're too small. He doesn't just mean the doorway.

"Anyway, thanks for everything," he says, getting up. He unknots the ribbon and takes the bottle of champagne, of course, the bastard. "I'll be in touch about when you can get me back the paintings you have in storage." He passes me the balloons.

"Oh," I say as he gets to the doorway. "Can I ask what gallery you're moving to?"

"Certainly," he says. "Phillip Tench." And he leaves.

That's that then. Once again, it's spinning out of control. I hold the edge of the desk. I pick up my bag and look out of the window. It's dark. I know I need to go, but I can't make myself move towards the door. I'm frozen to the spot.

34

TEN YEARS AGO

I pick up my bag and look out of the window. It's dark. I need to go, but I can't make myself move towards the door. I'm frozen to the spot.

There's a noise on the landing and I turn round and see Daniel standing in the gap of my open doorway. He's smiling. But then he sees me holding my stupid Hello Kitty rucksack and his face falls. His eyes dart round the room and it's obvious I've packed all my stuff.

"What's going on?" he says in a shaky voice. "Where are you going?"

"Nowhere." It's a stupid lie because he can obviously see I've packed up.

"You can't leave," he says. "What will I do if you leave? What will happen to *me*?"

"I'm not leaving," I say. I can't bear how upset he's getting.

"Liar!" he spits at me. His eyes are shiny where I think tears might be coming. But maybe they're angry tears. He looks furious. His mouth goes tight and I can see his neck all

NEVER LET YOU GO   211

strained where he's clenching his jaw. I go stiff and hold my breath and realise I'm tense because he looks like he might hit me or something.

"It's Dad, isn't it? He's making you go."

I try not to react.

"I knew he would," Daniel says, almost in a whine. "I knew he'd make you go because he wants to hide what he's up to. He doesn't want you to know. When you're out of the way, he'll have no one to stop him getting me. I could hear your voices, talking in the kitchen. I knew it was about me."

I don't tell him about Henry. I know Daniel likes me and I don't want to upset him or make him jealous or anything. I remember how he got when he saw me and Henry together in the kitchen that time.

"He spoils everything," he says in a dark voice. I can't tell if he's talking to me or to himself.

Suddenly he leaps forward. I jump back, thinking he's going to attack me, but he grabs hold of my hand and squeezes it so hard that it hurts.

"Take me with you. Please. Please!"

I can feel my knuckles crunching together.

"You can't leave me here on my own."

I pull my hand away because of the pain, and I see he looks hurt.

"Something really bad will happen if you go. Something terrible. I know it."

He looks properly terrified. I feel awful.

"Look, Daniel, I didn't want to say anything," I say, "but I'm just going to stay with my friend Shaniqua for a couple of days. Her boyfriend died suddenly and she needs some help. The boyfriend we said we wouldn't talk about. That's why I didn't tell you." I feel bad lying to him, but he's so upset I need to calm him down. He just stands there, staring at me.

"A couple of days?"

"Yeah," I say. "I don't want to stay any longer. You know why."

I see him puzzling it through. His forehead wrinkles up like a little old man while he works it out.

"Okay, that makes sense," he says. "Sorry if I hurt your hand."

"It's okay," I say, giving him a smile. I lean over and put my arm round his shoulder. "It'll be okay. It will." We stand there like that. But it feels awkward. Maybe because my body knows I don't really believe it.

"I'll say goodbye before I go." I let go of him and he gives me a sort of puzzled look and goes out of the room.

It was hard leaving before, but now it feels even harder. I promised myself I'd look after Daniel, and I really will. I just can't now. I want to help him, but I can barely help myself. I have to get myself sorted first, and then I'll come for him. I know I'm letting him down right now, but what can I do?

I shouldn't lie to him. But I can still feel the ache in my hand, how he got hold of me and wouldn't let go. I should go and talk to him properly. But if he knows I'm leaving forever he'll never let me go. It'll turn into a scene, and that's worse.

I pick up my things and go downstairs and find a pad of paper and a pen in a kitchen drawer. I want to try to explain things to Daniel, but I don't know how to say what I'm thinking and feeling in a way he'll understand.

Daniel, I start writing. I think long and hard before I work out what to put next.

When I'm finished, I fold the paper and put it in an envelope and lick it closed. I walk quietly up the stairs. I know I promised him I'd say goodbye before I leave, but I can't. I just can't. Instead, I put the envelope just outside his bedroom door where I know he'll see it.

I sneak back down the stairs again. I go into the kitchen and pick up my stuff. I walk into the hallway and open the front door as quietly as I can. I step out onto the path into the night, pulling the door closed quietly behind me. I walk off, wondering what Daniel will think when he gets my note.

I've written just one sentence.

I'm sorry.

35

NOW

"I'm sorry."

"No," says Daniel, "don't worry. We can go there another time."

We walk away from Andrew Edmunds without eating. All I can think about is the last time I was there, and Phillip Tench smarming away at one of my artists. Now he's stolen another one.

We've found ourselves a quietish pub round the corner. I sit there, fuming, my head racing in an angry muddle. Just when I thought I was back on track, I can feel it's all going to slip away from me again. Tench seems determined to destroy me.

After a couple of minutes Daniel reappears with drinks. "Here," he says, depositing them on the table, "beer and crisps. That's what I call a proper dinner."

I chug a big gulp of beer and try to steady my temper.

"Right," says Daniel, "tell me what happened."

I fill him in on my conversation with James arsehole Balentine.

"What an absolute shit," says Daniel when I've finished. He seems as angry as I am. "Him and that bastard Tench. Self-serving pricks." His voice has got loud. I notice a couple of people at a nearby table looking round. One looks particularly pissed off, like he might say something about the volume, but then he spots Daniel's scars and goes back to his drink, as if Daniel's looks somehow give him a free pass. The angry bloke whispers to his mate, who looks over. They're not the only ones. When I'm in public with Daniel I'm hyper-aware of people looking at us. Daniel never seems to notice. Or maybe he's had so many years of it he's become immune.

"Let's sell them," he says.

I don't understand. "Sorry. Sell what?"

"The other paintings," he says. "JB's. The ones we've got in storage."

"We can't do that," I say. "He wants them back."

"Well, he can't have them. We transported them, we stored them, they were all offered to the gallery as part of the exhibition." He sits back in his chair and pops a crisp in his mouth. He crunches on it with a confident half-smile on his face.

What he says sounds convincing. But it can't be right, can it? "No, we can't. I mean, they're JB's paintings."

"Yes," says Daniel pedantically, "which *he* consigned to *you* as his representative."

"I don't know." I can feel myself wavering in the face of Daniel's supreme self-assurance. "Is it ethical?"

"Fuck ethics," he exclaims. "Is it ethical to poach other gallery artists? Is it ethical to shit all over a woman who's just given you the most successful show of your career? These bastards can't treat you like this. You deserve better."

His anger bleeds into me. There was a time I'd've smashed Balentine's teeth out of his head with that bottle of champagne I gave him. But I'm a different person now.

"Think about it," says Daniel. "You've got, what, thirty-five paintings in storage? We could sell all those at twenty grand a pop. That's seven hundred grand, just sitting in a warehouse. Do you really want to hand that to JB and Tench without a fight?"

Christ, it's tempting. I'd love to get one over on those bastards. And the money wouldn't hurt either. "But is it even legal?"

"I dunno," says Daniel. "Let the lawyers argue it out. Meanwhile, sell as many paintings as you can. By the time they do anything about it, you'll have sold them. You can give JB his fifty per cent. He won't give a shit whether it's you or Tench who's sold them."

Jesus. Am I going to do this?

"Yes," I say. "Yes. Sod it. Let's go for it. Let's do it!"

I gulp my drink. I feel a huge adrenaline rush of excitement, but also a wobble of fear. I look at my hand holding my drink. It's shaking.

· "It's okay," says Daniel, sensing my anxiety. He leans forward, pushing the empty crisp packets to the side. He takes hold of my hand. Not for the first time our burnt hands intertwine like two limbs from the same creature. His thumb gently strokes the smooth skin of my scar.

"It's okay," he says again. "It's okay. It's me. I've got you."

36

TEN YEARS AGO

"It's okay. It's okay. It's me. I've got you."

I bury my face into Henry's chest. I can feel the scratch of his suit jacket against my cheek. I close my eyes and let him pull me in tight, with his arms wrapped around me. I want him to squeeze me so tight all the air comes out of me. I feel how I haven't felt for a long time. Safe.

"Come on. Come in," he says, letting go of me and leading me through the hallway. We go into the living room and sit down on a massive leather couch. The room's painted dark green, and you'd think it'd be all dull and depressing, but it's not dingy at all. It's really cosy and comforting. The walls are covered with paintings and drawings. I guess they must be by people from the gallery Henry owns. There's a little metal statue on the table next to the sofa of a man's head. I'm nervous and don't know what to do with my hands, so I pick it up to look at it and realise it's a statue of Henry. I guess one of his artist friends must have done it. I try to imagine being the sort of person someone would ever want to make a statue of.

Henry sits on the sofa next to me. He puts the statue down and takes hold of my hand. I look down at our hands wrapped around each other like two hands from the same person. "I can see you're upset," he says. "What's going on?"

I don't know what to say or where to start. I've thought of telling him stuff before, but if I blurt it all out now I'll sound like a proper loser. But I don't want to keep all these secrets anymore.

"I have to tell you something," I say to him. "But don't be angry. I think you'll be angry with me."

He doesn't take his hand away, but there's a tiny shift in how he's sitting. He's gone all tense. "Yes," he says. The word sounds longer than normal. "What is it?"

"That stuff I said about me taking a year off before university. That's not right. I'm not going to university."

"It doesn't matter," he says, smiling. "You're bright and sparky. It doesn't make any difference to me whether you're going to university or not."

"I didn't do well at school, see. I had a lot of family trouble and it messed up my studies."

"I'm sorry to hear that," he says. "I hope things are better now."

"Well," I say, "not really. They're not. My mum died a while back and I got taken into care."

"Oh God, Ariana," he says, putting his arm around me, "that must have been terrible for you. I'm so sorry."

"It was okay," I say without thinking. I'm used to not talking about it. It's something I block out. But now I *have* to talk about it. It's hard. "Some of it was fine," I say. "Other bits weren't great and I ended up running away."

"Oh no. Poor you," he says. He still doesn't get it.

"I mean, I ran away pretty recently," I say. "A few weeks ago. I'm–" I can't say it.

"What?"

"I'm not nineteen. I'm seventeen."

He lets his arm go from around my shoulder. He leans back from me. He looks at me with this weird look on his face, like he's confused. His face kind of creases up. "Seventeen?" he says. He's staring at me like he's trying to match the word with what he's looking at.

"I'll be eighteen in two months," I say hopefully. It's not long. That'll be okay, won't it? He can wait two months.

"Oh God, Ariana, I don't know," he says, getting up and shuffling round the room. "I'm thirty-five, for God's sake. It was bad enough when I thought you were nineteen. But seventeen?" He goes high-pitched and his face screws up like he's tasted something sour. "I feel like... I don't know. It feels wrong. I don't want to take advantage."

"You're not," I say, jumping up, "you're not!"

I hope he's going to hug me again, but he doesn't.

"I think you should go home," he says. "It's a lot to take in. I need to think about things."

"Right, sure." I feel like an idiot. He doesn't want anything to do with me.

"Do you need a lift back to Vivian and Jeffrey's?"

"No, it's fine, I'll walk." I grab my bag and head for the door. I just want to get away.

"I'll call you later," he says, as I race out of the house and down the path.

Shit. Shit. I've messed it all up. Why didn't I tell him sooner? And why does it matter anyway, if we love each other? It doesn't make any difference how old he is or how old I am.

I walk along the pavement fast, wanting to get away. I haven't even told him most of the stuff I needed to say, about Liam and the key. Liam getting killed. About Jeffrey, and how he hits Daniel, and how Jeffrey must have killed Liam. Him burning evidence in the garden. And how Jeffrey stole my ID. How he's thrown me out to stop me knowing more stuff. All the thoughts spin around in my head in a blur. It's too much, and I feel lost. Henry was supposed to be the one to help me. Now I'm on my own.

I don't know where to go. I can't go to Shaniqua's. I don't know anyone else. I've walked fast and a long way, and I'm near the park. I think about the benches I've sat on sometimes, when I've been out with Henry or I've come down with Daniel on his bike. It's dark now and the park gates are closed, but there's a section of wall I know near a bus stop and a big tree.

The glass in the bus stop's been broken for ages. I stand on the red plastic seat and step onto the frame. I've pulled the sleeves of my jacket down over my hands in case there's any bits of broken glass. Once I'm up, I grab one of the tree branches and manage to pull myself up onto the wall. I throw my bag over, then jump down onto a patch of mossy stuff.

It's weirdly quiet in here, and less windy than on the road. Away from the street lights it's really dark, all dark green shadows, like Henry's living room, but creepy rather than cosy. I walk round the path until I find the benches I was thinking of. They're off to one side under some trees. I sit down and try to work out how to get comfortable. I put my bag down on the bench and use it as a pillow. I take my jacket off and lay it over me, the one Poppy ripped, but it's too small and doesn't cover me properly, so I put it back on again and button it right up to the neck.

Now I've stopped walking it's cold. The leaves are rustling above me even though it's not that windy. I'm freezing. Somewhere far away I can hear voices. It sounds like two people arguing, a man and a woman. I can't work out whether they're on the road or inside the park.

It starts me thinking about who else might be here. I can't be the only person round here who doesn't have a place to stay. What sort of people need to sleep in a park? They're probably desperate. I've got money in my bag.

I sit up again and split my money into two piles. I put most of it back in my bag but I hold twenty quid in fivers in my hand. I figure if someone comes at me, I can get up and run, and throw down the money I'm holding. While they pick up the notes, it'll give me a chance to get away.

But what if someone isn't interested in money? What if they're interested in me?

I'm freezing, and now I'm too scared to sleep. This was a stupid idea. I don't feel safe. I get up and shove the money I'm holding in my pocket. I grab my bag and start walking. But when I get back to the bit of wall I jumped over, I realise like an idiot that there isn't a tree this side. I can't reach up to get out. I'm trapped in here.

I can hear the man's and woman's voices again. They're all echoey, like they're a long way away in an empty swimming pool or something. The woman makes a sort of screech, and I can't tell if she's laughing or screaming.

I start moving faster, round the edges of the park, looking for somewhere I can climb out, but it's all too high. I come to some gates, but they have massive spikes on the top. They're impossible to get over. I keep walking, feeling more and more scared.

Eventually I come to a bit where a tree has been cut up. There are thick logs and fresh sawdust on the grass where someone's sliced it up with a chainsaw. It must have blown down in a storm or something. I manage to roll one of the slices of tree to the edge of the wall. Then I go back and get another one. It takes all my strength, but I manage to get one of the logs on top of the other one. When I stand on them, I'm just about able to reach the top of the wall. I have to throw my bag over the wall and hope there's no one on the other side who'll nick it. It takes me a few goes, but at last I'm able to scrabble up the wall and onto the top of it. I swing my legs over and catch my breath a bit, then jump down. I bend my knees, like they used to tell you in PE when you jumped off the ropes, and I get down onto the pavement without hurting myself.

IT'S one in the morning when I arrive back outside Vivian and Jeffrey's. All the lights are off. Everyone must be asleep. I'm so cold now I can't sleep outside anywhere, even if it was safe. I go to the fake rock Daniel showed me that time and slide the plastic cover back. The spare key is still inside. I let myself in quietly through the front door.

I feel scared being here, but it's better than anywhere else. It's better than nowhere at all.

I don't know what they'll have done with my room, and anyway, it'll be too noisy if I go up the stairs. I don't want anyone to wake up and know I'm here. I creep up the hallway and through to the kitchen. I know where I can go without them hearing me. I head into the back of the house and come to Jeffrey's office. The door is closed. I turn the handle and open it without making a sound. I step in and close the door. It's almost completely dark in here. A bit of light peeps in past the blinds at the window. I walk slowly across the wooden floor, worried it might creak, but it doesn't. I find my way to the big grey sofa.

I put my bag down on the floor and lie down. I take my phone out and make sure it's switched to vibrate, then I set the alarm for five o'clock. I tuck the phone in the breast pocket of my jacket, so I can be sure it will wake me. I need to be up and away before anyone knows I've been here.

I close my eyes and think about trying to get some sleep.

I don't know what's going to happen tomorrow. But for now at least, I'm safe.

37

NOW

For now at least, I'm safe.

That's what I keep telling myself as I sit here in the conference room of *Perry & Sanders Solicitors*. Safe for now.

But a lot has happened in the last couple of days. The morning after my terrible meeting with James Balentine, Daniel and I started making sales. It was absurdly easy. Everyone knows the show is sold out, so that makes the paintings all the more desirable. People always want what they can't have. We told everyone we'd managed to get our hands on just one more JB painting and they practically took our arms off for it. By the end of the first day we'd sold five. And by lunchtime of the day after we'd sold three more. Never in my wildest dreams did I think the gallery would be as successful as this. It was exhilarating.

But the good feeling didn't last. That afternoon the post came with a letter from JB's solicitor demanding the immediate return of all his work in storage. The tone wasn't JB's at all. It wasn't bluff Yorkshire bluster so much as nasty veiled threat. It had that slimy shit Phillip Tench's fingerprints all over it.

Daniel looked at it and just shrugged. "We can't return what we haven't got," he said and got back on the phone. Within twenty minutes he'd sold another painting on condition he could get it to the buyer in twenty-four hours. Christ knows what the rush was. Daniel said he needed the van to take it to Cornwall. He'd be gone for a couple of days. He grabbed his bike and the van keys and left.

I was more worried by the letter than Daniel. It felt like trouble. I figured it would be a good idea to have a solicitor as well and got straight on the phone to Nigel Perry.

So here I am, sitting at the vast oak conference table set up in confrontational battle lines. Nigel Perry is on my side, sitting opposite Phillip Tench. I knew the little shit was behind it all. The two of them are dressed in similar suits, and each has the same build and shiny bald head, like Tweedledum and Tweedledee. Tench has a dull-looking woman with him, his lawyer, who is introduced as Samantha something. She's wearing a horrible sage-coloured dress and has lank, mousy hair and oval plastic glasses the wrong shape for her bony face. She looks like an emaciated owl. She hasn't made eye contact with me the entire time we've been here, which is twenty awkward minutes.

We're all waiting for JB, of course. You'd think something like this would put a rocket up his arse, but apparently not. I figure he's deliberately late, playing one of his bullshit macho power games. After half an hour, Tench phones him. I enjoy watching how twitchy he gets. He came in here all oily and smug, but with each passing minute he looks like he's losing his cool. We all hear the call go to voicemail.

There's some awkward whispering between Tench and owl-woman.

"Ahem," coughs Nigel Perry theatrically, interrupting them like a teacher getting the attention of naughty children. "Given your client has chosen not to attend this meeting, I think we should assume this matter closed for the present. I'm sure we all have things we need to be getting on with." He shuts the notepad in front of him with a passive-aggressive finality.

Tench and the owl get up.

"So delightful to have met you," says Nigel as he shakes Tench's hand. It's amazing to watch Tench get out-smarmed at his own game. They leave.

"I suspect that's not the end of that," says Nigel, once we have the room to ourselves. His cheery smile has gone. "I don't know what your arrangement was with Mr Balentine, but given they've sent you a letter asking for the return of the paintings, we can assume he doesn't believe he consigned them to you for sale."

"He asked me to ship them to London and I've been paying to store them," I say. I can hear how angry and stressed I am.

"It's a bit of a grey area. We'll see," is all Nigel offers.

I'm nervous about getting in trouble, but I'm also pissed off and I don't like being messed about. "What happens if I sell the paintings anyway?" I ask.

"Hmmm." He sits there mulling it over. "It could go either way." He takes a sip of his coffee and curls the fingers of each hand into the other. "You *could* argue the paintings in storage were technically part of the body of exhibited work. But you might struggle to convince a judge they were intended for sale without clear written agreement."

I haven't the faintest idea if there's a contract, or if there's ever been one. We certainly didn't do a new one for this show. Not for the first time, I realise I'm hopelessly out of my depth.

"You could be liable for the unlawful selling of someone else's property."

"Unlawful?"

"Oh yes. Very much so. It could be a criminal matter. Plus, it's probably not very beneficial for your reputation." He gives me a knowing smile. "My advice would be to not sell the paintings at this stage."

"Right," I say. "Thanks for the advice." I don't tell him I've already sold half of them. We'll cross that bridge when I have to throw myself off it.

I walk back towards the car. The last time I was in that office I discovered I was facing financial ruin. Now I might be facing a whole lot worse. I feel like it's spinning out of control and I can't keep hold of it. A wave of panic runs through me. I notice how fast I'm breathing and my heart is racing. My legs feel wobbly and I have to stop for a moment outside a shop, lean against the wall and catch my breath.

It's all going to shit.

Jesus. I feel like I'm suffocating.

38

TEN YEARS AGO

I feel like I'm suffocating.

Jesus.

It takes me a moment to remember where I am. On the sofa, in Jeffrey's study.

The house is on fire. A huge swirling cloud of black smoke clings to the ceiling. I roll off the sofa and crawl to where I think the door is. But it's just a wall. No door. I've lost myself. I'm trapped.

Jeffrey. He's done this. Daniel was right. Jeffrey was burning evidence in the garden and now he's burning everything. Everyone.

"Help! Somebody help me!" I scream at the top of my voice, over and over. But when I stop screaming all I can hear is the roar of the fire. It's deafening. No one's going to hear me. No one knows I got back in the house. No one is coming to save me. I'm going to die.

There's a huge crash and a mass of bright light. I feel sharp stings on my body and realise I've been hit by pieces of flying glass. The room flashes orange with flames. Then something has hold of me. It's a hand. A blanket soaked in water is thrown over my head. I see orange light through the blanket as I'm dragged across the room. It gets brighter and the water starts to steam round my head. My hands feel like they're on fire. I'm screaming in pain.

Then it gets darker and colder and I hear something else – sirens, fire engines.

"Ariana," someone says near me. I collapse, gasping and coughing, and pull the hot blanket off my head.

I'm alive.

My hair is burnt and it stinks. My hands are agony and horribly red. There's a fireman next to me, covered in greasy black soot. "How do you know my name?" I say. He ignores me and puts a mask over my face and I start to breathe easier.

I'm on the grass verge outside the house. There are flashing blue lights and the house is a ball of fire. I was inside that. People are standing about in pyjamas, crying. Two people in uniform rush away carrying someone draped in black. It's a person smaller than them, a kid.

I know it's Daniel.

Daniel said my name. He was the one in the house. Daniel saved me. He rescued me. I should be dead, but he saved me.

They're lifting him onto a trolley by an ambulance. I want to see him. I have to know how he is. I try to stand, but as I put my hands on the ground to push myself up, I feel a terrible pain. My hands are more red and now they look swollen.

A medic comes over from one of the other ambulances. "Hello." He moves the mask off my face. "Can you tell me your name?"

"Ariana." I'm not coughing now I've had the oxygen.

"Are you having trouble breathing?"

"Not much," I say. "It's my hands."

"Right, I'll give you something for them. Did you lose consciousness at any point?"

"No."

"Are you hurt anywhere apart from your hands?" He has a kind voice.

"No, it's just my hands. They really hurt." Big blisters are starting to come up. They look awful.

"How do they feel?" he says.

"They're burning. They're agony. Please."

The nurse starts taking the top off a plastic bottle. "Okay," he says, "this might sting a bit." He begins to squirt water onto them. It's cold. It stings like fuck. When he stops pouring the water it burns more. It hurts worse and I can feel how hot my hands are.

Another nurse comes over and they walk me to the ambulance and sit me inside. They put a needle in my arm and tell me it'll help with the pain. They hang a bag up next to me and I begin to feel woozy. One of the nurses holds my arm as the other one starts putting bandages on my hands. It's like he's rubbing me with sandpaper.

A siren starts and I see Daniel's ambulance drive off. I want to know if he's okay. I try to ask, but they've put the mask on me again and I can't take it off because of my hands. I feel trapped, and I have a sudden flash of being trapped in that burning room. I feel incredibly scared and completely alone.

I wish Daniel was here.

When we get to the hospital, it's a blur. The nurse from the ambulance tells the doctors what happened, and then the doctors do some tests on me, take my pulse and other stuff.

They tell me what they're doing but I still feel woozy and the pain in my hands makes it hard to concentrate. They put another bag of liquid on the tube going into my arm. They uncover my hands and wash them again and put more bandages on. It's agony and I don't understand why they are taking the bandages off. I beg them to stop but they do it anyway. They give me an injection of something.

I'm in a bed in a room. Different people come and go, all wearing paper gowns and masks. They have gloves on and paper hats over their hair. I'm not sure what they're doing or why there are so many of them. They get the bed in place. Eventually they go out and for the first time since I came out of the fire, I'm on my own.

My hands are agony, and I feel scared and incredibly sad.

After a while two nurses come in dressed in the same gear. They stand a long way away from me by the door. They whisper to each other and then one of them speaks to me.

"Ariana."

It's not a nurse. It's Henry. I start to smile.

"How are you feeling now?" he says.

I realise it isn't Henry after all. His voice sounded a bit the same, kind and soft, but it's not him. It's just one of the doctors. I feel very flat and low.

"Please try to get some rest," he says. "Good rest is what you need. I'll come back and see you in the morning."

They start to go out.

"What happened? How is everyone else?" I ask. "How's Daniel?"

"Do you mean the boy from the house?"

I'm dreading the answer.

"He's alive," says the doctor.

Oh God. I was sure he was dead.

"He's alive," says the doctor again. "We're looking after him now. He's here."

Relief floods through me. Jeffrey tried to kill Daniel, but he hasn't done it.

Daniel's alive. He's alive and he's here.

Daniel is in this hospital.

39

NOW

Daniel is in this hospital.

He called me an hour ago and asked if I could pick him up. He was vague on the phone and I don't know exactly what's happened, but it's not like him to ask for a favour, so it must be serious. I've closed the gallery and come as quickly as I could. I park up and head into the main reception.

"Hello. I'm looking for a patient being treated here. Daniel Willens."

"Do you know the ward?" The blank-faced receptionist sits behind a wall of glass. She doesn't look up from her computer screen. I hate these places. I've spent too long in them. They make me feel anxious and on edge.

"I'm afraid not, no," I say, as politely as I can manage.

She starts typing. After half a minute she stops. "Can you spell that?"

"W-I-L-L-E-N-S. Daniel."

More typing. "He's not here. Are you sure it's this hospital?"

I see why they have protective screens now. I'm just about to lose it when I hear a voice behind me.

"Ariana."

It's Daniel. He has his left arm in a sling and a crutch under his right arm. He's got an ugly purple bruise around his right eye, the cloudy one. Like that time I found him when his dad hit him. It's practically swollen shut.

"Christ," I say, hurrying over to him. "What happened to you?"

"Bloody accident while I was on my bike. Transit van one, bike nil."

"God, you were lucky," I say. "Well, not lucky, but you know what I mean."

"Yeah," he says. "It could have been worse. Nothing broken other than my bike and my dignity."

"Come on," I say, "let's get you in the car."

I take Daniel's arm and help him limp out to the car park.

"I'm glad you appeared when you did. The idiot on reception couldn't find you on the system."

"Oh," he says. "Maybe because they'd discharged me? Anyway, we found each other."

We get in the car. It's a bit of a performance with Daniel's stiff leg, but we manage it eventually. I have to lean over him to help him buckle his seat belt. His face gets buried in my hair.

I get in and we drive off.

"Thanks for coming to get me," he says.

"How are you feeling?" I ask. "It looks pretty nasty."

"I know," he says. He puts his hand up to his swollen eye. "I hope it hasn't ruined my good looks." He laughs. That's a good sign, I guess. Though I wonder whether joking about

his appearance so much is a defence mechanism. "Bit embarrassing really," he says. "The bike's a write-off. I never made
it to Cornwall with that painting."

"What d'you mean?"

"I never even made it to the van. I was cycling to pick it
up when I got knocked down."

"I don't understand. How long have you been in
hospital?"

"Two days."

"Jesus, Daniel, why didn't you let me know?"

"I didn't want to be a bother. I'm fine. Don't worry about
it." He winces a bit as he leans back in his seat.

"Where do you need to go?" I ask.

"Can you just take me home, thanks."

"Are you sure? Will you be able to cope like this? Do you
want to stay at mine for a bit?"

He looks like he's really thinking about it. Eventually he
shakes his head. "I can't. I'd like to, it's a lovely offer, but
there's stuff I've got to do at mine. But thanks."

"Okay, if you're sure."

He gives me the address and we drive in relative silence.
I'm not sure if he's sleeping or just quiet. He lives in Ilford,
outside of London technically, in Essex. The route takes us
past Canary Wharf and then onto some three-lane highway I
don't recognise. Eventually we hit the North Circular. Then
the satnav takes us off, through bland suburbia, up high
streets that all have the same mix of Costas and chicken
shacks and vape shops. Christmas lights are already up in
some windows, but the cheap festivity just makes it more
miserable. Then onto drab residential back streets with rows
of Victorian terraces and semi-detacheds. It takes nearly an
hour and a half.

"Do you cycle this every day?"

"Yes," he says. "Different route. And it's quicker on the bike. About fifty minutes."

Finally we turn into Daniel's road. It looks like all the others. It's getting darker now, and a few of the houses have lights in the windows.

"Which one's yours?"

"That one." He points to a slightly shabby semi-detached. It's a big house. None of the lights are on. Does he live here alone? How can he afford it? He must have got compensation when the rest of his family died, or insurance for his old family house or something. I don't know how these things work. It feels too awkward to ask. Maybe there's a weird scheme for crime victims where they give you money when your dad tries to murder you...

"Thanks very much," he says, unclicking his seat belt and reaching round to where we've put his crutch on the back seat. There's a finality in the way he says it that makes it clear he isn't inviting me in. I get out and help with his door.

"Okay then," he says. "I think I probably need a couple of days off. I'll let you know."

"Take as long as you need," I say.

He looks at me seriously. "I'll be there. I want to help you."

"Okay," I say. "Hope you feel better soon. Let me know if there's anything I can do." I lean into him and give him a hug. Then I realise I must be crushing his bad arm and let go. But if I've hurt him he doesn't say anything. "Bye."

I watch him limp into the house. I wait until I see a light go on in the hallway, then I head off. Not for the first time, I'm struck by what a mystery he is to me. I've always thought of Daniel as this incredible person who can do anything. But right now he seems pathetic and sad.

Fortunately the drive back is quicker, heading into town while the rush-hour traffic is heading out. I get home about half past six.

I grab the post from the mat and go through to the kitchen. The house feels empty. I'm still not used to Henry not being here and wonder if I ever will be. It felt lively for a few days when Cassandra was here. It's doubly quiet now she's gone.

I wish I hadn't thought of Henry and Cassandra at the same time.

It's too bright and cold in the kitchen. The whole house is cold. I go through to the living room and switch on the lamps, and turn the dimmers down to a low, comforting glow. I make up a fire in the fireplace and tend it until I have a couple of logs burning nicely. I lean my hand on the weird, spiked metal fire surround. It reminds me of the gates in the park I used to go to years ago, pointed to stop people climbing over. Slowly, I feel the metal begin to warm.

But still I don't feel cosy. I imagine Daniel, rattling around alone in his house in Ilford, while I'm on my own here. I think about calling him to see if he's okay. But I know it's just because I feel lonely. I won't allow myself to do it. It's pathetic. So I don't call.

I go to the fridge and grab a bottle of wine. I haven't done any proper shopping for days and I'm not convinced there's anything to eat. I'll phone for a takeaway later. I sit at the counter and take a sip of wine. I've been dreading the bills for weeks, though I feel less anxious about them now there's money coming in from the gallery.

But the first envelope I look at isn't a bill. It's a solicitor's letter addressed to me as director of the gallery. It must have come here as the registered business address. Even before I open it I know what it's going to be.

And I'm right.

It's an official letter from the firm Owl Woman said she came from, but now she's representing Tench, not JB. It says Tench is JB's formal agent and demands the return of all the paintings in storage. It threatens legal action if I don't return them by the end of the week.

But of course, I can't return most of them, because most of them are sold.

Tench has got me. He'll never settle. He isn't just going to ruin me financially now. It's not just about money. He's going to have me put in prison.

I feel lost.

And then I realise I feel lost without Daniel. He might have started all this, but every time I think things are going wrong, he comes up with an answer.

Daniel will know what to do. He'll have a plan. I just have to wait for Daniel to come back.

40

TEN YEARS AGO

I feel lost without Daniel. I just have to wait for Daniel.

They're keeping me in for a couple more days, but say I'll be fine. My hands are still in bandages, but when they change the dressings I can see the blisters have gone.

After days of asking, they've said I can visit Daniel. The nurse leads me down the corridor and to a room on the same floor as mine. Outside the door they make me dress up in one of the stupid paper outfits all the nurses have been wearing, with the mask and the elasticated paper hat.

His room's like something out of a science fiction film. It's all white and clean and there are plastic curtains hung everywhere, like a tent. The nurse tells me I have to stay outside the curtain, which is about three feet away from the bed. The plastic looks stiff and cloudy, but I can see Daniel behind it.

I know he's been burnt worse than me, but I'm not prepared for this. He's lying on his bed almost head to foot in bandages. He has a tube coming out of his arm hooked up to a bag of solution over his bed. The tube runs through a kind of machine. I know it's to hydrate him and give him something for the pain. Morphine probably. I was on morphine for the first couple of days, but now I just take pain tablets. The fact Daniel's still on it means he must be bad.

I look at the bandages on my hands and remember how painful they were. Then I look at Daniel and try to imagine how unbearable it must be to have burns all over his body. He looks so tiny. He's just a little boy. It's too much to get my head round.

"Daniel?" I say. I whisper it. I don't want to disturb him. "Daniel. It's me, Ariana."

There's a long silence. Then his head moves slightly. He can't look towards me, but I think maybe he's heard.

"Who's there?" His voice is raspy and very quiet. He sounds woozy, like he's just woken up. It'll be the drugs too. He has a bandage over his right eye and he can't see me.

"It's Ariana," I say again.

"Ariana." It's all he says.

"Can you remember what happened?" I ask. I don't know how much the doctors will have said.

"Fire," he whispers. "Mum and Dad and Poppy are dead." He gives a big sigh. I don't know whether he's sad, or it's tiring to talk. "It's just us now."

I've got closer to the plastic curtain to hear him whispering. Now I whisper myself. "How did it happen?" I don't want the nurses outside to hear me. "Did your dad start the fire?"

"I went in his study," says Daniel. "He hit me... Then I found him setting fire to the house." He's talking slowly, taking a break between sentences to catch his breath. "I locked him in... I tried to get to Mum and Poppy... Stairs were on fire... I got out..."

I can hardly hear him now. "How did you know I was in the house?"

"Heard you screaming... Had to get to you..."

I still don't understand how he did it. "But the house was on fire, Daniel. You went back in?"

"Had to get you..." is all he says. He lets out another sigh and I can tell the effort of talking has knackered him completely. He whispers something but I can't hear it.

"I'll come back tomorrow," I say. "Get some sleep. Thank you, Daniel. Thank you. Thank you."

I leave and go back to my room.

No one's said anything about Jeffrey. They wouldn't believe it anyway. They wouldn't believe he tried to kill his whole family. They'll just think it was an accident. No adult ever believed me when I said stuff, and no one will believe Daniel. There's no point telling.

Daniel's right, we just have each other and the stuff we both know that no one else knows about.

From now on, it's just me and Daniel.

41

NOW

It's just me and Daniel. He limps in, still smarting from his bike accident, the bruise around his eye all shades of red and purple and yellow. "Like one of JB's paintings," he says, slumping down at the desk.

The run of JBs show is over and all the work has been taken down from the walls and shipped to the buyers. Even the large work has gone, the doorway knocked out and repaired again by a builder I found online. It wasn't cheap, but it was worth it to get everything out of here. Now the walls are stark and empty.

We go through the figures – which JB paintings we've sold from the ones in storage and for how much. We work out how much we'd have to pay to get them back. The demand we've created has come back to bite us in the arse. It'll cost significantly more to buy them back than we sold them for. Even if I *can* buy them all and keep Tench and the police off my back, I'm ruined.

I should never have listened to Daniel about selling those extra paintings. But what's the point of tearing into him?

Even if I got persuaded by his confidence and carried away on his charisma, I can't blame him. It's *my* gallery. I agreed to it. Idiot.

My phone goes. It's Nigel Perry again. I've been ducking his calls for the last couple of days, assuming he must have bad news. But I can only avoid him for so long. I answer.

"Ariana? Nigel Perry here."

"Sorry I haven't returned your calls. I've been a bit busy," I lie.

"Any news about James Balentine?" he asks.

"I don't know," I say. "I assumed that's why you were calling."

"No, nothing," he says. "I suppose they haven't found him yet."

"Found him?" I'm confused. "Found who? What do you mean?"

Daniel looks at me with a puzzled expression. I switch my phone to speaker and put it on the table so he can hear.

"James Balentine," says Nigel emphatically, as if he's talking to an idiot. "His solicitor contacted me. Apparently he went for a walk two days ago, as he does every morning, and he hasn't been seen since. His wife informed the police and they notified the Mountain Rescue service. They've been searching in grids with dogs and drones, but no sign of him so far."

I remember the wild countryside we drove through on the way up. How bleak it was. Two days out there can't be much fun.

"They're doing a televised appeal later today. But after forty-eight hours, the prospects aren't too good, I imagine."

Daniel makes a kind of wincing face. I know what it means. He thinks JB's a goner.

"Nigel," I say hesitantly, "I don't want to be crass. Obviously finding JB is the most important thing. But what does this mean for me? I mean, are there any implications for what's going on with those paintings?"

"That's what I'm calling you about," he says. "Apparently Mr Balentine hasn't signed any formal contract with Phillip Tench or his gallery. Mr Tench isn't empowered to act on Mr Balentine's behalf. The paintings belong to Mr Balentine himself. Or, if anything were to happen to him, to his estate. His wife, presumably."

The call ends. Daniel and I sit in silence for a moment. Finally, he speaks.

"Two days out there?" says Daniel. "That's the last we'll be hearing from him. I'm sorry, but it's true."

I know he's right. I have a strange mix of feelings. I never liked JB, and I liked him even less when he left the gallery for that nasty little shit Phillip Tench. I'm relieved his disappearance has got Phillip Tench off my back, at least for now. Deep down I'm hoping JB won't be found alive. I daren't say it out loud. It's too awful. I know it makes me a terrible person.

Daniel just looks at me. I'm convinced he knows what I'm thinking.

Later, we search the internet and watch an appeal for people to get in touch if they have any info on JB's whereabouts. Mrs JB is sitting behind the policeman who makes the appeal. She looks frail and tragic and even more ghost-like than when I met her in Yorkshire.

Immediately after, Daniel says he's going to get on the phone to sell the last of the JB paintings. It feels crass or tactless somehow, but Daniel is fired up by all the news about JB's disappearance. He thinks we should make hay while the sun shines. He limps around the gallery rabbiting away on his phone, his face animated in his enthusiastic sales pitch. He seems manic. I can't hear what he's saying, but his bruises combined with his scars make his exaggerated expression look tortured, like a tortured animal.

"Sold another one," he says, striding over to me with a huge grin on his face. "Thirty-five thousand."

"Jesus." The money is amazing. But something about pushing things higher and higher feels dangerous. It's like Icarus getting too close to the sun. Then I catch myself having that thought, and remember Daniel's already been through the fire. It feels tactless to even think it.

"They'll keep going up," he says. "They know when the news comes out he's dead, the prices will really rocket. They're getting in fast before the price hike."

He's right. If these are the last paintings JB ever made, if there is a finite supply of them, then their value goes up. That's just how the market works. And yet the way he says it makes me shudder. I struggle to put my finger on exactly what Daniel's doing wrong. But it feels like he's dancing on JB's grave. It makes me uncomfortable.

Maybe Daniel's lived so long with death in his life he's immune to the shock of it. Henry's death is so recent. It feels so raw, in spite of what happened between him and Cassandra. I can't just shrug off this JB stuff like Daniel does. I guess if your entire family dies in a fire, the only way you can carry on is to protect yourself from the reality of it, insulate yourself from your feelings.

For the first time since his reappearance, I feel myself pull away from Daniel. We're on different trajectories again, heading in different directions.

He takes my hands in his.

"We're doing it," he says. "We're making it work. I always knew we could. Right back then I knew. Liam couldn't get us, or my dad, or JB, or Tench. Even the fire. Together we can do anything."

He doesn't let go of my hands.

"How many of the paintings in storage have we sold?" I ask.

"Nearly all of them!" he says in triumph. He thinks I'll be delighted with the achievement.

He doesn't know the reason I ask. Because when the paintings are sold, this will end. It will have finished and I can move on. Move away. This feels too close. Too intense. I don't know what Daniel thinks is happening, but this is too much. I need space. I need to create some distance. I feel like I'm on the edge of something terrible, some vast black hole that I could fall into. I need to step away. I need to protect myself.

42

TEN YEARS AGO

I need to protect myself. I could die if I don't. Hospitals are full of sick people. People here must have all sorts. But all I've done is catch a cold. It's mad to think, but a week ago they were so worried about infections even this stupid cold could have killed me. My hands are much better now and they're close to letting me go home.

Not that I know where home is.

They know me as Tracey Jones here, not Ariana Simpson. They've told Craig I'm here and there's talk about me going back to Rob and Julie's. But sod that. There's no way I'm going back there. I'm so close to my eighteenth birthday now, I reckon I'll get out of it. I know they have places for care kids to move into and I'm gonna make Craig's life hell until he gets me in one of them.

Anyway, because of this cold I need to protect myself, put on a gown and two masks to be safe and a paper hat and shit. Daniel's still in special isolation and if he got my cold it'd be really dangerous.

"You're not going anywhere," says Precious when she

comes in. She's the nurse who's been looking after me. She's bossy but she's all right.

"Why not?" I say. "I'm fine." Even as I say it, I can hear how bunged up I sound and how raspy my voice is.

"Back in bed, lady," says Precious. "We got patients on this ward you could kill with that snotty nose of yours."

So I'm trapped in this room. It's shit. It's so boring. There's a telly, but if I have to watch one more episode of *Homes Under the Hammer* I think I'll kill myself. And anyway, I promised Daniel I'd see him every day. I can't let him down. I just can't. It's like the most important thing ever.

The door opens again and I assume it's Precious. I'm ready to leap up and argue about how I'm fine to see Daniel.

But it's not Precious.

It's Henry.

"Hello," he says. He sounds shy.

"Hello," I say back as casual as I can, like I'm not really fussed. Like he's just anyone.

"I can't come any closer," he says.

"You can if you put the right gear on," I say. I sound angry with him, like he should know about the protective gear. But I know inside that's not really what I'm angry about. And I'm not really angry either. I'm making out I'm angry to hide how hurt I am. I don't want him to know I care.

"I'm sorry," he says. "They didn't tell me I had to wear anything." He stands there looking awkward. "I'm sorry about everything," he says. "When I heard about the fire I felt dreadful. I feel so guilty for sending you away that night. If I'd known, I would never have done it. I wanted to come and see you as soon as I heard, but they wouldn't let me."

"Don't worry about it," I say. I don't know why I'm being

such a snarky bitch about it, but I keep acting like I don't care, even though I really do.

He looks like he might cry.

"I've messed it all up," he says. "I made a mistake. I should have let you stay. I don't know what I was thinking about, worrying about what other people might think. As soon as I thought I might have lost you, I realised what an idiot I've been. Am I too late?"

"For what?" I say.

"For us to be together," he says.

I leap off the bed and run towards him. I hug him. He pulls back a bit.

"Aren't we supposed to stay apart, because of infections?" he says.

"Don't worry," I say, "I'm fine now. The worst that will happen is I get snot all over your suit."

We laugh and hug and I feel unbelievably happy. Henry's lovely and I know I love him, and he's going to look after me, he says. I know what he means. We're different ages, but it doesn't feel like it in some ways. We've found each other and we're right for each other, and the age thing doesn't matter.

We sit and talk for a while. He asks me how the care stuff works, and I tell him I'll be able to work it out how I can live with him. I have no idea yet myself, but I'll make it work somehow. Even if I have to hang on 'til I'm eighteen, that's only a few weeks. It'll be okay. I know it will.

Then we talk about the fire, and why Jeffrey started it. I don't tell him about Liam, but I tell him lots of the other stuff Daniel told me. Henry looks really shocked.

"Christ. I knew Jeffrey was an arsehole," he says, "but that's unbelievable. Poor Vivian."

He looks at the floor and goes quiet, and I wonder if he's thinking about when he used to date her years ago. I want to ask, but I don't. Then he looks up.

"And those poor kids," he says, and lets out a massive sigh.

I want to say something, but I don't know how to. It's such a big thing, me and Henry getting together. I don't want to mess it up with something else big. But I can't not ask, so I decide to just say it.

"Can Daniel come and live with us?"

Henry looks at me. He has sad eyes.

"Oh Ariana," he says, and I already know he's going to say no, but he keeps talking anyway. "It's wonderful that you want to look after him, but it wouldn't be right. Can you imagine what it must be like to have lost his whole family? How he must feel to know that his own father tried to kill him?"

"But he rescued me. He saved me," I say. "I owe him."

"The kind of help he's going to need, we can't give him," says Henry. "I don't just mean here, medical stuff. I mean professionals, counsellors... Help to cope with what's happened to him. What's been done to him."

I don't argue. Henry doesn't get how the system works and what it does to kids. He thinks it can make them better. There's no point telling him about what it's really like. Unless you've been there, you don't know. I make a silent promise to myself that I won't drop it. I'll keep working on Henry. I won't let Daniel down.

"They won't let me see him today, but I promised," I say. "He'll wonder where I am. Will you take him a note if I write it?"

"Sure."

I hunt around on my table until I find a bit of paper, some leaflet about patient rights and how to complain. It's blank on the back. Henry lends me a pen. It's awkward to hold it with the bandages I still have and my writing looks a mess.

Dear Daniel.
I have a cold and they won't let me come today. I'm
sorry.
I know I already said it, but I can't believe how brave
you were saving me. I want to say thank you for
saving my life. I will do whatever I can to pay you
back. I will make sure you are ok.
I promise I won't let you down. I'll look out for you.
Always. I'll never let you go. I promise.
I'll see you again very soon.
Ariana x

I feel better about things knowing Daniel's going to get my note. I fold the paper over and give it to Henry.

He smiles. "I'll take it in a while," he says.

"Can you do it now? Please. I know he'll be waiting." I can't bear him thinking I've let him down.

"Okay," says Henry. "Sure."

Then Henry goes out of the room.

43

TEN YEARS AGO

Henry goes out of the room.

He pauses in the corridor and puts his hand lightly against the door. Ariana is on the other side of this door. Ariana, with whom he has fallen hopelessly, inexplicably in love.

It worries him what his friends and family will say. And if it isn't what they say, it'll be what they think. He's in his thirties and she's seventeen. It's the sort of thing he'd otherwise be appalled by... and somewhere inside, he still is appalled by it.

He knows he's going to have to park that feeling, find a way to push it down, stop thinking about it. He'll have to give it time. It's all very new. What he knows for sure is that when he heard about the fire, and thought Ariana was dead, his life was ruined and he had lost the best thing that would ever happen to him. Like realising you desperately wanted a painting only after it's sold to someone else. A whole path of his life had closed off and the road he was supposed to take had gone.

And when he discovered she was alive, he knew in an instant that he wanted to be with her, for always, whatever the challenges or difficulties. He'd got so used to being on his own he almost missed it. How absurd, he thought, to let embarrassment get in the way of happiness.

Happiness. He realises with some surprise that's what he is. He's happy. Even the idea that he is happy makes him happy, and he gives a little chuckle to himself. The independence he prided himself on for so long was just a sanitised way of describing his loneliness. Everything feels possible now. A whole new beginning.

"Henry?"

The voice calls him back from his thoughts. He turns and finds a young Asian doctor he vaguely recognises staring at him.

"Henry Clough, right? It's Asif. Asif Malik. We met at your gallery a couple of years back."

Now Henry places him. He was a student doctor at the time. He took a shine to one of the paintings in a show but couldn't afford it. Nice chap. Henry gave him quite a discount and let him pay in instalments.

"Asif. I remember. You bought a James Balentine painting."

"I did," says the doctor, flattered to have made an impression. "You were very kind to me."

"Well, you were very enthusiastic. Paintings are like puppies. You can't keep them all, but you want to see them go to a good home."

"Well," says the doctor, "we love it."

The men smile at each other. They've exhausted the extent of what they have in common. The doctor looks past Henry at the door he's just come through.

"Are you visiting Tracey?"

There's a brief pause while Henry recalls that Ariana is admitted here under her real name.

"I am, yes," he says.

Another pause.

"She's my niece."

He doesn't know why he feels he needs to add the lie. He needs to accept what's going on between them. He can't keep inventing these absurd justifications.

"Right," says the doctor. Henry notices his smile has gone and wonders whether there's bad news coming, whether Ariana's condition is worse than she knows. "Does she know the other boy, the one who came in at the same time?"

"Daniel?" says Henry. "Yes. She was living with his family before, well, before the fire."

The doctor looks round shiftily. "Do you have a minute?"

"Yes," says Henry, becoming increasingly worried.

The doctor takes Henry's elbow and leads him up the corridor. They go past a few doors, all of which seem to be small rooms like Ariana's. They stop outside a door marked *Multi-Faith Room*. The doctor knocks then looks inside.

"In here," he tells Henry.

Henry follows him into the room and closes the door. The room is uncluttered, with a few chairs and cushions. It's painted in a neutral magnolia. There isn't a window, but the lighting is soft and warm. There's a little curtain over the glass panel in the door for privacy. He hadn't realised how noisy it was in the corridor, but now he's in this room he's struck by the silence. It must be soundproofed or something.

There's a table on one side with an assortment of books,

the Bible, the Quran, the Torah. There's a little statue of a Buddha. It looks like a religious maniac lost his faith and took everything to a car boot sale. Henry assumes they haven't come in here to pray. He looks quizzically at the young doctor.

"I've got two kids myself," says the doctor, dropping his voice. "They change your life. You'd do anything to protect them. Anything."

"I'm sure," says Henry. He has no idea what this has to do with him. "Is there something you wanted to tell me about–" he catches himself just in time, "about Tracey?"

"You didn't hear this from me," says the doctor, "but keep your niece away from that boy."

"From Daniel?"

"From Daniel, yes." The doctor sounds urgent and nervous. He keeps one eye on the door. "I shouldn't be telling you this. He's traumatised. He has a history of issues in the past. It should have been picked up much sooner. He's been seen by a school psychologist."

"Ah," says Henry, with some relief. He knows all this from Ariana. "I know a bit about the family history. The dad was abusive. It's no wonder the boy has issues with a parent like that. And I guess it's only going to get worse now his father has attempted to kill him in that fire..."

It feels good to discuss this with someone. Henry felt guilty saying no to Ariana about Daniel living with them. But it's good to get it confirmed by a professional.

"No," says the doctor, "you don't understand. I've seen his records. In the incident at school, he nearly blinded another boy. And the fire at the house. The father didn't start it. The police think the boy did."

"The boy?"

"Yes. They think he started the fire. He killed his whole family. He's not well enough to be moved right now. But when he is, the police are taking him."

Henry feels himself frozen. He can't comprehend what he's just heard. He knows what the words mean, but he can't find a way to let them bed in so they make sense.

Daniel?

Daniel murdered his family?

He's twelve.

"I must get on," says the doctor. "You didn't hear it from me, but remember what I said. Okay?" He opens the door to leave.

"Thank you," says Henry, out of automatic politeness.

When the doctor has gone and Henry has the silent room to himself, he sits down on a wooden chair and tries to process the changes of the last few days. Signing the lease on a new gallery. Learning Ariana is seventeen and a runaway from a care home. The fire. Vivian dying and thinking Ariana might be dead. Deciding that he is going to make a life with Ariana. And now this, about Daniel. The arsonist. The murderer who nearly killed Ariana.

He looks at the table, the Bible and Quran and Torah. The Buddha. They don't help him. None of it makes sense.

Henry walks out into the corridor, which seems even noisier after being cocooned in silence. He'll go home, he thinks, and see what tomorrow brings. Maybe they'll allow Ariana home tomorrow. But even that feels complicated now, after the elation of her saying yes. He feels a bit anticlimactic and flat. He's sure it'll be okay when he sees her again. It's a good thing, he tells himself.

It's only as he reaches out to push open the double doors at the end of the corridor that he realises he's still holding a piece of paper in his hand – Ariana's note to Daniel. He's been too gentlemanly to read it so far, but in the current circumstances it seems only sensible to take a look.

He unfolds and scans it.

Thank you for saving my life.
I'll look out for you. Always.
I'll see you again very soon.

What the hell is he going to tell her? The truth will devastate her.

She doesn't need to know right this minute. Stick to the plan. Go home, and see what tomorrow brings.

Just before the doors at the end of the ward stands a row of colour-coded bins with foot-operated lids. He goes to the nearest one, orange, steps on the pedal and drops Daniel's note into it. He removes his foot from the pedal and the lid closes. It's only then he notices the sign above it. *Toxic Waste.*

Whatever happens, he knows the single most important thing is to keep Ariana away from that sick little bastard, that evil monster Daniel, until the police can lock him up. This thought makes Henry feel better about the whole situation. The truth is, Ariana's lost, she's run away, and he has rescued her. He's doing a good thing. Noble almost.

It's a moment of startling clarity.

The most important thing he can ever do is make sure Ariana never, ever sees Daniel again.

PART 5

44

NOW

The water is hot and relaxing. The room smells fresh. I've lit some candles and turned the main light off. I push the bubbles to one side and get in.

I've done it. I'm a success. In less than three months, I've taken a failing gallery, turned it around, and sold thousands of pounds' worth of art. Against all odds, I've paid off most of my debts and secured my future in this house.

I should be happy.

But I'm not.

The last ten years of my life have been about trying to build a version of myself that's good and true and honest. I've survived my family, and being in care, what happened with Liam and my almost fatal encounter with Daniel's toxic father. I've escaped a fire that almost killed me. I've survived the death of my husband, the discovery of his infidelity, and I've saved myself from financial ruin.

But this last part doesn't sit right with me. This business of selling JB's paintings for massively inflated prices while he lies injured or dead somewhere on the moors. Paintings which I know he never meant for me to sell. I've crossed a line, selling those paintings. I've put everything at risk. It isn't right. The first time I encountered Phillip Tench I knew he was a creepy shit who'd sell his grandmother if he thought he could make a profit. But is what I'm doing so different? I've become Phillip Tench.

I slosh the water about and scoop some bubbles towards me. I listen to the guttering of the candles and watch the shadows flicker on the ceiling. I've set the bathroom up to relax. But I can't relax. This is putting a sticking plaster on a gaping wound.

I pull the plug out and dry myself off. I put on pyjamas and head to the computer to search the news. There are no updates on JB. He's been missing for a week now and it doesn't take a genius to work out the prospects don't look good. It's terrible to even think it, but JB going missing has saved me from scandal and financial ruin. JB's bad fortune has been my good luck. But I can't enjoy it.

Daniel hasn't been at the gallery for a couple of days. I was intrigued by his mysterious disappearances at first. Then they annoyed me. Now it feels like a relief. I'm sure he thinks he's been helping me, and in many ways he has helped – but his relentless drive has pulled me in a direction I don't want to go. All this JB business. I have to put the brakes on. I have to pull back.

Fortunately, we've arrived at a natural break. Yesterday, the final JB painting was sold. It looks like it's over. I close my laptop and go back up to the bathroom to clean my teeth.

I look into the mirror at the face staring back at me. Who is this person who's done these immoral, unethical, illegal things? Is that me? Is that who I am? I don't want it to be. I make a promise to myself here and now that's the last shady deal I do.

I clean my teeth, head into the bedroom, slip under the covers and turn off the light. An orange glow of streetlights creeps in around the side of the curtains at the window I can no longer look out of without seeing Henry. The orange warms the room, but it's unsettling. It reminds me of Daniel's heat lamps and the fire in Jeffrey's study.

I'm not sure how I'm going to have the conversation with Daniel. He's a million times brighter than me and he always has an answer for everything. If I practice what I'm going to say, if I get it perfect, Daniel won't be able to find a way into my head and persuade me.

Daniel, I need to tell you something, and I know it's not what you want to hear. But I'm closing the gallery. I've been thinking about it for a while, and I can't keep doing this. It's gone from a disaster to a success, which I could never have done without you. But it's just not me. It was Henry's thing. It was never mine. The truth is, I'm not happy here. I'm twenty-seven. I have my whole life ahead of me and I have to do something with it. I don't even know what's next for me yet, but it's not this.

This doesn't mean I don't want you in my life. I'm so glad we found our way back to each other. We'll still see each other, and you'll always mean so much to me. We'll always be friends, no matter what. But I need space to figure out what my life is supposed to be. The life you saved, which I need to do something with, to make your saving me worthwhile. I hope you can understand.

I say it over and over in my head, moving bits, tweaking

thoughts, until I have it perfect. It's clear and solid and doesn't feel like there are any gaps for Daniel to creep into, like the light coming around the curtain. *I hope you can understand.* It becomes a kind of mantra in my head until I fall asleep.

45

NOW

I get up early and go over the speech in my head. I'm pleased I've remembered it overnight. I leave for the gallery and decide to practice it out loud while I drive.

I immediately stumble. What seemed to flow in my mind becomes a stuttering, gibbering mess once I hear myself say it. It's stilted and painfully rehearsed and sounds like a feeble set of excuses. It doesn't remotely convince me, so it's never going to convince Daniel.

I don't know why I get like this around him. In one way he's always given me incredible confidence. But in another, he makes me feel hopelessly incapable. Something about how brilliant he is makes me feel utterly insignificant. I feel tiny in his shadow.

I rethink everything and decide I'm over-explaining. I don't have to justify myself if I want to step away from the gallery. I don't need excuses. I need to say it plain and simple and then stick to the bare bones of the facts.

Daniel, I'm closing the gallery. It's just not me.

I say that several times out loud. It's better. It's direct and to the point. And if Daniel offers up any sort of objection, I can resist by staying firm and sticking to my guns.

Daniel, I'm closing the gallery. It's just not me.

I park in the eye-wateringly expensive car park. I'm early and everything's quiet. The Christmas street lights have been put up overnight, but they're not lit. Just tatty wire outlines, like ghosts of Santa and reindeer. They make everything look depressing. I walk to the gallery. I want to get myself settled and relaxed before he comes in.

But when I get there, the lights are on. Daniel's already arrived.

Even more disturbing, the walls that were empty yesterday are now hung with five medium-sized pictures – all new JB paintings. I don't understand how that's possible. I've spent hours rehearsing and refining a speech, and in ten seconds the rug has been pulled from under my feet.

Daniel emerges from the office and smiles at me. "What do you think?" he says.

"What the hell, Daniel?" I'm on the edge of completely losing my cool. "I thought we'd sold all the paintings in storage."

"Yes. These are different ones. New ones."

Now I'm really confused. "What do you mean?"

"I was thinking about those paintings we sold," he says. "I know you're worried you could be in trouble. I went home and felt bad about it. I pretty much pushed you into it."

He did push me, but there's something about how he frames it that winds me up. It's *my* gallery. It was *my* decision. I'm furious with myself for not trusting my instincts and putting my foot down. It's not as if I'm incapable of asserting myself. How did he manage to do that?

"Anyway," he goes on, "I realise you need serious money

in case JB shows up and you have to buy the paintings back. So…" he says, smugly. He makes a grand sweeping gesture with his arm at the paintings on the wall.

"Where did these come from?" I ask, forcefully.

"Mrs JB," says Daniel. "I called her to check if there was any update on JB, but really I was fishing to see if she had any more paintings around. She's convinced JB's gone for good and she's going to end up penniless. I told her how much money we could get for her with any new paintings. I went up to see her yesterday. I didn't want to tell you in case it didn't work out."

"You emotionally blackmailed her into giving you these?" I picture that timid shadow of a woman, terrified she's a widow and scared into giving up any hope her husband's coming back, desperate to make some money while she can. I remember how she looked at Daniel when we first went up there, how she physically recoiled from his scars. He's effectively frightened her into handing these paintings over.

"It's all legit," he says. "She was practically falling over herself to give them to me. Once we cleared his studio, she went through the house taking all his old paintings down. She even helped me load the van."

I don't like how he's laughing. I'm not exactly JB's number-one fan, but I know how it felt when Henry was killed. I think of that poor woman, beside herself with worry, and Daniel gloating as he piles all these paintings into a van.

It's the first time in my life I've questioned what Daniel is doing. It's clever, but it's cruel and it's cold. I suddenly feel a distance between us, and it makes me all the more certain I need to step back from the gallery, and from Daniel himself.

"Daniel," I say, "I'm closing the gallery. It's just not me."

I wait for him to argue back. He thinks for a few seconds.

"Maybe you're right," he says. "That might be a good idea."

I anticipated him arguing with me. What I didn't expect was to be thrown by him *not* arguing.

"This was Henry's thing, really, not yours," he says. "Henry's gone. You have to move on. If you leave this behind, it'll be easier to find what you want to do next."

"Yes," I say, relieved. "Yes, that's it exactly." I should have known Daniel would get it. It's almost as if he's seen straight into my head. I feel myself relax. I've been unfair to him. "Thanks."

"What we should do," he says, "is hit the phones hard and sell these new paintings as quickly as possible. Get it finished."

"Oh." I hadn't anticipated any more selling. "Can't you just... take them back?"

"No way!" says Daniel. "Think about it. Let's say JB shows up alive. You'll have to buy all those other paintings back. You need the money. These are your insurance. Plus, his wife is relying on us to get as much money for her as possible. She gave them to us because she wants us to help her. Yes, you're helping yourself, but you're helping her too."

I'm conflicted. Rehearsing in the car on my drive in, I was utterly convinced I'd find a healthy distance from the gallery and from Daniel. Now here I am with more paint-ings, getting into a whole round of selling again. On the other hand, what Daniel says makes sense. I would be helping JB's wife out. And God knows I might need the money.

"Okay," I say, "we'll do it."

I leave Daniel to make phone calls to buyers who missed out on the last paintings we had. I tell him I need to plan a strategy with the other artists for winding up the gallery and wander out to a coffee shop.

But the truth is, my need to put space between myself and Daniel has got even stronger. Once again, I feel tied to him in a way I don't wholly understand but don't seem able to escape.

I find a corner in a weird little place on Saville Row that seems to be a coffee shop and clothes shop combined. Anyway, it's quiet and I grab a flat white and a croissant and sit at an empty table tucked away behind a rail of tweed suits that remind me of ones JB used to wear.

Used to wear. I'm already thinking of him as if he's dead. I know they're still searching, but it's been days now and still no sign. I look on a Facebook page someone has set up about him. There are a million theories. Maybe he's lost his bearings and wandered miles in the wrong direction. Maybe he's fallen down a ravine, or into a peat bog.

I imagine his wife, sitting in that miserable kitchen, reading what I'm reading. I recall my own sense of desolation, waiting for news from the police about the joyriders who killed Henry, the lack of certainty not allowing for any kind of closure. I feel bad for her.

I remember the wife called me on JB's mobile the first time we spoke. On a hunch I dial his number.

"Hello?" It's her. The voice sounds more frail than I remember it. Older.

"Hello. Is that..." I search to recall her name. "Elizabeth?"

"Elspeth. Yes?"

"Hello, Elspeth. It's Ariana Clough here."

Silence.

"From JB's gallery in London."

"Yes?"

I have no idea if she knows who I am or not. I wonder whether I've caught her having a sleep.

"I just wanted to call and see how you're doing. I've been thinking about you a lot, and JB, of course."

"Oh, I'm alright, dear," she says. "It's a bit of a worry that they haven't found JB yet, but they're bound to soon. He'll be holed up somewhere safe for sure."

"Oh. Well, that's good," I say. From what Daniel told me, I thought she'd given up hope. Her jolly optimism isn't what I was anticipating.

"He knows those moors like the back of his hand. He was born around here, you know. He always has a flask of whisky for emergencies, and a slab of Kendal Mint Cake in his jacket pocket. Jimmy's as strong as an ox. I'm not worried."

The human brain does strange things under pressure. It's a kind of shock, I suppose. She's delusional. No one can be on those moors for this long and not be dead or in terrible trouble. But it's not my place to correct her.

"I'm so glad you're well, Elspeth," I say. "It's important to stay positive. I'm sure you're right about JB being home soon. And meanwhile, we'll do our best to sell those paintings for you."

"Paintings?"

"Yes, the ones Daniel collected from you."

"Oh yes," she says, "that poor burnt boy. I thought you'd sold all those ages ago."

She's confused. "No," I say, "not the ones in the show. The ones Daniel collected this week."

"This week? I think you're mistaken, dear. No one's collected any paintings this week. That charming Mr Tench came here a few weeks back, but as JB told him at the time, there were no new paintings since you and the boy with the horrible scars took them all down to London a month back."

I hang up and wonder what's going on.

Maybe Elspeth is confused. She's crazy to think JB's just going to wander in and demand she put the kettle on. So maybe she's crazy about everything else. Maybe she's got it wrong and Daniel collected the new paintings this week.

But I don't think so. She seems incredibly clear on the timeline and when she last saw Daniel.

In which case, where have those paintings come from?

And why is Daniel lying to me?

46

NOW

Daniel murdered JB.

It's the only thing that makes sense.

He murdered JB and hid his body somewhere, or buried him on the moors. We sold all those paintings in storage, then Phillip Tench threatened to sue me and the only way to save us was if JB never asked for them back.

So Daniel killed him.

And then what? He broke into their house and stole the new paintings? These are smaller than the ones we had in the show. JB said he was going to work on a larger scale from now on. So these ones must be older paintings, ones JB had up at home maybe. Daniel killed JB, then broke into their house. If you murder someone, you might as well rob them too.

"Hello?"

I practically leap off my seat in shock. But it's just the waiter.

"Another coffee?"

"Er, no," I stutter, "thanks."

He retreats behind the counter. I must have been sitting over my cold coffee for an hour. But now I've been jolted out of my spiralling thoughts, what I've just been imagining strikes me as absurd. Daniel, a murderer?

And yet I can't quite shake it.

I need to find out what's really going on. I hurry out of the shop and gallop back to the gallery.

"Did you kill JB?"

"What?" Daniel looks utterly stunned at what I've just blurted out. As he spins round, I see he's holding a mobile phone to his ear. "Andre," he says calmly, "I'm so sorry, someone's just come in. Can I call you back?" He hangs up.

"Did you kill JB? Is that why he's disappeared? Did you steal these paintings from his house?"

"Whoa, slow down." He holds his hands up in surrender as if I'm about to shoot him. If I had a gun I probably would. "Sit down a minute. Let's talk about this."

He sits at the table. He looks small and frail. He looks like... Daniel. I can't imagine him murdering anybody. His strained expression pulls his scarred face tighter. He sighs and looks away for a moment. I can only see his cloudy eye, which remains expressionless.

"How could I have murdered JB?" he asks. He sounds sad. "I was in hospital in London when he disappeared. Remember? You picked me up."

Of course. That's right. He was knocked off his bike and in hospital for two days. I picked him up and drove him home. I'm such an idiot.

"Sorry. I don't know what I was thinking."

But there's still a nagging question.

"Daniel, where did all these paintings come from?" He

goes to speak, but I stop him. I don't want him lying to me again. "I already spoke to Elspeth Balentine."

He chews his lip for a moment.

"Okay," he says, "I'll tell you. I don't think you'll like it."

I dread what's coming. "Tell me." I want him to get on with it fast, like ripping off a plaster.

"I've been going round the student art shows, looking for people you could take on if any other artists walk. I met this guy I thought was a promising painter. We went to the pub. We started talking about JB. I was pretty drunk by this point. I asked him if he'd be able to copy a JB painting."

"You got him to forge one?"

Daniel gives a laugh. I can't tell if he's embarrassed or amused. "This is weeks ago. It was more of an academic exercise."

"What do you mean?"

"Look, I don't want to come over as rude, but JB's a fraud. They're just mindless daubs of paint slapped about. They're shit. I wanted to see if this guy could do the same. We went back to his digs and had a couple more cans of beer and he knocked out a painting in about an hour."

I look round the gallery. "He did all these, did he?" If Daniel hadn't told me, I'd never know they weren't originals.

"When I knew you might need more money, this seemed like an easy way to make some."

"Jesus, Daniel!" At least he's not a murderer. But this is serious. My head's spinning. "Look, I know you were trying to help me. But this is more than selling a few paintings we have in storage. This is forgery. It's fraud. This would mean prison for sure."

He looks down at the table. I'm so used to feeling like

he's the grown-up, I'm taken aback by how young he looks. Like I'm his mum, telling him off.

"We can't do this," I say.

"Too late. We already have."

He looks directly at me. It's hard to tell if his mouth is pulled tight by the burn scars or if there's a hint of a smirk on his thin lips.

"I thought it would be an interesting experiment to mix a couple of the fakes in with the paintings in storage. No one noticed. You didn't notice either. We sold them for the same price as the others."

I hold the edge of the table. I feel like I might fall over if I don't grip something solid.

"So, I really think it would be best to keep going," says Daniel. "I mean, what are you going to do? Ask for your forgeries back? No, let's keep going as we are, keep running the gallery together and sell these for as much money as we can."

He is. He's smiling.

"I always knew you'd make it work. You're amazing."

He rests his hand on mine where it holds the table. I recall what he told me about everything spinning at millions of miles an hour. I feel sick. Nothing is solid. The table. My hand. His hand. I look at his hand on mine and I think about the atoms of him merging into the atoms of me.

"Oh," he says, "and I found this."

He reaches into his pocket and takes out a piece of paper. I read. It's an email, from JB to me, confirming he'd given us permission to sell all of his paintings we held in storage.

Any works you have in storage after the show I
consign to you for sale purposes.

But I never got that email. It's a fake. It's as fake as the paintings on the gallery walls.

"So that's a relief, isn't it?" says Daniel. "That's Phillip Tench off our backs anyway."

He must have faked the email himself. But the way he looks at me, with utter conviction, makes me wonder for a moment whether he truly believes what he's saying, like that time he pretended he'd been on a school trip to see the Vikings. He's such an utterly convincing liar, maybe he even convinces himself.

"We make a great team," says Daniel. "I always knew we would. I can see us making a real go of this gallery together. The perfect partnership."

He looks at me with a beaming smile on his strange, distorted face. He looks so happy.

"It all feels like it's coming together, don't you think?"

But I just stare into his cloudy expressionless eye, a milky dead nothing.

47

NOW

"Thanks for meeting me."

"No worries," says Cassandra, coldly. She's nothing like the bubbly girl from the gallery. She's distant and aloof, holding herself in reserve. I'm not surprised. I'm amazed she's here at all, in this hip little East London cafe she's picked. Near where she lives now, I presume.

"I know you must have found it odd, the way I asked you to leave the gallery and leave my house."

She doesn't say anything, just raises an eyebrow and toys with the spoon on her saucer. Her hair is scraped into a ponytail and she's wearing one of her mini-skirt suits. Her back is straight and rigid. She must do Pilates or something because her posture is perfect. Only the occasional chink of her spoon against her cup gives away any sort of nervousness.

"I'll try to explain as best I can," I say. I slide a piece of paper across the table. It's the printout of the email Cassandra sent JB, including the size of the doorway his painting wouldn't fit through. "Did you send this?" I ask.

Cassandra picks the paper up and glances at it. "Probably. I always sent artists the gallery measurements." She drops it casually on the table.

"The measurements are wrong," I say.

"Well, I don't understand how. I just copied and pasted the email we always sent. Maybe Henry measured them wrong." She stares at me confrontationally. Chink chink goes the coffee spoon. She's nervous or she's furious.

"I checked emails you sent to other artists," I say. "The measurements are all correct in those."

A flicker of confusion goes over her face. Maybe she thinks I'm trying to catch her out. But I don't want to let on yet that it's not her I'm trying to catch.

"I don't know about that," she says. "Like I say, I just copied and pasted the old emails."

"And what about this?" I ask.

I slide another piece of paper across the table. It's the email I found between her and Henry. She picks it up between finger and thumb with disdain. But then she looks harder. A puzzled, tortured look flashes across her face. She hunches forwards over it and loses her cool, rigid composure.

"What's this?" she asks. She seems genuinely confused.

"You tell me," I say.

"Is this some sort of joke? I never sent this." She almost shudders at the idea. "Never."

I believe her. If Daniel could fake the email from JB, then he could fake these messages between Cassandra and Henry too. He was on that laptop all the time. He's smart. He'd find a way. Though why he wanted to ruin Cassandra in my eyes or destroy my memories of Henry, I don't understand. I take the printout back and put it in my bag.

"I'm sorry, Cassandra. I thought that email was real, but

I don't now. How I handled it all was horrible. I was vile to you."

"Where did it come from?" she asks.

But I'm not ready to talk about that. I duck the question. "Did you find somewhere else to live? Where are you working now? Do you need help with anything? A reference or something?"

"I'm fine, thanks," she says. The guard has gone up again. She looks at her watch. "Actually, if that's everything...?" She shifts her weight, clearly about to stand up.

"Sure, of course," I say, standing up myself. We both put jackets on in awkward silence.

"Was it Daniel?" she says, out of nowhere.

"What makes you think that?" I ask.

"I dunno," she says. "Something about him. He draws you in. He's so... magnetic. You forget what he looks like. Or maybe you don't. Maybe that's part of it. I fancied him like crazy, you know?"

"Yes?"

"Yeah. I know it's bad to say it, but it's hard to imagine it now. His face and stuff. If I picture him, I can't believe I fancied him. You know what I mean? He's repulsive. But he kind of... hypnotises you."

I do know what she means. I've felt it myself. The irresistible charismatic pull of him.

"We went on a date once," she says. "Well, I thought it was a date. I asked him for a drink. You get a lot of guys hitting on you if you're a pretty girl in a gallery. But he was different. He never flirted with me once. I'm not a raving egomaniac or anything, but it was weird. All he did for the entire date was talk about you."

"Me?"

"Yeah. He's obsessed with you. He was always charming and polite, but I got the feeling he didn't like me. Didn't like me moving in with you."

She stops gathering her stuff up and looks straight at me. For the first time in our meeting she's not angry or guarded. She looks worried. But I suddenly get the sense she's not nervous for herself. She's nervous for me.

"It's like he wanted you all for himself."

48

NOW

Once we leave the cafe I go and sit in my car, trying to make sense of it all. All the awful, untrue things I've been feeling about Henry. And what else? Daniel's been lying for months. I trace back through everything since he showed up at the gallery, trying to unpick the lies from the truth. But it's impossible to tell what's real and what isn't.

My phone buzzes and when I look, it's a message from Daniel.

Are you free? Any chance you could come to my place? D x

I'm in East London and not that far from Daniel's. Does he know that? It seems like a weird coincidence he's messaging me right now, when I'm only twenty minutes from where he lives.

Is he watching me?

I look out of my car window and scan the road I'm

parked on. Ordinary houses. There are a couple of people walking up the street. Some of the gardens have walls and shrubbery where a person could hide. At the end of the road is a shop, and there's a figure standing outside in a dark jacket with a hood up. I can't see at this distance whether it's Daniel or not. But as I'm watching, a woman comes out of the shop holding a child by the hand, and the man outside joins them and the group walks this way. It's not Daniel.

This is ridiculous. I can't cower here in my car, scared of passers-by. Why the hell would he be watching me?

What does Daniel want? He seems to be doing every-thing possible to make money for the gallery. Perhaps if he hacked into those email accounts he can hack into my bank account as well. What if he's got a whole string of crimes in his past? I have no idea what he's been up to for the last ten years. I'm beginning to doubt our entire friendship and everything I've ever thought about him.

But even if that's true, would he rob from me? From *me*?

I have a sudden horrible thought. Maybe he doesn't *need* to hack my bank account. He's already got access to my laptop. Jesus. I open the banking app on my phone and look up the balance.

I'm relieved to see all the money is still there. I go into my settings and change the password just in case. My secu-rity questions have answers he couldn't possibly know, about my mum's maiden name and my school. He doesn't even know my real name, or anything about my past. But by now I'm doubting everything and I change those too, just in case.

I can't unpick Daniel's lies from the truth, but I know he's lying.

The saving grace is that Daniel doesn't know I'm wise to

him. If I can keep that a secret, try to act normal and carry on like I trust him, maybe I can figure out what the hell he's up to.

I text:

Sure. On my way now. Ariana x

I find his address in Waze and start the car.

When I get to the house I park a few doors up the street and prepare myself. I can't let him realise I know he's lying. I think about Daniel and how convincing he is when he tells a story. I try to get myself into that state of mind. *We're friends,* I say to myself in my head. *We're friends. We're friends.* I look at myself in the rearview mirror and say it. I smile, and look at myself, and pretend to be somebody else.

We're friends. We're friends.

"Ariana. Great! Come in." Daniel holds the front door open for me. The light is on in the room at the end of the passageway behind him, but there's no light in the hallway itself, and it's gloomy. I walk in and he closes the door behind me with a solid click.

"Sorry," he says. "The bulb's gone."

From what I can make out, the walls are painted a reddy-brown colour, and the wooden staircase has been stripped back to dark hardwood. There's a door set into wooden panelling, to a cellar presumably, with Daniel's new bike leaning against it. Another door at the end opens onto the kitchen.

"How long have you lived here?" I ask casually, trying to resist the tension I can feel inside me.

"A couple of months," he says. "I rented it furnished.

They've tried to do all the period colours. It's like living in a Farrow & Ball catalogue."

I follow him past his bike into the bright kitchen.

"Ariana," says Daniel, "this is Zane."

A man is standing at the table. He's about nineteen, painfully thin, with long greasy hair and round tortoiseshell glasses. He raises his hand awkwardly and wiggles his fingers in a small wave. "Hello," he says in a nervous nasal whine. I notice he has paint stains on his tatty black t-shirt, and small, hard flecks of dried paint cling to the hairs on his forearm.

"Zane's leaving," says Daniel. "You've just caught him. He was bringing some more paintings round." Daniel points over near the fridge, where some wrapped canvases lean against the wall. So Zane is Daniel's forger.

"You're a student?" I ask.

"Er, yes," says Zane. "First year Fine Art at Goldsmiths."

"Thanks," says Daniel, cutting across him. He takes some money from his pocket and peels off a few notes then hands them to Zane. As he takes the money I can see his hand is shaking slightly and his fingernails are bitten down to the quick. Daniel puts his hand lightly on Zane's shoulder, ushering him from the room. Then Zane turns back towards me.

"Maybe I could bring some of my own work to –"

"Perhaps," says Daniel, interrupting.

He smiles in a way that's intended to be charming, but now I know what I do about Daniel, I see him in a different light. The mouth pulled tight in a grimace. The horrible scarring. The dead, staring eye. I see what I was pretending all this time wasn't there. He scares me.

Maybe he scares Zane too, because he stiffens under Daniel's touch and cowers away as he retreats up the dark hallway. I hear the front door close and Daniel comes back into the kitchen. "Do you want to see the place?" he asks.

I don't. But in an effort to seem normal, we head off and he gives me a guided tour of the house.

"It's Victorian, 1895," he says. "The couple who own it are working abroad for a year. It's still got all their stuff. It's perfect for me. I pay next to nothing."

We go into the room next door. It's a formal dining room. It has a large wooden table with two place settings, cutlery and wine glasses.

"No one wants dining rooms anymore," he says. "They're all knocked through. You can stay for dinner if you'd like."

"Perhaps," I say. But I mean it like Daniel meant it about Zane bringing his own artwork to the gallery. 'Perhaps' as in 'no way'. There's no way on God's earth I'm staying for dinner.

We head into the lounge. The room has all the period features, coving and an ornate ceiling rose. There's a real fireplace. The room is dominated by a vast modern sofa.

"Cosy, isn't it?" says Daniel. "I'll show you upstairs."

We go back into the gloomy hallway and up the darkened staircase. As we head deeper into the house I'm all the more aware I really want to get out of here.

"Where were you before you moved here?" I ask.

"Oh," says Daniel casually, "here and there." He doesn't add any more.

We arrive on the landing and he opens a series of doors. "Bathroom... Bedroom... Office..." He swings one final door open. "Master bedroom," he says. There's a silence as we look in at a large bed, but we don't go in.

"Then there's this," he says, leading the way up a

narrower flight of stairs. "Proper little Aladdin's cave, isn't it?" We come to another door and into another bedroom. "Guest bedroom with en suite," he says. It's a plain room, with a high ceiling that follows the slope of the roof on both sides and four large skylight windows. "Nice, right?" he says.

"Yes," I say. I don't know what to add.

"Anyway, that's the house," he says and leads the way out of the room.

I'm relieved we're heading downstairs again.

"I was thinking," he says, "it must be weird for you in your house, with all Henry's things. His paintings and drawings and his little bronze statues. Hard for you to properly draw a line and move forward.

"You haven't been to the house, have you?" I ask, trying to reassure myself I'm not misremembering.

"Only outside, to drop you off in the van," he says. "No, I'm just imagining. But what I was going to say was, you could come and stay here for a bit, if you wanted. See if that helps."

We're back in the hallway now. It's dark, and the light from the kitchen is behind him, so he's in silhouette almost. I can't see his scars anymore, and his eyes are just two darker hollows in his shadowy face. You'd never know he had been in the fire at all.

He's close to me, and he speaks softly.

"You should give up that place with all those bad memories. You could stay here, with me. We're the only two people who've ever really understood each other."

There's something else in his tone. Something more than just friendly.

"When we met there was a big age gap between us," he

says. "But now that gap isn't significant. It's less than the gap between you and Henry."

Oh God. Where has this come from? Has he always felt like this? Is this why he wanted to destroy my memories of Henry? I knew he had a bit of a crush on me as a kid, but this is different. I feel him grasp my hand in the gloom.

"You were really only a kid then yourself," he says. "We were lucky we found each other. People like us know the right way to bring up children because we've seen the wrong way. We make a great partnership. Not just with the gallery."

I stand there stiffly, hoping he can't feel the resistance in my hand as he's holding it. I don't know what he'll do if I turn him down. I'm overwhelmed by the feeling that I don't trust him.

"That fire we went through," he says. "We should be dead. But we're not. When you come through something like that, it makes you aware of just how precarious life is. It makes you certain you can't waste a second. I know you feel it too."

He squeezes my hand harder. I can't see his expression. His face is just a dark shadow against the light.

"It's a lot to think about," I say. "Let me think about it."

"Of course," he says. He lets go of my hand. A wave of relief goes through me and I step back towards the front door. "It's late," I say. "I must go. But I'll think about what you said." I turn towards the front door and make to leave. But as my hand lands on the lock his voice stops me in my tracks.

"Ariana."

I turn back towards his shadowy form in the kitchen doorway.

"Aren't you forgetting something?"

"Am I?" I say. I can hear the nervousness in my voice. "What?"

"The paintings," he says lightly. "I'll get them for you."

I wait in the hallway with my heart thumping out of my chest while he disappears into the kitchen. I can hear him moving something in the other room. It seems to be taking him longer than I'd expect. It's probably only been thirty seconds, but in my desperation to be out of here it seems like an eternity.

"Ariana," he calls from the other room.

"Yes?"

"They're a bit awkward. You couldn't give me a hand, could you?"

I can only see his shadow on the floor, moving slightly and then standing perfectly still. My hand is resting on the lock of the front door. It feels like sanctuary and I don't want to let go. I don't want to walk up the dark corridor and back into the house.

"Ariana?"

"No, it's fine," I say, turning the knob and opening the door. "I'm in a hurry actually. Bring them into the gallery."

"It'll just take a minute," he calls.

"No, it's fine. I'll see you tomorrow." I hurry down the steps and away from the house. I'm halfway across the road when I hear him at the door.

"Okay, see you tomorrow," he sing-songs casually.

I scurry to my car, fumbling the keys. I get into the driver's seat and close the door, then lock it. Only then do I look back at the house. Daniel stands in the doorway. The street light illuminates his scarred face. He smiles at me with his twisted grin, then steps back into the darkness and closes the door.

My hand is quivering. I'm too shaken to drive.

Is he watching me?

I crane my neck to look. But the lights aren't on in the rooms at the front of the house and all I can see is the dark expanse of glass at the window.

It's impossible to tell.

49

NOW

I replay the conversation in my head. Did what I think just happened really happen? That stuff about me going to live with him? A partnership? Children?

He's delusional.

I've often wondered what happened to him in the past ten years, but now I think I know. He's gone mad. It's not the right term, I'm sure. But that's what it feels like. Totally mad. And it makes complete sense. The fire, his family, everything he's been through. It's more than anyone could cope with. Who wouldn't be damaged by having a father who tries to kill you? Not just damaged on the outside, but on the inside too. Better to be like me, and have no father at all, or one who ignores you entirely and doesn't care whether you live or die. Better than having one who actively wants to destroy you.

Daniel scares me. I try to imagine what being in that fire must have been like for him, that poor twelve-year-old kid who suffered so much. For weeks I've looked at him and admired the way he's risen above it, the way he grabs life with incredible self-assurance. I thought it was brilliance, or confidence, or bravery. But now I see there's an arrogance to it. A frightening aura of entitlement. The fire twisted him. It twisted and broke the house, and it twisted the flesh on his face and body, and it twisted his mind as well.

I need to get away from the gallery, and as soon as possible. Once I'm driving I make a call. "Nigel Perry, please." Holding music kicks in, something classical I know but can't name. I'm too wound up to find it relaxing. After a couple of minutes, Nigel comes on.

"Nigel. It's Ariana Clough. I've decided to sell the gallery. I know you oversaw the lease. Could you find out how much it'd cost to get out early?"

"Of course. I'll ask Erica to hunt out the paperwork and we'll give you a call in the next couple of days."

"Thanks."

"Oh," he continues, "did you hear the news about James Balentine?"

"No," I say, dreading what might be coming next. "Have they found him?"

"No," says Nigel. "They're scaling down the search."

In truth, I have a sense of relief. With JB gone I won't be in trouble for selling those paintings in storage. I want to ask Nigel if I'm right to think this, but it seems too selfish, so I don't say anything. I just give a quick goodbye and ring off.

I'm just turning the corner when I spot someone at a bus shelter on the other side of the road, peering at the list of routes. His back is to me, but I can tell from his build and hair it's Zane. I make a split-second decision and swing the car around. I pull up and wind the passenger window down.

"Zane?"

He turns and peers into the car, then there's a flash of recognition on his face and he looks horrified.

"Get in," I say.

"What do you want?"

"I need to speak to you," I say in a firm voice. "Get in."

He just stands there. Lights flash in my rearview mirror and I see there's a bus wanting to drive into the stop. "Come on!"

Zane lurches forward and gets into the passenger seat. I pull off.

"Where are you going?" I ask. "I'll drive you back."

But he doesn't tell me the address. All he says again is, "What do you want?"

"The paintings," I say. "I know what Daniel's made you do." I drive in whatever random direction we're going, wondering if I should just pull over. Out of the corner of my eye, I see Zane chewing on the raw skin at the side of his tattered fingernails. "It's okay," I say. "We have to talk to the police."

"I'm not going to the police!" he says in horror.

"It's alright," I say, doing my best to sound calm. "We can tell them you didn't want to do it, that I had nothing to do with it, that it was all Daniel."

"It *was* Daniel," says Zane. "He's a fucking nutter. Jesus, what a freak. I don't just mean to look at. He's deranged."

"It's okay," I say. "We can go together."

"I shouldn't be talking to you," Zane says. "He told me if I said anything to you he'd kill me. He meant it. He's insane." There's real fear in his voice. I feel myself driving too fast. It's all too heightened in the car. I lose concentration and cut someone up at a junction and they honk at me. I need to slow down before we have an accident.

"Listen, Zane," I say, "we'll go together. To the police.

You can tell them you did the paintings against your will, that–"

"I'm not telling them I did the paintings!" He sounds outraged. "No way am I telling them that."

"I know you're worried you'll get in trouble," I say. "But we can work it out, I promise."

"I'm in too deep," mutters Zane, more to himself than me. "I needed money but I'm in over my head. I'm in too deep. I need to disappear."

I can tell he's properly scared of Daniel. God knows what Daniel has done to intimidate him into this state. I get the impression Zane's going to stick to his story about not doing the forgeries whatever. Maybe he's more scared of Daniel than he is of the police. But I must persuade him. Zane's the only one who knows it was Daniel who wanted the forgeries and not me. If I'm going to save myself, I need Zane.

We come to another junction on a busy high road lined with shops.

"Listen," I say calmly.

But before I can say anything else, Zane swings the door open and throws himself out of the car. I'm slowing for the lights but I'm still doing about twenty miles an hour. I hear him cry out in pain through the open door as he hits the road. The car behind hoots and there's a screech of brakes. I lean over instinctively to grab for the open door, but as I do I swerve badly to the left and my wheel hits the kerb with incredible force. There's a bang as the tyre bursts or the axle breaks or something. I slam on the brakes and come to a halt. The passenger door flies fully open before bouncing against its hinges and slamming shut.

Fuck. I could have killed myself.

I undo my seat belt and get out. The car behind is still honking. A couple of pedestrians come over to where I am. "Are you alright, luv?" asks a woman who's got off her bike just behind me.

But I don't answer. I'm staring over her shoulder back a hundred yards up the road where someone is helping Zane to his feet. He waves them away and limps onto the pavement, then hobbles off and into the crowd.

He's gone.

50

NOW

I wake up with the light streaming onto my face where I haven't closed the curtains. I reach for my phone and feel a terrible spasm of pain run up my neck. It's so violent that it stops me in shock and I daren't move again, even to breathe. Eventually I take a gasp of air and feel every single muscle in my back contract in agony.

I knew I'd jolted my neck last night, and I felt achy as I waited for the RAC to take the car away. I was stiff and awkward as I got in the Uber, and by the time I got home I felt extremely uncomfortable. But I thought I'd sleep it off. Not in my wildest imagination did I expect to feel like this.

Inch by inch, I manage to lift the phone where I can see it. 6 a.m. I sink back into bed as gingerly as I can, with my hand wrapped around the phone, the hard edges of the case pressing into my fingers. I should lift it up again. I should lift it up and call the police and tell them about Zane and the pictures. I should tell them about Daniel.

But I don't.

I lie there until the need to pee makes it impossible to stay in bed. I shuffle myself to the side and swing my legs around until I can get my feet on the floor. I take a deep breath and slowly raise myself to a sitting position, then pant like someone in a medical drama having a baby. I don't remember searing pain like this since I was in hospital for my burns. I get one hand on the bedside table and the other on the bed and force myself to standing.

In the bathroom, the idea of lowering myself down onto the toilet is daunting, but I somehow manage it. When I'm done, it's only by sheer force of will I get up and back into the bedroom. I go to the wardrobe and remove the first thing I can reach without straining. It takes me half an hour of painful manoeuvring to get dressed. I'm exhausted by the effort.

The stairs terrify me. I grab the rail so hard my knuckles go white. After every two or three steps I need to take a rest. Eventually I make it to the bottom. I lean against the wall by the front door and call an Uber.

It's half an hour before I get to Accident and Emergency. I check in, fill out a form and then sit in the busy waiting room. It feels weird being at this hospital. This was where I picked Daniel up when he had his bike accident, and now I've had an accident of my own. I don't believe in fate, but there's something about the chance overlap that bothers me.

Just as I'm thinking this, my phone rings. It's Daniel.

"Hey, Ariana. I'm at the gallery, but it's closed. Are you okay?"

"Um, no, actually. I'm at the hospital." For the first time I feel okay about my injury, as it's an excuse not to see him.

"Christ. What happened?"

"Car accident. I'm fine. I had a bit of a prang on the way home last night."

"God, are you okay?"

"Yeah," I say. "I'm in A&E. But only as a precaution. Nothing broken other than my car and my dignity."

"Jesus, Ariana, why didn't you let me know?"

"Honestly. I'm fine. Don't worry about it." I wince a bit as I shift in my seat, and a sharp pain shoots up my neck. It's all I can do to stop myself shouting in agony, but I don't want to let Daniel know how bad I am.

"Do you need me to come and pick you up?" he asks.

"No. Seriously. I'm literally leaving now," I lie. "I'm just waiting for my prescription to be filled."

"I'll come. It's no trouble."

"No," I say, a little too firmly. "I've already called a cab. It's two minutes away."

"Okay," he says, doubtfully. "If you're sure."

"I am, thanks. They've told me I need to rest, is all. I'm going to take a couple of days, then I'll give you a ring."

"Well, okay, if you're sure." He's reluctant to let it go. "I hope you feel better soon. Let me know if there's anything I can do."

"I will. Bye." It's a relief to ring off.

It's three hours before they call my name. For the entire time I wait, I watch the entrance to A&E, convinced Daniel is going to appear. But he doesn't.

The doctor asks lots of questions. He gives me a thorough examination and sends me for an X-ray. I'm relieved to learn nothing is broken. It's whiplash. He sends me home with pain medication and a neck collar like a dog that's had an operation. It'll help immobilise my neck for twenty-four hours. I'm to rest for a day or so, but he tells me I need to get moving if I can. Basically, I'll seize up like a rusty engine if I don't ditch the collar and move about a bit. I should be fine in a couple of days.

Though I'm in pain, I'm grateful for the time to think things through and get my head together, free of Daniel's oppressive influence. I lock the doors, order a shopping delivery and bunker down in the house for three days while I recover and try to make a plan.

But as my body heals, my mind becomes increasingly cluttered. I find I'm going over and over things, sinking further into a kind of desperate hopelessness. My desire to fix my life after Henry died has drawn me into this fraud with the forgeries, this criminal act. I went along with things I shouldn't have. I let myself go down this path. I'm as much to blame as anyone.

Daniel. I always thought he was such a good influence in my life, but he's not. He's a terrible influence. He's like one of those kids they separate you from at school because they lead you astray, but infinitely worse. Is it his fault? Is he so charismatic that he's irresistible? Or is it me? Did I follow along because I have a weak character?

Whichever it is, it stops now. I have to get him out of my life. I have to go to the police, whatever the consequences.

Maybe there's a way I can explain that it wasn't me who made the forgeries happen. That it was Daniel, putting pressure on Zane. That I only found out about it when it was too late.

But who's going to believe me?

I need Zane. I was right in the car. I need Zane to come to the police with me. He's as much a victim of this as I am, I'm sure of that. I remember how terrified he was. I need to get Zane.

By eight I'm up and dressed. I try eating something, but there's so much at stake I'm too nervous and have no appetite. The car's still being repaired, so I walk up and get the tube. I travel East, thinking about the last time I was on this side of London, three nights ago, in Daniel's house. There are ten million people in London, but I still feel nervous, like he'll single me out and know I'm here. I get off and take the overground down to New Cross Gate, and come out a few minutes' walk from Goldsmiths Art College, where Zane said he studies. I don't know if being at Gold-smiths was a lie, or even whether his name really is Zane, but I don't have anything else to go on.

The place is swarming. Goldsmiths is bigger than I was anticipating, a massive university with loads of different departments. I realise immediately the foolishness of the errand I'm on. There must be thousands of students here, split across loads of different buildings. I sit on a bench, puzzling out what I'm going to do next. I watch the crowds carefully and start to notice individuals. Most of them are in their early twenties, but there are a few older people too, mature students maybe, or staff at the university, or just commuters taking a shortcut across the courtyard. A lot of people look just like me. I don't need to feel conspicuous.

I get up and move to the middle of the large open concourse. There's a signpost with arrows pointing towards various buildings. I search on my phone and find the name of the building where the school of art is based and head that way.

I hover in the foyer, pretending to look at a display of life drawings while I keep an eye on the people coming and going. There are fewer students here but it's still busy. If Zane passes through here I'll see him, but it's all a bit haphazard. I could be here all day and not encounter him. Maybe he hasn't come in today at all. After fifteen minutes I bite the bullet and approach a couple of girls as they leave the building.

"Excuse me, do you by any chance know a chap called Zane who's in the first year?"

The girls look at each other with blank expressions. "Which course?" asks one.

"Fine art, I think."

"Sorry," says the girl. "We're film and moving image." They smile apologetically and head out.

I try the same thing with a couple of other people and get the same blank responses. Maybe Zane was a false name. I could ask in the college office, but they'll want to know who I am and it'll all get complicated. A girl wanders this way holding a large art folder under her arm.

"Hi, there. I wonder if you can help me. You don't know a lad called Zane, do you? First-year fine art?"

"Zane? Sure. His studio's up these stairs. Turn left, and it's at the end of the corridor."

"Okay, thanks."

The girl heads off in the other direction. No one's about and there appears to be no security at all. I head up the stairs and to the end of the corridor. As I approach I hear tinny dance music coming from an open door. There's a little card on the wall by the side of the door.

Matthew Jones
Zane Hendricks

I poke my head into a large room which has been subdivided by temporary walls made out of hardboard. A young man is in the first room, sitting in a tatty armchair, reading a book. Matthew Jones presumably. He looks up briefly, but when he doesn't recognise me he goes back to his novel. I skirt the edge of his studio and peer through a gap in the stud wall to the studio behind.

There's an easel supporting a half-finished garish painting of a naked woman. A few other equally unattractive paintings are dotted around the room. Other than that, it's empty. No Zane.

"He's not in today," calls a voice over the partition wall. I wander back round to the lad in the armchair. "He hasn't been in all day."

"Oh, okay, thanks. Do you think he might be in later?" I ask. "I'm his aunt."

Mathew just shrugs.

"His aunt?" says a voice behind me. I turn and see a scruffy-looking man in his forties. He has a thick jumper with an ugly pattern and longish ratty hair. I'd assume he was a student if he wasn't so old. Something about his look reminds me of JB, and I guess he's an art teacher. "Zane? You're his aunt?"

"That's right," I say. I've got to brazen it out now and hope the lie sticks.

"Can I have a word in private?" asks the tutor. He sounds cross or disbelieving. Shit. Have I messed up, coming here?

"Of course," I say, as lightly as possible.

I follow him out of the studio and along the corridor. I walk behind as he goes down the stairs, past the door where I came in, and along another corridor. Then he turns a corner and goes down another narrow staircase to the basement. The stairs are dark and there's no rail, so I trace my hand along the wall to feel my way. He stomps ahead of me and flicks a switch. Fluorescent lights stutter into life, illuminating one end of a large room filled with strange sculptures – odd abstracted human forms made from twisted metal and plastic. The oversized figures disappear into the shadows at the darkened end of the room. It feels like we've interrupted some strange secret meeting here in the dark. It's eerie and unsettling.

"Sculpture are off on Wednesdays," he says.

"Right."

"Do you know how to get in touch with Zane?"

"Well," I say, "I was in this part of town and I just thought I'd drop in to see him if he was here, in his studio. We hadn't arranged anything." I can hear myself talking too much, the over-elaboration of the bad liar. I make myself shut up.

"Well," says the tutor, "if you see him, can you tell him he's missed supervision three times in a row and if he does it again, he'll need a formal discussion about his future on the course."

"Three times?"

"Yes. He's a good attendee normally, but he's missed meetings the last three days in a row. I'm prepared to cut him some slack, but he's pushing things too far."

"Oh. Right. I'll be sure to tell him when I see him."

"Good. Thanks."

The tutor moves and I follow, up the stairs and back to reception.

"Look," he says, his tone softer than before, "he's a nice kid. This isn't like him at all. If he's got some reason for not being here, any issue he'd like to discuss, it's better if he comes to us about it rather than just vanishing. Thanks." He wanders off.

I head back out into the courtyard. Zane said he might disappear, and he has. He's in the wind. I won't find him now. I can't get him to come to the police with me. And there isn't anyone else to back up my side of the story.

I'm on my own.

51

NOW

"Christ," says Daniel. "Why didn't you call me? You look awful."

We're in the gallery office. There's a glass of water and a packet of Ibuprofen on the table. I'm wearing the neck brace again and I've deliberately not put on any makeup so I'll look more pale and tired than usual.

"Are you sure you should be in today?"

"I don't know," I say. I'm putting on a feeble voice, but I mustn't overdo it. I don't want to sound like a kid phoning the school secretary faking a sicky. "Maybe you're right. I should go home. Sorry to have dragged you in."

"It's fine," he says. "I had to bring these in anyway." He indicates three fake JB paintings leaning against the wall.

"You head off," I say. "I'll take five minutes to clear my head and then I'll lock up and head home. I'll get a cab and go back to bed."

"Sure you don't want me to help you get back?"

"No, honestly," I say. I ditch a bit of the voice in case I seem too feeble to leave. "I'll be fine."

"If you're sure," he says, standing and picking up his jacket. "But I'll call you later to see how you're doing."

"Thanks." I force a smile.

"Maybe I can pop round, bring you a takeaway or something," he adds speculatively.

"Let's see how I feel," I say. No way. No, thank you.

I give it ten minutes after he's left. I get up and move across the gallery slowly, like someone in pain. I pick up the three paintings, shuffle through the door and lock up. I stand in the street by the doorway as if I'm catching my breath. Then I walk about fifty yards, put the paintings down and lean against a shop window for a moment. I figure if Daniel's watching he'll fly to my aid, make up some story about having forgotten something at the gallery or whatever. But he's not going to miss an opportunity to look like my knight in shining armour.

I lean there for a minute before I figure I'm safe. Then I pick up the paintings and walk to the expensive car park. The garage dropped my car at home yesterday. I put the paintings in the boot, get into the driver's seat and remove the neck brace, tossing it in the back. I put the address in the satnav and head off.

The art restorer has called me several times about the JB painting I left, but I haven't wanted to think about JB, so I ignored the messages until yesterday.

It's half an hour before I pull into the courtyard at the back of the mews house where Matilda works. It's getting close to dusk and it has turned decidedly chilly, so I get my jacket out of the boot. It's lying by the JB forgeries Daniel just gave me. I grab the paintings and lock up.

Matilda swings the stable door open and invites me in. The space is half artist's studio, half science lab. There's a reception area with a sofa and coffee table and a vase of flowers. She must have rich clients who come through here, and presentation is all part of her business.

"Sorry I was so hard to track down," I say.

"No worries. I've enjoyed living with it for a while," she says. She looks across to a wall where a couple of paintings hang on display, one of which is JB's. "Let me show you what I've done."

While she pulls on white gloves and lifts the painting down, I unwrap the Zane fakes.

"There's a couple of other paintings by the same artist I'd like you to look at, if that's okay," I say casually.

"Of course," she says. "We'll take a look in a bit."

I carry the forgeries over and lean them carefully against the table opposite. Meanwhile, Matilda places the real JB painting on an angled easel, a bit like an architect's drawing board. She has a magnifying glass on a pivoted stand which she swings it over. It's like something a dentist would use. I'm not interested in this original. It's the fakes I've come to find out about. But I don't want Matilda to sense there's anything wrong, so I let her do her stuff on the real JB first.

"The surface was pretty dirty, so I gave it a thorough clean. There were several areas where the canvas showed wear, particularly at the corners." She turns the painting over so we're looking at the back. I remember guiltily just how long I had it bashing about in the boot of my car. "I lined the canvas to support it. Took it off the frame and patched it from behind. And I applied new keys to make sure the corners were stable, then restretched it."

She's extremely thorough. If anyone's going to spot those other paintings as fakes, it's someone who's spent weeks looking at a real JB.

"As for the paint surface," says Matilda, turning the whole thing over to face us again, "where there was flaking, I used adhesive to attach the paint layer back onto the canvas. In small areas paint had been knocked off altogether and I did a little inpainting to replicate."

I stare through the magnifying lens at the surface of the painting. "I can't see anything," I say. "Which is a good thing, obviously."

"I can show you," says Matilda. She swings a lamp over. "This is a UV bulb. Retouched areas fluoresce differently under black light." Matilda clicks on the UV lamp.

Immediately I can see little speckles around the edges of the painting. It looks like it's been dusted with glitter. They shimmer like little fish scales.

"You can see the bottom left corner where a section of paint cracked off almost entirely. May I?" She steps forward to reposition the magnifier. I move back to give her more space.

As I do, I notice something about the forged paintings leaning against the table opposite that sends a cold chill down my spine.

Matilda leans in close to the magnifier, studying the surface of JB's painting intently. "You can see where this green swirl comes down and meets the blue that the paint itself has been laid on quite thickly and..."

She's talking, but I don't hear anything else she says. It's just a blur of noise and I can't concentrate. In fact, I'm not looking at JB's painting at all. I'm staring at one of Zane's forgeries. Where the black light spills across the room, there are marks clearly visible on the surface of the fake that were invisible before.

One single word in large block capitals.

HELP.

"THANKS VERY MUCH," I say to Matilda over my shoulder as I hurry across the courtyard, clutching JB's painting and the three hastily wrapped forgeries.

"Are you sure you don't want me to look at them?" she calls after me. "I have time."

"No, it's fine, thanks," I say, hurling them into the boot and leaping into the car so I can get them away from that black light as quickly as possible. I drive round the corner, and once I'm a couple of streets away I stop. It's getting late and most shops will be closing, but I search on my phone and find a B&Q that isn't too far out of my way. I look on the website. It's still open and they have what I want in stock.

Once I'm home I park the car and hurry into the house clutching the paintings under my arm. There's a lamp I can use in the sitting room. I dump the paintings on the sofa, then unscrew the bulb and replace it with the ultraviolet one I've just bought. I turn off the main light so the room is almost completely dark. Then I switch on the lamp.

The room lights up with a kind of eerie underwater glow. Objects radiate a haunting, fluorescent light, alien and other-worldly. The white blouse I'm wearing is almost dazzling in the purple-blue light that seems to shine out of me, and flecks of fibre speckle my black trousers like needles. Dust hangs in the air like a million tiny stars.

I look down at my hands, which are glowing. It must be the hand cream I use to protect my scars. I kneel on the floor, reach across and unwrap one of the forgeries. Writing leaps out from the painted surface.

HELP.
I am being forced to make these paintings against my
will.
A man called Daniel is forcing me to do this.
I am being held prisoner.
Please contact the police.
PLEASE HELP ME.

Everything is written in a desperate, urgent scrawl. Daniel must have tracked Zane down and now he's holding him against his will somewhere, forcing him to make these paintings. It's insane.

I put the first painting aside and look at the other two. As with the first, they're a mass of urgent, pleading secret writing.

HELP ME.
I don't want to do this.
Please tell someone.
HELP HELP HELP

They're tortured and upsetting and I turn off the lamp so I don't have to look at them anymore. I stay here, in the dark, for a long time. What should I do? Zane sounds terrified. I should go to the police.

But I'm a part of what Daniel's doing. It's my gallery. Zane made these forgeries for me. Some have already been sold in my name. And now I'm implicated in something far worse. Kidnapping? False imprisonment? Torture?

How can I possibly explain I'm not involved?

It's completely dark now. I go up to bed. I close my eyes,

but in the darkness all I can see in my mind's eye is that glowing writing.

HELP. HELP ME.

52

NOW

I'm woken by a knock at the front door.

I'm immediately anxious it's Daniel. Now I know what he's done to Zane, I keep wondering what he's capable of doing to me. I could get up and creep to the window, try to see if it's him down there. But I don't want to be seen. And anyway, it's the window I don't look out of. There's another knock. I wait, holding my breath in the silence.

After a moment I hear an engine drive off. Perhaps it was someone who's delivered something and left. I'm so on edge, even a simple delivery is making me terrified.

I put on a dressing gown and tiptoe downstairs, looking to see if there's a shadow of anyone against the glass in the door. But no one's there. Slowly, I unlock the front door and open it.

There's a large cardboard box.

I peer down at the label and see it has Daniel's name and address as the sender. It's square, about two feet wide, and my first thought is that it's going to have Zane's head in it. My mind races with what I should do. I can feel my heart beating faster and my anxiety growing. I lean down and lift it tentatively.

It's a massive relief when the box is light, too light to contain a human head. But I'm no wiser what's in it. It's so light I wonder if it holds anything at all. Maybe he's sent me an empty box as some sort of sick prank, just to mess with my head. I carry it inside cautiously, as if I might be handling an unexploded bomb. I go into the living room and put it down carefully on the sideboard. The top is held down with brown parcel tape, and I scratch my fingernail under one end, then start to rip it back.

Slowly, I begin to lift one of the cardboard flaps. Then I fly backwards in terror as something emerges from the box.

A balloon.

It's just a balloon. And then another. Two round, silver helium balloons, on twine, attached to a fancy decorative weight in the box. The balloons read GET WELL SOON.

This can't go on.

I dress, grab what I need and get in the car. I have to look up where I'm going. I could have phoned, but this feels like the sort of thing someone's going to need to discuss in person.

"Hello," I say when I get to the reception desk. "I'd like to report a kidnapping."

Maybe it's because I'm weirdly calm that the whole thing is handled in a very quiet, polite way. Or maybe they just don't believe me. Anyway, the desk sergeant takes my name and asks me to explain why I'm there again. I sit on an orange plastic chair in reception while he contacts someone.

There's another man waiting, a guy in his forties in a poorly cut suit and drab tie. His legs are crossed and his trousers have ridden up, revealing a bit of pasty shin above the top of a frayed sock. He's holding a file of papers and scribbling notes with a sour look on his face. I guess he's a solicitor. I'm almost certainly going to need one and I half wonder whether I should ask him for a card, but then the desk sergeant calls him through and so I don't.

I should be feeling nervous. This is what I've been fretting about for days now – the police discovering my involvement in something criminal. But I don't feel nervous. I feel relief. Relief to be free of this crippling anxiety that's overwhelmed me. There are worse things than being in trouble with the law.

After a few minutes, another man in a suit takes me through to an interview room. I follow him, holding the fake paintings I've brought. I explain my story. Daniel working at the gallery, JB's disappearance, Zane and the forged paintings, Zane's disappearance, and finally the messages on the front of the fakes. He sits and listens without reacting, but when I get to the bit about the secret messages in invisible ink I see a look cross his face. It could be surprise or scepticism. I'm aware, hearing myself say it out loud, how outlandish it all sounds.

When I've finished, he asks if I'll excuse him for a moment. He's gone for some considerable time. I just sit here and wait. I get a weird flashback to the room I sat in that day I got caught shoplifting. The day I ran away and everything started.

I wonder what's going to happen next. Is he going to come back and send me home? Is he going to arrest me? He's closed the door on his way out and I wonder whether he's locked it, trapping me in here. I have no intention of leaving, but I have an urge to get up and check the door. It occurs to me how suspicious that would look, me fiddling with the door handle just as he comes back, and it makes me laugh. Nerves probably. I stay in my seat.

Eventually the detective comes back in with another detective, holding a torch. It has dark blue glass on the end, and I recognise it as a torch the police use to inspect stolen bikes for postcodes, like the one Daniel used years ago to show me what he'd written on Jeffrey's study walls. They unwrap the forged paintings and scan them with the UV torch, revealing Zane's protestations and cries for help. They mutter to each other, but my brain is suddenly whirring on something else. The torch that Daniel had years ago. The pen he once showed me where he security-marked his bike. His bike now, leaning in his hallway against the cellar door.

"Zane's in his basement," I say. "The basement in Daniel's house."

There's a brief discussion and then the detectives leave, more animated this time. I'm asked if I'll wait. I agree, and I'm taken to another room. I'm happy to wait, because I need to know what happens. I know they're going to rescue Zane and get Daniel and I need to know what comes next.

It's hours before someone comes back and explains it to me. The station goes on high alert. The messages on the paintings are taken extremely seriously. Zane has been reported missing by one of his housemates and his family hasn't heard from him for three days. Enquiries are made into Daniel. An armed response unit is gathered. Three transit vans loaded with officers zigzag through London traffic, sirens blaring and blue lights flashing, making their way to Ilford. The tension in the van is palpable.

When they're a mile from the house they turn off the sirens and approach in convoy at a normal pace. The operation is a delicate one and they don't want to warn Daniel of their arrival. It's vital they don't spook him and give him a chance to run. He's a kidnapper, he's dangerous, and they want to make sure they catch him.

Two streets away they stop and make a detailed plan. They have photographs of Daniel and Zane, which they study. They want to be sure they know the hostage from the kidnapper. Officers are sent to the front and the rear of the house. A unit goes to the front door while another secures the back. They burst through the front door, guns at the ready, and call for Daniel to make himself known with his hands up, but there's no response. They do a detailed sweep of the ground floor, which is empty. They edge their way upstairs and that's empty too.

Just the top floor now. They inch their way up the narrow staircase and push open the door to the guest bedroom. It's empty.

All that remains is the basement.

They tentatively open the door. It's dark on the stairs. An officer reaches around and flicks the light switch, but the light doesn't work. Torches are switched on and pointed down the stairs into the darkness below. The steps are old and narrow and face towards a wall at the bottom so it's impossible to see most of the cellar. The officers point their weapons and shout again for Daniel to show himself. He doesn't appear, but there's some kind of noise and possibly a voice, but it's muffled and distant.

Everyone remains on high alert as the first officer creeps his way cautiously down the stairs into the pool of light cast by his torch. It stinks down here, of shit and piss and body odour. It's often like this at crime scenes, with the stench of decay and death, and the nauseating reminder of human mortality. You never get used to it. At the bottom of the stairs he swings round fast, gun raised, to see the rest of the cellar.

Three or four lights on stands are dotted about the place, all unplugged. A bicycle, upended so it sits on its saddle and handlebars. Behind that, items of art equipment. Easels with half-finished paintings, dozens of completed paintings leaning against one wall. The floor is littered with empty tubes of oil paint. And against another wall, laid out on shelves, hundreds of blank canvases.

They hear another sound and the officer moves his torch to the shadowy corners of the room. There's a low fold-out bed with a couple of tatty blankets, shoved against a wall with some thick pipework, probably part of the original plumbing or a disused heating system. Padlocked to the pipework is a heavy chain which trails down onto the bed, ending at a shackle that's attached to a man's leg. The man looks filthy, his lank, greasy hair in an untidy clump. He has a ball-gag over his mouth and makes pained, muffled moans. He holds his handcuffed hands up to shield his eyes from the dazzling torchlight.

An officer goes over to the bed and releases the ball-gag.

"Zane Hendricks?" he asks.

"No," says the man in a hoarse, rasping voice. "James. James Balentine."

The house is secure. The victim is safe.

The perpetrator is nowhere to be found.

53

NOW

I'm waiting in a tatty probation office in a run-down building in Cambridge Heath. It's the God-forsaken arse-end of London that's populated by galleries, and I've walked past a couple getting here from the train station. But I'm not here for any of that.

It's been a week since the raid on Daniel's house. Nigel Perry has been representing me with the police, and the full story is starting to come together. Apparently, James Balentine was on his morning walk when Daniel ambushed him. He managed to overpower JB and get him into the van. He tied him up, drove him to the Ilford house and somehow dragged him into the cellar. That's where he's been all this time, shackled up and forced to make paintings for days on end, or handcuffed and gagged in total darkness. He found a UV security pen near Daniel's bike and made his secret messages.

Apparently JB put up quite a fight. He had a walking stick and gave Daniel quite a battering. Those must have been the injuries Daniel said he got falling off his bike. They think Daniel deliberately injured himself more to convince me he'd been in a car accident. There's no record he checked into the hospital at all. I thought he had an alibi for the time JB disappeared, but they reckon he just hung around in reception until I arrived to pick him up.

Zane's body has been found hidden in Epping Forrest, a few miles from Daniel's house. Zane never was in the cellar. In fact, he never painted any forgeries at all. The lad he shared a studio with confirmed Daniel met Zane at an art school show, but the best theory is that he just paid Zane to pretend he was faking the paintings, presumably to stop me suspecting he'd kidnapped JB. When Zane got spooked, Daniel must have tracked him down somehow and killed him to keep him quiet.

Nigel thinks they won't come after me for selling the paintings we had in storage. The irony is, since the story hit the news, JB's work is even more sought after. He's recuperating at home, but he's sitting pretty on about thirty paintings Daniel made him do. Phillip Tench has started a bidding war for them, apparently. Nigel went for a meeting with Phillip Tench and said he had a JB painting up in his gallery already, with a UV bulb above it, switching on and off.

HELP ME.
I don't want to do this.
Please tell someone.
HELP HELP HELP

I really don't understand the art world and I'm glad I'm getting out. I should have the gallery wound up by the end of the month. I'm not sure what I'll do for money, but I'll survive. And of course, I have Henry's old JB painting to sell. Not a bad investment after all.

"Hello. Thanks for coming to see me." Robin, Daniel's probation officer, leans round the door. "Do you want to come with me?"

I follow him up a corridor and into a small meeting room. There's a table and two chairs and a framed photo of some mountains on the wall. It's basic. Robin slides a little plastic tile on the sign outside the room so *UNOCCUPIED* reads *OCCUPIED.* He closes the door and places the large briefcase he's carrying on the floor.

"I wanted to discuss Daniel with you," he says. "I want to apologise that I might have put you in harm's way."

"I appreciate that," I say, disarmed by his honesty. I've had my fair share of dealings with people in these jobs, and it's the first time anyone's ever admitted a mistake.

"The truth is, I was thrown by your name, and I didn't dig further. We had no record of contact with an Ariana Clough. If I'd known you were Tracey Jones and you knew Daniel from his youth I'd never have let him work at the gallery or be anywhere near you."

"I'm not sure I understand," I say. "I know this kidnapping business happened, but I don't see how it relates to what Daniel did earlier, the drug possession."

Robin sighs. He looks at the table for a long time, then at me. He holds my gaze until it becomes uncomfortable. "You were in care yourself, weren't you?"

"Yes," I say. "A long time ago now."

"I saw your file. I hope you don't mind. I had to, as follow-up on Daniel's case. You didn't have an easy start. And then you met Daniel..."

He trails off. But the way he says Daniel's name makes it

sound like meeting him must be the worst thing that could ever happen to a person.

"The story Daniel told you, about a prosecution for drugs, was one he and I agreed in order to protect his interests. Daniel was actually prosecuted for something considerably more serious, which he did as a child."

I feel myself flush hot. There's only one thing he could mean. I dare hardly think it. "Tell me."

"You didn't hear this from me," he says, looking intently at me again. He's trying to be sure he can trust me. He slides his chair backwards and leans down to his briefcase. He takes out a file. I know it's Daniel's, and that I absolutely shouldn't be seeing it.

"This will all come out," he says. "It's bound to. You should know that Daniel set the fire at his family home. He was responsible for the deaths of his family. He murdered them."

The moment he says it, I know it's true. It hits me with blinding clarity. Of course it was Daniel. I feel myself holding the edge of the table, holding on against the spinning of the room which Daniel told me about. When did he tell me that? Was it ten years ago, or just last week? Everything seems to blur into one moment.

"Daniel's been in the system for a long time," says Robin. "There were several incidents at school as well as home. Opportunities were missed. Then there was the fire. He was prosecuted for arson and murder, but it was recognised at the trial that he has very complex mental health issues. There isn't full agreement on his diagnosis. Some reports suggest he has Narcissistic Personality Disorder, or possibly Antisocial Personality Disorder. A decision was made to detain him at a specialist secure mental health unit for young people."

I'm rewinding everything, trying to piece it all together. My brain is flying at two million miles an hour, trying to reconcile this reality with everything I thought I knew.

Robin thumbs the corner of Daniel's file in a manner that gives away his discomfort. "He had a whole range of therapies. By all accounts he responded well. He's a clever man, fiercely intelligent. Maybe his brilliance got in the way somehow, I don't know. But in time he was moved to a less restrictive unit, then underwent gradual reintegration into society. I was part of the team facilitating his release."

"And the first thing he did was come to me," I say.

Robin shifts awkwardly in his chair. "As I say, perhaps his intelligence got in the way. He's clever. He wasn't assessed a high-risk client at this stage."

"Oh, wasn't he?" I say, unable to stifle a laugh of astonishment. "Well, it seems that assessment wasn't entirely accurate."

54

NOW

He's disappeared and they don't know where to find him. He doesn't have bank cards they can trace, just a little cash from work he did for me. His only phone was pay-as-you-go with no contract, which they found at the house. He's vanished.

A chill runs through me. I tell myself it's the cold weather drawing in and go into the living room to make up a fire. After a while, the logs catch and it starts to crackle, glowing red and kicking out heat. But the chill doesn't leave me. The bit of me that shivers at the thought of Daniel still out there somewhere.

There have been bulletins on the news and reports in the papers, as there often are when they want the public to stay away from a dangerous criminal, or help if someone spots the suspect somewhere. The photofits and drawings are usually pretty nondescript. But of course, that's all different with Daniel. Most people don't look remotely like him. It's easy to build up the story of an evil perpetrator on the loose when he's as frightening to look at as Daniel is. A monster.

Even knowing what he's done, the stories demonising

him don't tally with the person I know. The police advise me to be wary, and Robin tries to explain the way Daniel's damaged mind works. But I'm not scared. Everything I know Daniel has done, however destructive to others, has always been to protect me. I stare into the mesmerising glow of the fire. He won't harm me. I know it. He loves me.

Am I being stupidly naive? Is this how his kind of magnetic charm works? Cassandra said he hypnotises you, and maybe she's right. Maybe I'm somehow under his spell. He has a kind of power over me I don't understand.

I have a vague, half-remembered thought about something Daniel once said, something about having power over people. It starts to come back to me, but it's too outlandish to contemplate. It can't be true, surely. With a rising feeling of dread, I switch on the lamp. Nothing. I take the lamp from the living room to the kitchen and plug it in. Nothing. Then I climb the stairs slowly and head to my bedroom. I turn my face away from the window as I close the curtains. The room is in semi-darkness as I plug in the lamp. I know what's coming. My hand is shaking as I switch it on.

The bedroom explodes into life.

Beloved. Prime Mover. Chosen One. Creation's Fire.
Goddess. Keeper of my Soul. Sacred Flame. Angel.
True Light. Muse. Salvation. My Everything.
Saviour. Forged in the Flames.

Every inch of wall fluoresces with a wild, glowing scrawl. The ceiling too. It's mad. I have no idea when or how he got in here. I imagine myself, night after night, sleeping in this room, and all the while this was staring down at me. His secret, invisible hold over me.

There's a knock at the door.

I'm utterly convinced it's Daniel. But why would he knock if he's able to just get in? Who knows how his warped mind works? I have to know, and so I do what I haven't done for weeks. I cross the room to the window, pull the curtains and peek out.

To my relief, it's just a motorcycle courier. I can see down onto his helmet where he stands on the path and I notice he's holding another box, a smaller one this time. I know immediately Daniel's sent me something else and wonder what it could be. I'm not surprised he's trying to make contact. I expected it. I head downstairs, wondering what bizarre object awaits me in that box.

I open the door and the courier hands me the package, then thrusts a clipboard and pen my way, with a delivery note I have to sign. I put the box on the hall table, dreading to think what the hell I'm signing for. I turn to take the clipboard and pen.

The courier has stepped into the hallway.

He pushes the front door closed and lifts up his smoked visor.

It's Daniel.

It's a shock. And at the same time, I'm not surprised. I knew he'd come. "What do you want?" I ask.

"You know what I want," he says.

And I do. He wants me.

"I think we should talk, don't you?" he says, calmly. "Why don't we go through and make ourselves more comfortable? We should discuss the future."

I lead us through into the living room. I can't imagine what he means by the future. Surely he doesn't have a future worth talking about, given what he's done. But the things he's done in the past make it hard to understand how he's standing here now. Yet here he is. The past and future both seem to be focused in this moment right now, like the sun's rays focused through a magnifying glass, intense and dangerous.

Daniel removes his crash helmet and puts it on the sideboard next to the balloons he sent.

"How are you feeling?" he asks.

"Better," I say. It's bizarre to be making small talk.

It's as if he senses my mood. "You can talk to me," he says. "I know there are things I haven't been entirely honest about. This seems a good time to clear the air." A wry smile plays across his thin, crooked lips.

"Okay," I say. "Let's do that." The list of things I want to ask is enormous. I don't know where to start. I wonder whether he'll be honest with me anyway, or how I'll know, as he's so expert at making lies sound like the truth.

I notice he's holding the box he brought today. "I assume that's empty, just a clever way of disguising yourself?"

"I suppose I am quite easy to recognise from a photofit." He laughs. "But no, there's something in it. It's for you."

He passes me the box. I open it. Inside is a small locket, the one I've noticed him wearing on a couple of occasions. "Did this belong to your mother?" I ask.

"It did. But I don't keep it for sentimental reasons. Well, not with her anyway. I took it well before she died. It was just something I needed at the time. Open it."

I press the clasp on the side of the silver case and it clicks open. On one side is a photograph of me, from ten years ago. In the other half is a clump of hair.

"Where did you get the photograph?" I ask.

"It was from that ID card of yours," he says. I took it to a print shop and they made a copy."

"So your dad never took my ID. You did? For this? And when I noticed it gone, you put it in his office so it'd look like he'd taken it, not you?"

"Yes." He sounds proud.

"And when did you get the hair?"

"When I was putting the ID back. Initially I just wanted the photograph. But when I came into your room at night, you looked so peaceful as you were sleeping, it felt like you wanted me to have it. So I cut some off."

I remember that time when I met Henry. I couldn't get my hair to stay flat. That must have been because of Daniel.

"I've always worn it next to my heart," he says. "Look."

He unbuttons his shirt from the neck down. It's the first time I've seen the horrific scars on his neck, like strings of elastic pulling his shiny skin tight. He pulls the shirt to one side and shows me an angry rectangular burn on the left of his chest, the size of the locket.

"From the fire," he says. "It got so hot. So you see, you're etched into my heart." He smiles again, a smug, self-satisfied smile, as if he expects me to be impressed by the scale of his devotion, and not how I actually feel, repulsed by his obsession.

"So you lied about Jeffrey taking my ID," I say. "What else did you lie about?" A thought strikes me. "Did you lie about him hitting you? Did you hurt yourself falling off your bike, and blame Jeffrey for it? Just like you pretended you'd been hurt in a bike accident when it was JB who'd hit you?"

He doesn't answer me directly. All he says is, "He wanted to hit me. He would have done, if he thought he could get away with it."

I see it now. He wanted me to dislike everyone else. He wanted to isolate me so I'd feel more lonely, more reliant on him. Just like he did when his lies put a wedge between me and Cassandra.

"Poppy never ripped my jacket, did she? That was you, wasn't it?"

He doesn't answer. He just smiles, pleased with himself.

"And Liam. That wasn't your dad. You found him somehow and killed him."

"To protect you," he protests, as if somehow I'm the mad one for questioning him.

"Your mum said something to me once. *Get away while you can. He's dangerous.* I've never forgotten it. I always thought she meant Jeffrey. But she meant you."

"She was a weak woman," he says.

"You burnt that house down and left them all to die."

"I came back for you," he says, sounding more like the petulant twelve-year-old than the grown man. "I was sad I had to leave my spiders and snakes. But I did it for us, so we could be together."

"No," I say, "you did it for yourself. You're the coldest, most selfish person I've ever met. You feel more sorry for your spiders than you do for your own family. You're grotesque. And I don't mean how you look. Grotesque on the inside."

A pained look fixes on his face. At first I think he's hurt. But then I realise he's puzzled. He genuinely doesn't understand why I'm rejecting him.

"But we're supposed to be together," he says. "There's nothing to stop us now."

I'm by the side table with the little statue of Henry. I

pick it up and study his face. Then it occurs to me. The worst thought of all.

"That burnt-out car. They never caught anyone because they wore gloves and didn't leave fingerprints. But you don't have any fingerprints, do you? It was you, wasn't it? You killed Henry."

He just stares at me, confused and aggrieved. "There's nothing stopping us now," he says.

He walks towards me slowly, then takes my scarred hand in his.

"We were always going to be together," he says calmly. He's no longer confused. He's happy. "We're like two planets," he says softly into my ear, "destined to live in each other's orbits forever. It's how the universe is made. It's inescapable. And now I've found you again, I'll never let you go."

I feel the bronze, hard and heavy in my hand. And then I strike.

55

NOW

Disoriented, it takes him a moment to remember where he is. In the living room at Ariana's house.

His eyes widen, searching for any sign of light. It's entirely dark on the right, of course, as it has been for the last ten years. But with his good left eye all he sees is darkness. Then he looks deeper and it comes into focus. Not darkness. Dark green. And a table lamp, at a strange angle. No, not a table lamp. A light fitting.

He realises he is staring at the ceiling.

His head feels muggy. Daniel lifts his hand to his head. He can feel the warmth and stickiness of the blood where Ariana hit him. He'll have a painful bruise there for sure, and might even need stitches if a sharp part of the statuette has caused a significant laceration. But a single blow is unlikely to have fractured his skull. He assumes she only hit him once. If she'd hit him more than once, he supposes she wouldn't have stopped until he was dead.

He tries to get up, but can't move properly. He may have a mild concussion which is impacting his balance. He feels a sharp pain in his right shoulder and presumes he landed on it hard when he fell unconscious to the floor. He reaches to feel the painful shoulder and his hand touches something surprising that shouldn't be there. Metal.

Daniel twists his head to look. A metal spike has pierced his shoulder blade and ripped through his jacket. He's fallen badly onto the fireplace surround and is pinned there. He tries to lift himself, but his scarred, withered limbs are too weak on his right side to lift his body weight.

He'll just have to wait until Ariana comes to help him.

He knows that there's a danger of shock with an injury like this, and keeping a patient warm is typically important. Thankfully, he has fallen near the fire and he can feel its heat radiating towards him.

He recognises the acrid smell of smoke. Not just wood smoke from the logs in the fireplace, but something else. He can see from the corner of his eye that in falling he has knocked into the companion set and some implements have landed in the fire, hitting a log, which has rolled across the hearth onto the carpet.

Tar. That's what he smells. The carpet must be synthetic. He's surprised a couple as urbane as Henry and Ariana haven't opted for a wool carpet. It's a shame in these circumstances, as wool would be charred by the fallen log but unlikely to burn. Whereas synthetic fibres are highly flammable.

Either his eyes are adjusting to the darkness, or the fire is spreading and the room brightening with an orange glow. Probably the latter. Smoke is beginning to swirl and cling to the ceiling in a black cloud. He can taste it now, plasticky and chemical. It's harsh in his nose, with an abrasive, biting quality. He knows the fire will have released a mass of toxic gasses from the carpet – hydrogen cyanide and carbon monoxide. Ariana will have to be quick if she's to save him from the poisonous, suffocating cloud.

And from the fire itself, of course.

She must have run out to get water, then realised the fire was too large for her to put out alone. Sensibly, she has moved to another space so she won't be overwhelmed by the smoke. She needs to be able to direct the fire and ambulance crews to where he is. She is most likely waiting for them on the street now. He'll no doubt hear the sirens soon.

The heat intensifies around him, and the smoke sinks lower. His throat burns with the taste of it. He notices the *GET WELL SOON* balloons on the sideboard, swaying from side to side on the currents of swirling, hot air. They bump together, and he imagines them as two universes meeting, his and Ariana's, or their past and their present, connecting, crossing over, or their past and their future. Anything is possible. Everything is possible.

The balloons are beginning to sink on their strings. The room is getting hotter, and the density of the surrounding air is increasing relative to the helium, reducing its buoyancy. Eventually, the balloons will sink lower until they touch the floor. The helium will expand and the plastic of the balloon will burst.

He imagines his family like balloons, the chemistry and physics of them in their burning rooms, the rubbery surfaces of thin skin containing tissues, blood vessels and organs, the gasses expanding and the fluids boiling and vaporising, rupturing and exploding. The human body is an extraordinary thing.

He feels himself getting uncomfortably hot. Painfully so. It's fascinating that his nervous system doesn't store a record of the original pain he felt. He has evolved beyond it. If his brain allowed full sensory recall, the experience could be traumatising. But he's aware his amygdala and prefrontal cortex have stored its emotional impact. He's reminded now of its intensity and unpleasantness.

Any moment now he'll hear the sirens, or Ariana will burst through the door and rescue him as he rescued her. He is utterly certain of that. He wonders which will happen first, Ariana's arrival or the balloons bursting. It amuses him to speculate which it will be. Wondering helps him pass the time while he waits. He's so lucky to have met her. Just the thought of it fills him with joy.

He waits, and watches the balloons sink lower, and lower.

EPILOGUE
TEN YEARS LATER

There's a distinct smell of burning meat.

I rush to the oven and open the door. A wall of heat hits me, and condensation forms on my glasses. I can smell the acrid smoke. I slide my glasses up onto my head and pull the tray out with an oven glove.

The sausages are ruined, each split down its centre, skin curled back and peeling away like burnt paper, revealing layers of scorched flesh. Fat clings to the metal tray in charred, blackened pools.

This is my one job and I've ruined it. Every year is the same. Tobias takes charge of the bonfire and fireworks, I take charge of the food. I go to the freezer and take out another couple of packets. They'll cook from frozen if I turn the oven down. It's a ritual. Phoebe will demand it. You can't have Bonfire Night without sausages.

Tobias wasn't familiar with Bonfire Night until he came to England. When Phoebe was born seven years ago on November 5th he couldn't believe it when the sky lit up with fireworks, as if they were just for her. Her own personal 4th of July, he called it. Every year since, he's insisted we hold this weird hybrid of birthday and bonfire party. He loves being the master of ceremonies, decking the garden out with balloons and streamers no matter the weather, planning the party games, designing an elaborate firework display, building a huge bonfire. Birthday cake and baked potatoes, candles and sparklers. Over and over in a loop.

Delighted screams draw my attention to the kitchen window. An excited gaggle of seven-year-olds gather in a noisy group with their parents. Tobias is about to start the display.

I stay inside to keep an eye on the sausages. I turn the lights off so I can see better into the darkened garden. The bonfire has really taken hold now. The group stand near it, but at quite a distance. It must be throwing out some heat. Even from inside I hear a loud crack as some piece of wood splinters. The fire shifts and throws a cloud of burning embers out, spiralling up on the hot air currents and blending with the stars in the clear sky above. I can hardly see Phoebe at all, and Tobias is completely lost in the inky depths of the garden.

On the fence at the side I can just see a bunch of birthday balloons picked out by the light from the bonfire. They seem to move as the flames dance and the shadows shift. They sway slightly in the breeze. They bump against each other and I think of Daniel and the alternative universes meeting each other.

There's one universe we're in, where my house caught fire, and Daniel didn't escape and was killed, and I met Tobias and had Phoebe and was happy.

The display begins, teasingly small, with Catherine wheels spinning in all directions, faster than it's possible to imagine. I grip the edge of the work surface until my knuckles turn white.

The balloons bump, and there's another universe where the house caught fire and I phoned the fire brigade and Daniel was rescued and returned to prison where they won't make the mistake again of releasing him.

Rockets now, shooting impossibly high, exploding over us in galaxies like a speeded-up birth of the universe, bursting, expanding, decaying and returning to darkness, all reflected in the kitchen window so I feel somehow like I'm inside the heart of it.

Bump, bump. I feel like all I can hear now is the balloons bumping together. Another universe where the house was destroyed but Daniel escaped and I met Tobias and had Phoebe and was always waiting for Daniel to appear again.

I hear them in the garden now. Shrieking. Yells and screams as the fireworks fly and the fire rages. There's the sound of a distant siren, hurrying to a fire somewhere, some bonfire-related domestic tragedy. Or possibly an ambulance, rushing across London with a patient inside, terribly burnt in a fire. Or maybe a police car, racing against time to some unfolding crime, not bonfire-related at all, but happening unnoticed in plain sight, the terrible screams masked by the screams of joy as the fireworks ascend. I listen again, but I can't tell whether the siren is moving farther away or coming closer.

Bump, bump. The balloons feel almost deafening now. So much time has passed, so many strange things have happened that it's hard to remember what's real and what's imagined, where the nightmares are so vivid that they make the past seem like the present. Where Daniel explains how the universe works and it all merges together and you can't be sure exactly what *has* happened and what *will* happen. Anything is possible. Everything is possible. And maybe it's all happening, all at once, right now, right this very second, and it's foolish to think you'll ever know what the truth is at all.

Bump.

END

THANK YOU FOR READING

Did you enjoy reading *Never Let You Go*? Please consider leaving a review on Amazon. Your review will help other readers to discover the novel.

ABOUT THE AUTHOR

Caleb Crowe is a British writer of psychological thrillers, and is fascinated by stories where extraordinary things happen to ordinary people, and the mundane is transformed into the menacing.

He's afraid of the sea, fearful in the countryside, panicky in large open spaces and terrified of small, confined spaces. He finds eerily quiet villages and bustling impersonal cities equally unsettling. There's nowhere, and no one, that doesn't possess some kind of dark, brooding anxiety just waiting to have the lid prised open and turned into a twisty, suspenseful, nerve-shredding story.

He lives in Manchester with his partner, two children and two cats, who probably have their own mysterious agendas. Whether he's navigating the urban jungle or wrestling with the daily challenges of family life, Caleb draws inspiration from the unpredictability of everyday existence.

Find Caleb on his website: www.calebcrowe.com

ALSO BY CALEB CROWE

Printed in Great Britain
by Amazon

57553901R00199